LOVE *Spells* TROUBLE

LOVE *Spells* TROUBLE

NIA DAVENPORT

BLOOMSBURY
NEW YORK   LONDON   OXFORD   NEW DELHI   SYDNEY

BLOOMSBURY YA
Bloomsbury Publishing Inc., part of Bloomsbury Publishing Plc
1385 Broadway, New York, NY 10018

BLOOMSBURY and the Diana logo are trademarks of Bloomsbury Publishing Plc

First published in the United States of America in July 2025 by Bloomsbury YA

Text copyright © 2025 by Nia Davenport

All rights reserved. No part of this publication may be reproduced or transmitted in any form or by any means, electronic or mechanical, including photocopying, recording, or any information storage or retrieval system, without prior permission in writing from the publisher.

Bloomsbury books may be purchased for business or promotional use. For information on bulk purchases please contact Macmillan Corporate and Premium Sales Department at specialmarkets@macmillan.com

Library of Congress Cataloging-in-Publication Data
available upon request
ISBN 978-1-5476-1296-3 (hardcover) • ISBN 978-1-5476-1297-0 (e-book)

Book design by Yelena Safronova
Typeset by Westchester Publishing Services
Printed and bound in the U.S.A.
2 4 6 8 10 9 7 5 3 1

To find out more about our authors and books visit www.bloomsbury.com
and sign up for our newsletters.

To my younger self,
I'm so glad we've never stopped dreaming.

LOVE Spells TROUBLE

Chapter One

The harbinger of hell doesn't live in the underworld—he's chilling at my mom's rescue. Don't get me wrong, Hades, an eighty-five-pound chocolate standard poodle and the shelter's longest-running resident, is cute as heck, but *he hates me*. Like *hates* hates me. And I've never done anything besides try to be friends with the demon dog. But His Majesty refuses to suffer my presence. He adores the other volunteers—it's really just me he has a problem with. Which makes it all the more problematic that I'm the only one here to give him a bath before his prospective Paws Parent comes in.

"Be a good doggy, please?" I slowly approach my nemesis's kennel, with my hands up, palms out, nonthreatening. I keep a smile on my face, and I pitch my voice friendly, peppy, and soothing.

Hades swishes his curly tail and glares at me. I have a

theory: I'm near sure Hades loathes me because he senses I'm a witch. And from what I've surmised, the snobbish, judgy poodle has a thing against witches.

"I should've called out today, too," I mutter when the dog scowls harder as I take another measured step toward him.

Hades sniffs the air, head held high and floppy ears pushed back, as if saying, *Yes,* witch, *you should've.*

I freeze in place. Hades earned his name for a reason when he came to Lucky Paws Rescue as only a one-year-old puppy six months ago. (Normally, we match our pups with good homes in a few short weeks, but Hades has the energy of a toddler, the snootiness of a king, and the attitude of a diva.) Bro is literally a whole demon. Not in the ferocious kind of way; Hades wouldn't hurt a mosquito. More so, in the himbo, uppity, difficult, I-don't-like-you-because-you're-beneath-me-witch-peasant sort of way. He allows belly rubs from everyone *except* me, and he purposely thwacks his tail, so it knocks into my leg—hard—every time we end up too close to each other. I wince, rubbing the skin below the edge of my shorts, already feeling the impending strike.

If it was any other day, I wouldn't have let Larissa, the shelter's co-director and adoption manager, dupe me into this job. All the other scheduled volunteers had emergencies and called out, and today of all days, Hades decided to roll around in a puddle of mud when Larissa took him on his morning walk. His Majesty picked the worst possible time to pull one of his usual stunts. According to Larissa, a fantastic couple and their son did a meet-and-greet with

Hades earlier in the week. They even filled out his adoption paperwork on the spot! Miraculously, Hades's antics didn't run off this latest interested family, and their son has an appointment to pick him up in about an hour and a half. I don't want anything to potentially jeopardize this adoption.

I throw my hands on my hips, toughening up and ready to do battle. Hades needs to let me give him a bath, and we need to take care of business in under ninety minutes. "You need to get over your problem with witches, already," I tell His Highness as I step up to his kennel. "Seriously, dude, you're like a hundred years behind the rest of the world." One hundred and five years, to be exact. Witches made their existence known in 1919, right on the cusp of the Roaring Twenties. Some even say it's what helped give rise to the explosion of economic and social change. A history that would be seriously cool and make me proud if it didn't give rise to the snooty Coven House system, which made us witches totally start to suck shortly afterward. Yes, I realize the irony of me being exasperated with Hades's attitude when most witches get on my last nerves, too. But that's beside the point.

"The offending witch is all you've got today, okay?" I stress what *is* the point to Hades. "Can we try to be friends?" If I was my mom, who founded the shelter, coaxing Hades into agreement would be easy. The Ancestors gifted her a Connection with animals. (Which is why she's a vet at the attached clinic, and a spectacular one.) She could walk in, soothe Hades with a little calming thought pushed his way, and immediately make the poodle forget that he thought she was a big, bad, Wicked Witch of the South. But... *le sigh*... I'm not Mom. The Connection the Ancestors gifted me is much less interesting and hard to explain.

"A member of your new family is coming soon to whisk you away to a cushy fur-ever home, Cinderella." I try reasoning with Hades to get him to play nice. "Trust me, you wanna look and smell all nice and pretty for him. If you make sure he *continues* to like you, you'll finally get out of here. Don't you want that? *It'll also get you away from me forever.*"

I swear the dog understands my words because he raises his head a fraction higher, as if he's some kingly lord considering my proposal. Then, he inclines his head to the side, bobbing it a bit.

"So that's a yes? To everything?" I ask with my hand on the door to his kennel. *Please let it be a yes so he doesn't clobber me.*

Again, he tilts his head, and I hope I'm not tripping and making things up and the motion actually does mean *yes* in poodle-speak. I open the kennel door, and good old Hades trots out, making sure to thwack my knee with his tail. I yelp and reach down to rub the slightly sore spot.

Maybe it was an accident this time? Or maybe the Demon Dog intentionally assaulted me!

I reach out to pat said Demon Dog's head, trying still to be friends. And he serves me the dog version of a side-eye. I snatch my hand back. "Right." I lay my hand against his peanut butter–colored collar instead. I touch it, not one hair on him, and lead him to a cozy adjoining room that houses bathing stations and an assortment of yummy-smelling shampoos, conditioners, coat oils, and fragrance sprays for our pups. It's our "Dog Spa."

As we walk, I catch a whiff of Hades's stink and wrinkle my nose. "Bruh, you smell atrocious," I let him know. "And look at your beautiful coat!" He lets me brush off a clod of dirt clinging to it. "You really woke up this morning and chose violence."

Hades makes a noise that sounds like a "harumph," and again, I *swear* the dog can legit communicate. Like perfectly understand human speech and talk back to you. But not even Mom can do that with animals, so I've got to be tripping.

We stop at the first bathing station in the Dog Spa. I kneel beside Hades, who isn't being *too* terrible with me today, and take off his collar. I turn the water at the station on, and it rushes into a huge oval-shaped tub. The water heater in the building is janky, and it takes water forever and three days to heat up. Luckily, I can use my Connection for this part. I wave my hand near the faucet and adjust the temperature myself by converting a little of the hydroelectric energy produced by the running water into heat energy. The flow of water gushing out of the faucet slows some when I do— the visible effect of borrowing from its hydroelectric energy. But water still fills the tub at a steady rate, and it's nice and warm.

My Connection comes in handy now and then, but it's not flashy at all. It'd only be cool if this was a comic and I was the hero starring in my own origin story. But in real life, a Connection to forms of energy isn't even a little thrilling. When you don't have a universe to save or a supervillain's butt to kick, it's only useful for mundane stuff like heating tubs for Demon Dogs who despise you.

A low growl sounds, and Hades is serving me a dog side-eye again.

"Okay," I say, giving him a cheery, hopefully comforting smile. "I should've figured you wouldn't like the use of magic in front of you. Sorry." Then I jut my chin out, because I refuse to be all the way disparaged by a haughty, hypercritical, prejudiced dog.

Can dogs actually be prejudiced? Is that even a thing?

"You needed and wanted me to do that," I drop a truth bomb on Hades. "You don't have the time it'll take to get a tub full of hot water the normal way, and you're too bougie to tolerate a cold bath."

He harrumphs again but doesn't growl. I guess he deigns to accept my use of magic when it's to his benefit and comfort.

I pat the side of the tub when it's near full. "Jump on in."

Hades clears the rim with a big leap, making a splash I jump back to avoid, and sits on his hind legs. I grab two bottles of shampoo—a Madagascar vanilla scent and a butterscotch scent. "Which one?" I hold them near Hades's nose so he can sniff them. It's my routine with the dogs I bathe. They like being involved in the process. Which I totally get.

I'd want to have a choice in the scent my coat was about to be drenched in, too. For example, if I was a dog and got bathed with something coconut smelling, I'd be pissed. I'd also vomit. I hate all things coconut in any and every variety.

Hades sniffs the butterscotch first, then the Madagascar vanilla.

"Excellent choice," I say when he nudges the vanilla toward me with his nose. "Madagascar vanilla lattes are my favorite. Madagascar vanilla Eggo waffles, too. Basically, anything Madagascar vanilla, I'm down for." I smile at Hades as I pour a pool of his chosen shampoo in my hand, trying to find common ground so we can get through his bath on cordial terms. I work the lather into his brown, curly fur, and His Majesty thumps his foot against the bottom of the tub. He leans into my touch; I guess since I'm pampering him and playing the role of shampoo slave, he can suffer my hand making contact with him now. I roll my eyes but also do a little happy shimmy with my shoulders. *Yes!* This isn't working out so bad after all. Hades hasn't waged an all-out war on me yet.

I'm covered in suds up to my elbows when I look up and see a guy step into the lobby. He's cute. Really cute. Scratch that. He's *fine*. The type of fine that demands I squint to get a better look and confirm he's real. He's tall (my type), with dark brown skin (my type, too), brown-black eyes (also my type), and curly hair cut low on his head (hair, I'm not picky about). Then, there's his face. With thick, black lashes, high cheekbones, and full lips, he looks like he stepped out of a fashion ad. Like one for Gucci or Prada or whatever it is rich kids wear.

He carries himself like a rich boy, too. His strides are long and confident, but lazy, like he has all the time in the world because everybody is on *his* time. And okay, bougie as hell rich boys are *not* my thing, but this guy is really, really, really attractive. So maybe, for him, I can make an exception. Especially since his attire doesn't scream obnoxious, rich jerk. Instead of the standard Bougie Boys Club uniform of khaki pants, a button-down shirt, and loafers, he's wearing gray joggers, a South Texas University hoodie, and a pair of special edition Starry Night Air Jordan Retro Ones that makes me jealous. *So maybe he isn't all that bad*, I conclude. He is wearing an HBCU hoodie, which gets him major points, and he has fantastic taste in shoes—he gets a trillion extra points for that since I'm a ridiculous sneakerhead.

It's then that I realize I'm staring, and that he's staring back at me as he pushes open the glass door to the Dog Spa. Has he been checking me out the entire time, too? A giddy thrill zips through me. He could be a fun summer thing. Not a boyfriend. Those, I've decided not to do headed into senior year. It doesn't make any sense. Things will just get deep, then I'll graduate and head off to Howard University, if I get in, and 99.9 percent of high school relationships *don't* survive moving on to college. My stats tutor from last year would cringe at my use of an arbitrary statistic, but I'm near sure I'm not too far off.

I shake my head because my thoughts have veered off on

a serious tangent—*and oh my God, I'm still staring!* My whole face burns, and I'm about to sputter something that'll sound like a good excuse. But Hades chooses the exact moment to call off our truce. With a raucous bark, he shakes vigorously, and the ton of water saturating the soaking fur of an eighty-plus pound poodle sprays me. I yelp and grab my hair. The reaction is too late and laughably futile. I was trying to be cute and wore my twist-out down today in gorgeous bouncy curls that brush my shoulders. The soapy water has drenched it, and I feel the strands turning frizzy beneath my hands. I direct some thermal energy into my hair, running my hands over the poofiness. The magical effort dries my hair, but without an actual brush, comb, and my Black Girl Coils hair care products, it doesn't help to set my curls back poppin' again.

My crop top and bike shorts are soaked, too. I look down at myself, and I'm a hot mess. But all the concern for myself flies out the window when I see suds covering the top halves of the cute guy's shoes. I lunge for him, not really thinking about what I'm doing. "Not the Starry Nights!" I shove him out of the puddle of water on the floor.

It doesn't do much good because sweet Hades has other ideas—again. He leaps out of the tub and flies at Starry Night Boy. Dripping wet, he puts his front paws on the bottom of Starry Night Boy's crisp shirt. When the boy squats so he's eye level with Hades, His Majesty shifts his paws to the boy's shoulders and slobbers a kiss all over his right cheek. The reckless, goofy behavior with prospective Paws

Parents is exactly why Hades remains unadopted. He's *extra* and *hyperexcitable* about everything.

"Your shoes!" I say, hoarse and wanting to cry for him. As Hades continues to drool all over the poor guy's cheek, more soapy, dirty water drips onto the shoes I stood in line at The Kicks Room for more than four hours to snag and didn't score. I looked online for my size afterward; they'd already ballooned up to fifteen hundred bucks, and there was no way in hell I could afford that. It took me three months of babysitting just to collect the shoe's one-hundred-and-eighty-dollar retail value.

I expect the guy to gape at the sneakers in horror, shove Hades off him, and curse up a storm. However, he doesn't so much as glance at them. "'Sup, my dude; I missed you, too!" He grins, throwing an arm around Hades to hug him. With his free hand, he scratches behind Hades's ear. Hades emits a happy yelp, and his tail wags furiously.

"Get down!" I cry at Hades.

"It's all right," the guy says. "It's blazing outside," he laughs to Hades. "I guess you knew I needed a cooldown, huh? Good looking out." He looks around Hades to me. "Sorry I came a little early. I know my pickup slot isn't for another hour, but I couldn't wait. Larissa pointed me back here. She said you were bathing him but should be finishing up soon and could help me with getting Hades ready to go."

All I can do is gawk at him for a second as my mind races

to switch from its preoccupation with the shoes to everything he's said. "You're . . . *the son?*" I clear my throat. "I mean the person in Hades's new family who is picking him up?" Truly, Larissa should've described him in greater detail; she wouldn't have had to work so hard to convince me to risk my life making Hades presentable if it meant I got to meet this boy.

He stands and continues to scratch behind Hades's ear, to the big beast's delight. "Yup." He gazes at Hades, smitten. "I love him. He's awesome; I can't wait to take him home! My parents filled out the app and all that, but Hades is gonna be *my* dog," he tells me proudly.

I blink. "Cool," I say, wondering what strange, distant planet he crash-landed onto Earth from. If he notices the buckets of water Hades continues to drip on his shoes, he doesn't show it. Most boys, most *anybody,* would be upset about their ruined sneakers. Especially a sneakerhead, which he obviously is. I motion to them wildly, unable to help myself. "Your poor shoes. They look trashed." The stars painted across the black suede tops and sides are light blue, teal, and white. The black suede might survive the water when it dries but the glittering stars are light enough in color that the mud-colored water has permanently stained them. The white soles are wrecked, too.

Finally, he looks down at the sneakers. He winces, but then says, "I'll live."

"Well, I'm slowly dying inside on your behalf. Those are freaking Starry Nights. My whole soul would be crushed."

Patting Hades's head, he chuckles. "You're in the kicks-obsessed club, too, huh?"

I nod. "Yup." I point down to the Nikes I'm wearing. "They're old and my I-don't-care-if-I-mess-them-up shoes now, but I got these limited edition, glow-in-the-dark Dunks two Halloweens ago." Well, they were really an All Saints' Eve present (which is a Halloween-adjacent witch holiday and also observed on October 31), but if I say that, then I have to relay the fact that I'm a witch and . . . that's getting into too much about me and my life with a boy I just met.

He looks the Dunks over appreciatively. "Nice." Hades finally drops down from his shoulders. He sits at the boy's feet—right on the shoes—and pants happily.

I raise an eyebrow. "You sure you want to take him home?"

A smile plays on the corners of the boy's (very kissable) full lips. He points to the *Volunteer* badge fastened to my T-shirt. "I'm pretty sure you're not supposed to ask me that."

Covering the badge with my hand, I say, "The Lucky Paws volunteer isn't asking. The sneakerhead was. And I gotta tell you, she's starting to grow highly suspicious of you." I give his destroyed shoes another aghast look. "I'd feel better about you becoming Hades's Paws Parent if you were at least a little pissed about the sneakers." I wave at him and his too serene nature. "You're too chill. It's freaky. Are you like a psycho or something?"

He sputters. "What?! You're not serious; stop playing with me, girl."

My lips twitch, but I stay in character. "I watch Investigation Discovery," I let him know. "You might be the dog owner version of those awful dudes who pretend to be dashing and charming and perfect until they marry their partner, then murder them."

He licks his lips. "Mmm. So you think I look good, huh?"

It's my turn to sputter. Matter of fact, I choke a bit. "I never said that!"

He strikes a pose, folding his arms over his chest and smirking. "*Dashing* means handsome, don't it?"

I shrug, admitting nothing. "That's one definition. But it can also simply mean to run fast."

"But you didn't use it as a verb," he returns, real slick-like. "Instead, you said *I was*—"

"It was just a joke," I say, shutting down the way he's about to call me out. Yes, bro is fine. But I can't look too thirsty, too early. So, I steer us away from the subject of my slipup and say, "If Larissa approved you, obviously that means everything is a one hundred percent go and you're good. Larissa has a freaky second sense that tells her on sight if prospective Paws Parents will be loving owners." If I didn't know for sure she wasn't, I'd think Larissa was also a witch with a Connection to a psychic gift. Within five seconds of a person walking into the lobby for their meet and greet, Larissa knows if they are decent folk, making the decision to either invite them back or tell them they don't meet the criteria to adopt.

Starry Night Boy smirks like he knows I'm full of it. But he only asks, "Do you want help while you finish my new buddy's bath?"

"Sure," I say, unable to stop the appreciative smile on my face. With Hades's massive self, I'll take all of it I can get. Especially when the help is as cute as Starry Night Boy.

Chapter Two

"What's your name, by the way?" I ask Starry Night Boy as we use plush bath towels to dry Hades once he's squeaky clean. (The Warden of Hell gets spooked by hair dryers. *Imagine that*.) Yes, I'm further scoping him out as potential summer fun. Even though, yes, I look like I got caught outside in a lightning storm after Hades's antics. But that hasn't stopped Starry Night Boy from checking me out, too. So I shoot my shot.

"Mekhi," he says with a grin that's lopsided, dimpled, and makes my knees wobbly. "But everyone calls me Khy."

"Got it," I say, playing it cool. "I'm Cayden. My friends do *not* call me Cay, though. I'd murder them," I deadpan.

The joke lands, and he laughs. "I think I like the sound of *Cayden* better anyway."

If decadent, super-tempting, triple-layer fudge chocolate

cake had a sound, it would be identical to the deep pitch of his voice when he says my name. And it seals things—even if he doesn't know it yet. I'm having all the fun with him this summer.

I speed up the work with Hades and project some of my magic his way so his thick, curly coat dries quicker. I chance the risk since Hades allowed me to use my magic earlier to serve His Majesty. When Hades is mostly dry, I sling the bath towel over my shoulder and slide my phone out of my pocket. "What's your number? We should hang out sometime," I say to Khy.

His eyebrows shoot up. He drapes the bath towel over his left arm, then a teasing grin blooms on his face. "I thought I was a psycho killer?"

I shrug. "That was so twenty minutes ago."

We both break into a laugh.

Khy AirDrops me his number, and I send him mine. When I accept his AirDrop, a picture of him in a wet suit while holding a surfboard pops up as his contact photo.

I wave the phone. "This is an interesting pic."

"Why? Because Black people don't surf?" He says it light enough, but there's a scowl to his expression that makes it clear it's an annoying quip he's heard a billion times.

"Not at all," I rush out. "My dad's a serious surfer. He competes in a few major amateur competitions a year and always beasts them. That's why I said it's interesting. He tried to get me into it, but being in the middle of an ocean with hundreds of feet of water beneath me scares me shitless, so no. I'll take snow and a pair of skis over a board any day."

"Wait. So you're cool with careening down the side of a mountain where you might smack into a tree but not with being in an ocean where there's literally nothing around you to splatter your guts against?" His face is aghast. "If you can't tell, I am not a fan of skiing. Ever." He bumps my shoulder with his. "But don't the two of us and our hobbies make a sick pair?"

I pop my lips, flirting back. "The Black girl who skis and the Black boy who surfs? We're a whole vibe, for sure."

"I like you," he says, chuckling.

I give him a shrug. "You seem cool, too."

He clutches his chest. "Ouch! Is that all I get?"

"For now," I say, slick. I'm not about to inflate Pretty Boy's ego. I'd bet my entire sneaker collection that it's already huge. It has to be, with that face and that swagger.

Just then, the door swings open. My mom strides in wearing a pair of pink scrubs (her usual attire whenever she's at the clinic or around the shelter). She's cradling Neyo, a gray pit bull who's the most chill puppy ever, in her arms. "Sorry I got here later than expected," she says, barely looking over at me and Khy. "I had a meeting with Auntie Nikki and it took longer than I'd planned."

Auntie Nikki is my dad's older sister. She's also my parents' financial advisor, and Mom only calls hanging out with her a *meeting* when they're discussing business-y stuff.

And by the tone of her voice, I can tell the meeting didn't go well. "Is everything all right?" I ask, worry suddenly gnawing at my insides.

Mom finally looks up at me and gives a bright smile—one that doesn't quite reach her eyes. "Everything is fine. We just had to discuss some boring budgeting things. Part of the eternal annoyance of *adulting*." Mom winks at me, finally smiling for real. Her awkwardness from before has completely melted away, so I decide to drop it. Maybe I was reading too much into it to begin with.

Mom turns her genial smile Khy's way and tips her head toward Hades, who's panting happily and gazing up at Khy as if he's the sun, moon, *and* all the stars in the sky. "Hello. I'm Dr. Jackson, the owner of this fine establishment," Mom greets Khy. "Thank you so much for giving Hades a home."

"Thank you for trusting me to do so, ma'am," Khy returns, the picture of manners. "I'm so stoked about it."

Mom bobs her head and carries Neyo—whom Hades could learn a thing or two from—to a bathing station. She settles the four-month-old, adorably chubby puppy into a tub and tells Khy, "Don't forget you've got a year of free vet care with our clinic. That includes all the immunizations, checkups, and sick visits. It's one of the many perks of adopting from Lucky Paws!"

As Khy nods graciously, Larissa, Lucky Paws' adoption manager, pokes her head into the room. "How's it going with Hades?" She smiles at Hades who's nuzzling Khy's chest as he drags the towel over Hades's head. "Seems like he adores you."

From her spot across the room, Mom mouths at me, *"He's a cutie!"* She tacks on a wink, and thank-the-freaking-Ancestors Khy is looking solely at Larissa. Otherwise, I'd try my level best to turn my magic inward and vaporize myself on the spot—just turn my flesh and bones into gaseous molecules that waft away.

I ignore my lovely mother; anything else might encourage her. I face Larissa and Khy and let Mom tend to her own business of bathing Neyo.

Khy swallows Hades up in a bear hug. "The feeling's mutual," he gushes to Larissa.

"I love that for y'all." Larissa does a shimmy/jiggle combo, then shoots Hades a thumbs-up. "You're getting out of here, boy. Hell yeah!"

Hades barks happily as Khy finishes drying his head and upper body. I do the same to Hades's lower body and tail.

"I'll take that," I say and hold my hand out for Khy's towel. I toss it and mine into a laundry bin nearby. I do not make eye contact with my mom again—nor will I as long as Khy is in the room. It's bad enough I can feel her scrutinizing the way we interact.

"Your parents just emailed over Hades's signed adoption paperwork," Larissa says to Khy. "If you'll come with me, I'll collect the rehoming fee, and you can bust Hades out of here."

Thank the Lord there's about to be space between Khy and my mom.

Khy smiles a goofy, joyful smile that makes him *more* cute. Before he follows Larissa from the room, he turns to me. "Talking with you was fun. I've gotta get my bud all settled in at home today, and I'm sure he'll be nervous his first nights in a new place, but what are you doing the day after tomorrow? Maybe if Hades is comfy by then, we can hang out?"

Mom chooses that moment to cough. Loudly.

Larissa ain't no better. She's a twenty-year-old pre-veterinarian student who usually feels like a big sister more than a boss, and sis doesn't even try to be low-key about looking between me and Khy with glee. She waggles her eyebrows and says for me, "Cayden should be free." She gives me a look that says *you better be free.*

Her and Mom's antics are ridiculous. Yet, they aren't wrong. I smirk at Larissa because she should know me better than to think my answer would be anything other than telling hot Starry Night Boy that I'm available—which I do.

"Yeah, that sounds fun," I reply.

Khy's smile gets even bigger. "Great. I'll see you soon."

Larissa walks him out, sending me a low-key thumbs-up behind his back.

Later, as Khy leaves the rescue with Hades excitedly trotting beside him, Larissa practically tackles me. "Girl, I see you and him being a whole adorable vibe! The way y'all were gazing at each other; it was giving *love-at-first-sight* energy!"

I balk because *love* is certainly not a word I'm interested in this summer. "Why are you like this?" I groan to Larissa. "Ain't no way I'm going there with any boy right now." And she knows why. In fact, she even encouraged my decision and told me it was smart.

But today's Larissa kisses her teeth and says, "I read energies to a fault, remember? And you were looking at the boy like—"

"Like I was picturing all the fun summer kisses I'm planning to enjoy with him, nothing more," I maintain.

She gives me a glib "okay" and points toward the window whose open blinds provide a clear view of Khy walking Hades across the parking lot. "You let me know how that goal turns out."

I ignore her and watch out the window as Khy unlocks a sporty, orange Porsche with a black racing stripe (because, of course) and opens the passenger door for Hades to hop inside. I even find myself appreciating this standard display of membership in the Bougie Boys Club. For starters, if summer flings, by definition, are casual and temporary, it literally doesn't matter. And more importantly, Khy being the kind of boy who drives a freaking Porsche proves what I stressed to Larissa *is* true. I'm not about to catch real feelings for him, and I haven't already started catching them, either.

Chapter Three

The next morning, I arrive for my shift at the other business that's tied with the rescue for first place in my heart. And although I *am* vain enough for it to be the reason, I don't only adore Cayden's Confections because it's named after me. I adore the bakery because it's owned by Jason Jackson, aka my dad, aka the world's best pastry chef (I'll fight anyone who disagrees).

The back entrance is unlocked like always, and I walk right in.

"Good morning!" I say cheerily to Dad. He's standing over a gigantic red KitchenAid mixer. As the whisk whirs around a shiny silver bowl, he intently stares at the contents.

Dad looks up when he hears me and returns my good morning.

I cross the kitchen space and hand him one of the take-out containers I'm holding. I detoured slightly out of the way and stopped by The Breakfast Kounter, a hallowed Third Ward institution, to pick up Dad's favorite (a bacon and cheese omelet with toast) and mine (the shrimp and grits with fried catfish). Dad heads to work as soon as he rolls out of bed, so I know he hasn't had breakfast, and the sugary goodness he whips up in the bakery, while stupendous, is not a hearty meal.

He opens his container and inhales gooey-cheddar, greasy-bacon bliss. "This is why you're my favorite kid."

I smirk. "I'm your only kid, Father of Mine."

He returns what I call a Dad grin: a smile that's all dopey and misty-eyed for his baby girl. "The sentiment remains the same."

"Sure. Sure," I say and hug him tightly. I love both him and Mom more than all the stars in the sky. Most of my friends aren't too fond of their parents a lot of the time, but I've avoided that phase so far.

Dad plops a kiss on my forehead, sits his food on the counter, then turns to the mixer and sticks a plastic spoon in the bowl. He scoops out a small amount of white icing and hands it to me. "Taste." There's a sly twinkle in his eye. We're playing the game where he refuses to tell me what he's concocted before I give it a try.

I eyeball the spoon. "No coconut, right?"

Dad gives me an insulted look. "I know my daughter.

I wouldn't give Cayden Maya Jackson coconut *anything*. Taste it."

I sniff the icing, making sure. Dad *really* likes putting coconut in stuff. And sometimes, he conveniently forgets the dash of coconut powder or the splash of coconut milk or the drop of coconut butter. But all I smell is sugar, pineapples, vanilla, and I think some kind of nuts. All things I love, so I eagerly bring the spoon to my lips. "Yummm!" I groan around it, in pure heaven.

Dad beams, delighted. "I'm trying out a new recipe for a pineapple vanilla rum cake. That's the frosting."

I wiggle my eyebrows at the mixing bowl. "Any rum in that icing?"

He snorts. "You wish."

I sigh. "Dang. I thought I was about to get wasted on a Monday morning. Start my week off right."

Dad gives me an unamused *Dad-scowl*, turning serious. "You thought no such thing."

I grin, giving him the spoon back. "You're right. I just like giving you a few extra gray hairs. Gotta keep the parenting gig entertaining for ya."

He fake coughs. "You mean stressful?"

"Love you, Father!" I blow Dad a kiss and head for the front of the bakery. A glance at the clock on the wall tells me it's 6:55 and the bakery opens at 7 AM. "Holler if you need anything," I call to Dad over my shoulder. "I'll order us some lunch later from The Jerk House!" It's a Third Ward favorite of Dad's; I can run over and get it on my break, and he never turns down jerk anything, so it'll ensure he doesn't opt to work through lunch.

"Thanks, Daughter of Mine!" he calls back. "I really appreciate you helping out this summer!" Dad's tone is steeped in gratitude, and it makes my heart twist in my chest. Business has gotten slow, and he needed to cut back on employee hours. I don't mind working the gig at all. Mom and Dad do so much for me that even if I didn't love the bakery, I'd still feel obligated to help him out. Me, him, and Mom are a tight unit. We always have been. We look out for each other, and we always have each other's backs. So this summer, I got Dad's back for sure. I offered to come in every day, but he wouldn't let me give up my Sundays at the rescue, and he insisted I take time to enjoy my summer. Which leaves me working only Monday through Thursday.

Up front, Dad has already stocked the glass cases below the bakery's counter. There are multiple flavors of tea cakes, brownie-bottom cheesecakes, red velvet cake, chocolate cake, coconut lime cake, Italian cream cake, strawberry tarts, gluten-free pecan pies, and some breakfast pastries, too. After resisting the urge to steal one from the case (the shrimp and grits I picked up is the only thing stopping me!), I start running through the start-of-day tasks.

I cross the floor, flip the sign hanging from the front door from Closed to Open, then I unlock the door. After that, I turn on the iPad and log into the Square app to take payments at the register, and I count the drawer for the morning. Finally, I turn around to make sure the coffee and espresso machines are already on and heating up. Dad got to that, too, before I came in.

The bell above the front door rings as I finish my breakfast. I pop my head up hoping it's a customer. We need a lot more of those these days. But it's only Mr. Charles, the mailman who's been working our neighborhood route since I was in diapers. He's getting ready to retire next year.

"Hey, suga!" Mr. Charles's Texas drawl is cane-syrup thick. He sounds exactly like Grandpop, Dad's dad, who was born and raised in Texas, too.

"How are you today, Mr. Charles?" I ask.

He scratches his forehead in the way old Southern men do when they're making small talk. "I can't complain. The Good Lord opened my eyes."

I nod and turn around to make the cup of coffee he gets when he comes to drop off the mail. Unlike the all-sugar and very little actual coffee concoctions I make for myself, he likes his *joe*, as he calls it, to be all beans and no sugar. Ick! Before placing his Styrofoam cup of night black coffee on the counter, I curl my hands more firmly around it and funnel a little extra thermal energy into it. Mr. Charles likes his joe extra *extra* hot, and the coffee machine decided to become a pain a couple of days ago. It's still functional, but the warming plate is janky and won't get as hot as it used to. After Mr. Charles's coffee is heated to suitable temps, I slide it and his usual slice of pecan pie in front of him.

He tries to hand me a ten-dollar bill along with our mail, per usual, and I wave him away, per usual. Dad issues standing orders to whoever mans the register that Mr. Charles's money is no good.

Mr. Charles huffs. He slides the ten bucks closer to me. "Tell yo' daddy to stop being stubborn."

"I do all the time," I promise Mr. Charles. "But it never does any good." I pick up the money and hold it back out to him.

Grumbling, Mr. Charles pockets it, collects his coffee and pie, and leaves.

I grab the stack of mail and go to place it in the mail caddy beneath the back counter. That's when I see it: a yellow slip of paper with the words **Late Rent Notice** in the caddy. I grab it, thinking what I'm reading has to be a mistake, but right behind it is a letter from *Marsden-Lindell Wealth Management*. Marsden-Lindell is the financial firm Auntie Nikki works at. And suddenly I remember how Mom was being weird yesterday when she mentioned she had a business meeting with my auntie. The way she'd smiled when saying everything was fine but still looked upset. Fresh worry sloshes around my stomach. Clutching the notice, I call out to Dad.

He pops his head out the swinging door. "Yes, Daughter of Mine?"

I hold the slip in the air. "What's this?"

He doesn't try to dodge the question with a plasticky smile like Mom did—he doesn't have the poker face for that. But he still plays in my face. He raises the wooden spoon in his hand and waves off my question. "Nothing for you to worry about."

I put a hand on my hip. "We don't lie to each other." I remind him of the Jackson Family Rule Number One. "Mom told me she had a meeting with Auntie Nikki yesterday. And now this? What's happening, Dad? Are we in trouble?"

Dad sighs. He must hear in my tone how desperate I am for straight answers because he cuts the crap and skips the part where he tries to treat me like a little kid who can't handle *adult* business. "I wasn't lying when I said this isn't something for you to worry about. But"—he sighs again and rubs the back of his neck—"we were late on the bakery's rent last month. We had to talk with your aunt about moving some money around."

My heart crashes against my chest. "So everything *isn't* all right like Mom said yesterday?"

He presses his lips together in the way he does when he wants to tell me the opposite of the truth to shield me from things.

"So that's a no?" I press, growing more concerned.

He gives a laugh that's forced—and transparently for my benefit. "It is, but I'll work it out. Rent on the place just went up this month."

"By how much?" I ask. Dad hesitates, so I ask again. "How much, Dad?"

"Two thousand dollars."

My stomach drops. "Is that much of a hike even legal?"

"That's what happens when capitalism meets gentrification," Dad grunts. "But with big money witches finding their prized, closed Coven communities crowded, we've now got witch-owned corporations turning an eye toward taking over neighborhoods occupied by regular folk to address witch housing shortages and other economic exigencies."

"Errrr, care to put that in nonbrainiac terms?" I ask Dad. I sort of get the gist of what my economics major and urban policy nerd father says, but not entirely.

"Sorry," Dad smiles. "You covered supply and demand in Econ last year, right? Think about it like this: among witches there's a high demand right now for more housing, more retail spaces, more eateries, more grocery stores, etcetera, that caters directly to their population. And the supply and availability of these things in their existing communities have become scarce since witchkind's numbers are growing as rapidly as the numbers of us ordinary people. So, they've got to find the land to throw more of these places up to meet their needs."

"Needs?" I cry. "Like those ridiculous outdoor mall and high-rise condo combinations, like The Spell Shoppes? Those are not *needs!*"

Dad bobs his head. "You're not wrong, kid. Unfortunately, cash and hobnobbing with the right government officials cinches whatever you want. And Coven witches play that game ruthlessly. The end result: Third Ward is getting hit with investors most people can't begin to fight back against. Coven-backed firms are buying up property, raising rents, and pushing us businesses—small or big—who don't cater exclusively to witch clientele out."

I wince, even though I have nothing to do with the types

of witches making things hard for Dad. Shady things like this are exactly why I've always struggled with being a witch. I am super glad my family lives outside of the Coven House system, which is comprised, 1,000 percent, of jerks. Even though witches no longer live in secret, they still choose to separate themselves from larger society, to a certain extent. They operate according to a maddening separate-from-and-better-than-you model. Not that I'm only now realizing it. My whole life I've known Coven witches think if you don't belong to a Coven House, you literally don't matter. It's the reason my mom's old Coven treated her and Dad (a nonwitch) so shitty when they decided to be together. It's why my mom went no contact with her parents and why we live outside of the Coven system. And now Coven witches are hurting my parents all over again. Sick over it all, I hug my stomach. "I'm so sorry, Dad. What can we do?"

"First, you have nothing to apologize for," Dad says adamantly. "Second, this isn't a *we* problem," he goes on. "It's a me problem, and you're doing more than enough already by giving up too many of your summer days to help out."

"I can give them all up," I offer quickly, returning to that former argument between us. "You can cut back on storefront payroll all the way, and I can come in every day." It's not like anybody would be losing hours and necessary pay. Dad's former full-time employee moved to Nevada at the beginning of the summer, and I convinced him to look for part-time staff and let me step in to fill the gap instead of hiring a new one. He hasn't hired a part-time person yet;

Mom has been helping out on the weekends when I'm off, and now I know why.

My stubborn, stubborn father shakes his head vehemently. "No." His tone leaves no room for argument. "You should get to enjoy your summer, too. Not be chained to the bakery every day."

I roll my eyes. "You're being dramatic. It's not that serious, and I want to help. I can have free time after I get off. We close at six. That's plenty of time to do other stuff."

"Cayden," Dad says. "Me and your mother are handling it. We've got things in the works to deal with the rent increase here and the one at the clinic." He grinds his jaw and abruptly stops talking.

My heartbeat kicks up another notch. "Both of your places are having rent increases at the same time?" That can't be good. It sounds like a potential disaster. "Will the businesses be okay? Will we be okay?"

He walks to me and plucks the late notice out of my hand. He gives me a hard, inflexible look. "Yes." He doesn't leave any room for argument about that, either. "We will be okay. We always are, aren't we? I mean it, this is nothing I want you to worry about. Mom and I are figuring it out. Promise me you won't worry."

"Cayden," he prods when I don't immediately make the promise, because he knows me. It's such a hard thing to do. How can I not worry when both my parents are struggling with something this huge?

"Cayden," Dad says again, and there's so much stress and

tension in his voice that I relent and just say, "Okay." I don't want to contribute to any more stress for him or Mom and if they know I'm worrying up a storm about this, it'll make them worry more about me worrying.

✦

Three hours and twenty minutes later, the bell jingles again. My cousin, Mercedes, walks inside. Dad and one of her moms, also an ordinary human, are siblings. We're the same age so we grew up really close. When I told her what I was doing for Dad, she insisted on working alongside me to help, too, and keep me company this summer. I can always count on Mercedes to be *ride-or-die* like that. It's why she's not only my cousin but my best friend.

    She nods what's up to me as she comes in rocking a white miniskirt, a sun-yellow blouse, flip-flops, and her box braids gathered high in a Beyoncé-bun. Gold hoops dangle from her ears. Mercedes stays flawless and gorgeous. She comes to stand next to me behind the counter, taking her place as my work partner for the rest of the day. Despite us being in a bakery, I feel severely underdressed beside her in my standard summer fit of shorts, cute sneakers (my kicks game is strong all day, every day, so I'm sporting a pair of grape-purple Nike Air Max 90s), and a crop top. My hair is also way less stylish than hers; I threw it up in a messy ponytail before I left the house. But despite the difference in dress code, people mistake us for sisters all the time. We both have Grams's dark brown skin, dark brown eyes, and high cheekbones.

The bell chimes, and it's a paying customer this time! I'm elated, but worry still gnaws at me after seeing that late rent notice; it's almost noon and this is our first customer since Mr. Charles. And it's also another one of our regulars. Which is good, but we need our dedicated patrons *and* an influx of new ones.

"Hi!" I say brightly to Mrs. Morris, putting my concerns aside.

Mrs. Morris orders her usual, a Texas-sized cheesecake brownie and cinnamon dolce cappuccino. She's an older woman who works as the dean's assistant at South Texas University, and she ducks into the bakery every weekday about this time on her lunch break.

"I got the cappuccino," Mercedes says. She walks to the espresso machine while I grab the cheesecake brownie from the display case. The dessert is room temperature and tasty as is, but I use magic to warm it up to extra yummy, fresh-out-of-the-oven levels before handing it over.

I ring Mrs. Morris up and thank her for her continued business. She asks after Mom and Dad and if I'm looking forward to senior year. When I tell her I am and that I plan to go to Howard after I graduate, she peers at me, wounded. Her New Orleans accent jumps out thick as she says, "What you goin' way ova there for? You got a perfectly good HBCU right chea' at home with South Texas."

"STU is fantastic," I assure Mrs. Morris. "But I wanna go away. I've lived in Houston my whole life." And it gets me far, far away from Texas Covens. Yeah, Washington, DC, has them, too; they're everywhere. But given my parents' history, I harbor extra-special grievances toward Texas Covens. Mom's old Coven is up in Dallas, but the Houston Coven was just as nasty to her and Dad when they relocated here.

Mrs. Morris sucks her teeth, but nods. The heavy New Orleans accent dwindles now that she's no longer incensed. "I guess. As long as it's an HBCU, I'm happy for you." She winks at me, takes a humongous bite out of her brownie, and hums contently. She eyes me with a knowing gleam. "You just warmed this right chea' up on the spot, yeah?"

"I did," I answer sheepishly.

Mrs. Morris raises her brownie in the air, as if toasting to me. "*Beeeybee*, I bet its neat for yo' daddy to have you around more this summer. Being able to slide folks freshly hot pastries on demand is quite the flex for a bakery!" She eats another mouthful of cheesecake brownie, then walks off to take a seat at one of the tables by the street-side windows. I stand up straighter, prouder, at Mrs. Morris's compliment. I might have issues with trash-fire Covens and all the BS they're about, but I *do* like—adore actually—having magic. Magic in general *can* be really cool when folks use it to help others out in big and small ways. It just so happens that most witches who belong to Covens are snooty jerks who wouldn't know what *community* means if it bit them in the butt.

After Mrs. Morris leaves, we get a few more customers before things turn dead again. Dad is making the bulk of his money these days from cakes he bakes for weddings, birthdays, and other special events. Which is great, but Cayden's Confections is Dad's baby, and he'd be crushed if he had to close the bakery front.

Please don't let Dad have to close down. Please let him and Mom find a way to afford the rent hike here and at the clinic. I put the desire into the universe with a hope that it'll manifest into reality. Expressed desires with intent behind them have power, and the Ancestors are always listening and making stuff happen for us. I make a mental note to repeat the desire and put it into the universe while burning a green candle (for prosperity) dressed with an oils mixture of wild orange, frankincense, clary sage, and patchouli (for abundance). For an added boost, I'll lay a pyrite (a powerful manifestation stone) beside my prosperity candle as it burns. Which reminds me ... I reach under the register to grab my purse and take out a small bag of on-the-go stones I keep with me. I drop a green aventurine (for attracting wealth wherever you want cash to grow) into the register. I'm sure Mom has already done the same for the vet clinic. Though, business there is booming. (Her clients know about her Connection with their pets and won't trust any other vet with their care because of it.) A rent hike on the clinic alone wouldn't be a problem, but a double rent hike, plus our mortgage, plus the bakery not doing so well, might stretch my parents thin.

"Everything all right?" Mercedes asks, nodding at the

register. She isn't a witch in the sense of having Coven roots and a Connection, but she keeps up with my practices and has become interested in the modern Black girl witch movement (BGWM) that's gained popularity outside the Coven House system and is pretty cool! Unlike the Coven system, BGWM isn't about long-lived family lines or who has what Connection. Instead, it comprises all types of women across the diaspora interested in exploring their cultural roots and the practices of their Ancestors that slavery and then post-slavery times labeled as "evil." I've been interested in it, too. I can't lie; I do sometimes really long for a community like that. I have my parents and the rest of my dad's family, obviously, but not belonging to a Coven means I don't hang out with other witches much. Not that I would want to, anyway, with the way they treat outsiders.

I tell Mercedes about our rent problems, and she scowls. "Fuck gentrification," she says, sounding a lot like Dad. "Damn. I really hate this. Is there something we can do to help? I mean something other than our summer shifts?"

"He said no. That it's not for me to worry about."

She gives me a *screw that* look. "Nah, we're doing more. We need to think of something else." Her eyes light up. "Maybe we can brainstorm some ways to drum up business for the place? I don't know, like a fun block party sponsored by the bakery?"

"A block party might be a good idea!" I say, getting excited. "Or wait... What about a cookout?" I squeal as the idea fully takes shape. "We could hold one in a park to spread community awareness; good BBQ and good desserts always brings folks out. And if we hold a rally against the damn witches messing up our neighborhood, we might be able to reel in some local news coverage! Gentrification is a huge topic, literally everywhere, and—"

"News coverage of an event where *Cayden's Confections* catered the desserts is instant publicity." Mercedes finishes for me. She whoops and slides her phone out of her pocket. "I'll start researching possible news and radio stations and how to reach out to them."

I do a happy dance; this idea might really work! "And when we contact them and explain the bakery might have to close down because of witch developers, we can toss in Mom and Dad's Coven history, too," I add. People also love a good underdog story, and the mess Coven folk have pulled might as well do something good for our family for a change. That part is me *squeezing lemonade out of lemons, suga*, as Mr. Charles would say.

"I'm with it all," Mercedes says, intently reading a web page on her phone. "We are doing this damn thing for Uncle Jason!"

"Errr... what are y'all doing for me?"

She and I both startle at Dad's unexpected voice. "Well, we were thinking," I start. "What if we hold a cookout and community rally and invite some news folks to cover it? Two birds, one stone. Save the bakery and make some noise."

"Y'all are amazing, you know that?" Dad says when I'm done. He swallows me up and then Mercedes in huge hugs.

"Ooh, now y'all really got me thinking," he says after he releases Mercedes. "I'm not gonna take over your project. But whatever you need from me to set this up, I'll make it happen. I'm gonna contact my frat brothers about providing the BBQ plates, and I'll talk to some of the other businesses in the neighborhood that have been impacted by The Spell Shoppes's construction. If we're doing this, I want to have them involved as well, so as many small-business owners as possible get the support they need."

Of course he thinks about the collective community first and solving his individual problems second. He wouldn't be Jason Jackson if he didn't.

A timer dings in the kitchen. Dad tells us how proud he is of us one more time before rushing off to go take something out of the oven.

My phone buzzes beneath the counter. I grab it and see a message from Starry Night Boy. Hell yes! This day is really on the upswing! If I can cinch him as a win for myself, I can do the same for Dad with the bakery. Clearly, I've got the special juice like that.

> Are you still free tomorrow? Hades should be cool. He's already right at home!

"Oooh! Who's texting you?" Mercedes nosily asks.

I don't even try to play off the Kool-Aid smile as I text Khy it's a go on my end. "This boy I met at the rescue yesterday," I answer, cheesing harder. "We've got plans to go out, and everything about him is spectacular. Look at this. He's fine and has a cool swag that isn't trying to be extra tough or whatever." I show her the picture Khy sent after asking about our date. It's a selfie of Hades snuggled up in his lap while he sits cross-legged in his STU hoodie on a comfy-looking, massive couch. Hades is dressed in the cutest *Lore Olympus* bandana. I giggle at Khy's humor in choice of attire and keep giggling at his next message.

See. No dog serial killer over here.

The next pic that comes is one of his—very kissable lips—twisted sideways as if to say, *Yeah, girl. You were on one. But we're good.*

Picking up the game, I take a selfie with my tongue out as my rebuttal, make sure it's cute, and press send. Before I know it, I'm clutching the phone to my chest like it's a bouquet of freaking roses or something while I'm waiting on his reply. I stiffen. Oh, helllll no. This is not what that is. Flirting is one thing. Thirsting is acceptable, too. But that supremely mushy move? *Summer fling: that's all he is*, I remind myself. Clearly, I'm tripping.

"Ugh!" I groan, giving myself a firm mental shake. I shove the phone at Mercedes. "Can you take this away before I embarrass myself *and* break my rule of not stumbling into anything serious headed into senior year?"

She doesn't follow directions. My delightful cousin simply stands there and pops her lips, a slick look on her face.

"Good luck with that, Sis." Her eyes swipe down the length of me, then back up. "From over here, you've already got it bad."

I flip her off. "Ha! Absolutely not," I snort. "We just met. It's impossible."

My phone vibrates, and why the hell does my heart skip some beats? Mercedes isn't right, is she? She can't be. That's ridiculous. My bizarre reactions are *only* thirst related. The boy is hot. Of course, I'm giddy talking to him and anxious to hang out. Nobody actually falls, in any manner, for somebody they only had one convo with that lasted for a measly half hour.

Do they?

Chapter Four

I stand in line beside my Summer Hottie—*nothing else*—at Maynard Manor, a year-round haunted house. According to the ticket I'm holding, it's the only one in Texas.

"This is . . . an unexpected choice for a date," I say to Khy. He offered to let me choose, but nah. Even hookups must pass certain tests. Pretty Boy Swag isn't enough to carry Khy beyond a first date and make him a shoo-in for the entire summer. He's gotta come harder. The pic with Hades was a start. But I need more solid evidence he isn't a raging jerk. This summer of freedom and fun before all the brutal SAT retakes, college apps, AP exams, and anxiously awaiting admission decisions that'll come with senior year is too precious to waste on some guy I'll end up itching to push off a cliff.

"I wanted to make a good impression with something unusual and fun," Khy responds, winning himself a second check in the *Not-a-Butthole* column. "I figured something less basic might wow you into saying yes to a date two." When he grins sheepishly, dimples punch deep into his brown cheeks, and my knees do that wobbly thing they did back at the rescue. I tell them to get themselves together, because *no. They may not go all wobbly over this boy.* While thirst is free to soar as high as it wants, wobbly knees veer too close to off-limits territory of the heart.

"And you concluded that a haunted house in the middle of June would achieve that?" I arch an eyebrow at the weird choice. It certainly is a first. I've never had a boy try to charm me with a haunted house date offseason before. When I'd told him to pick, I'd assumed we'd be doing something like dinner, or a movie, or an arcade, or a water park, or something normal. Not a haunted house when Halloween is eight months behind us. Though, I am interested and, all right, extremely excited. I like haunted houses way too much. From mid-September through October 31, I drag my friends to a different haunt every weekend. DemonWorld and its seven realms of hell has been the scariest so far, but FearFarm is a whole experience, complete with creepy Annabelle-like dolls chasing you through the woods. I never wanna leave either at the end of the night!

I eye Maynard Manor, wondering why I've never been here before and how it'll measure up to my favorites.

"I've learned that the unconventional impresses girls more," Khy says.

I snort. "So you've had a lot of practice with impressing girls?"

"Nuh uh. Nah. Nope." He shakes his head vigorously. "I am not walking into *that*. Don't want you to get the wrong idea about me."

I smirk. "Too late."

His above-reproach expression turns serious. "For real, though. I'm not that kind of guy."

Is he that type of guy, though? He is hot *and* rich. That's like a trademark player combo. *Buuuuut*, if this is only a summer thing and I'm not looking for a boyfriend, does it matter? The answer should be no, yet for some inexplicable reason I'm worried that he might be.

"I'll prove it to you," he says, brows furrowed earnestly. *Or it could be part of his game. Pretty rich boys* are *normally insanely smooth,* and *it's usually completely bogus.* "I promise I'm keeping it one hundred," Khy vows as if he's read my mind. "You'll see."

"Don't worry about it," I tell him, shaking off my apprehension. He and I aren't gonna get serious, regardless, so there's no need to hold him to boyfriend-level expectations.

We're still not at the front of the line. With Halloween four months away, the haunt has a lot of customers. "This better be good," I warn Khy in a teasing tone. "I'm a haunted house fanatic as much as I'm a sneakerhead."

He looks me over appreciatively. "Me too," he says as if smitten. And gah! Why does him looking at me that way make my stomach do flip-flops. *Stop,* I order it. *You're not allowed to go all heart-eyes-emoji over him.* "I come to this place at least four times a year. I promise it's good." Khy winks at me. It's the kind of wink only swoon-worthy TV heroes (like the Duke of Hastings on the *Bridgerton* Netflix show) can pull off. It should look corny in real life. It doesn't. My knees try to wobble again. I lock my legs tight. "And supposedly it's *actually* haunted," Khy finishes saying.

The statement gives me something concrete to focus on that's not his absurd, unrealistic wink, or his kissable wide lips, or the way his *BANZAI PIPELINE, OAHU* T-shirt clings to his chest, showing off muscles beneath the block letters. Nicely sculpted ones. *You're a teenage boy!* I yell at him in my head, growing irrationally angry. *Why do you have those?!*

"Are you an athlete?" I blurt out. I want an answer for the offending muscles.

He tips his head. "I swim competitively and play water polo."

Alrighty. He plays water polo, and he's rich, and he drives a Porsche. That brings us to a whopping sum of three standard requirements Khy's got for the Bougie Boys Club. His membership is practically diamond level. I really, really, really cannot stand rich jerks. And while that might be rooted in my dislike for Coven witches, regular old human snobs usually are no better. Globs of money, plus power, plus privilege have a way of making folks feel free to be awful.

I slide my hands into the pockets of my shorts, keeping it cool, however. I resist jumping to conclusions. To be fair, Khy hasn't done anything remotely jerklike. I afford him the benefit of the doubt. For now. "That's right. You said you surf. You're into water a lot, huh?"

"I am. I have a, uh, natural talent for water sports," he says, tripping over his words for a moment. He smiles with his whole face, big and wide. I swear to the Ancestors it drops a mic on the sun. His smile does gorgeous, oxygen-stealing, cardiac-arrest-inducing things to his face.

We finally reach the front of the line, and I wave my entry ticket between us like it's battle armor that'll shield me from being speared even more by that smile. The ghoul standing in front of a red velvet rope takes our tickets before unhooking the rope and ushering us through.

I focus on the thrill of experiencing a new haunt instead of Khy's dimples, or my response to them, or the fact that him choosing this date spot would make me consider him for boyfriend material in a hot second—if I was looking for one.

As we walk up steps that lead to a big porch, there's no cheesy, slasher-movie music playing, which is promising. The haunts that play dramatic music tend to be corny.

A second ghoul, dressed in an asylum patient's tattered, dirty rags, mans the front door. He doesn't speak when we approach. He silently pushes the door open and gives us a wide, deranged grin that's a touch sinister. Chills skitter down my spine, and I love it. Growing more excited, I step into Maynard Manor beside Khy. Like the poster beside the ticket counter said, Maynard Manor is an actual haunted house in Galveston, Texas. It was the home of a real-life man named Dr. Homer Maynard. Legend has it he was a twentieth-century psychologist who ran an asylum out of his house and performed illegal experiments on his patients. Supposedly, the souls of the patients Maynard's experiments killed are trapped inside his old house, and there have been actual ghost sightings around the manor at all times of day.

The first floor of the manor is as awesomely creeptastic as the estate from *Crimson Peak*—one of my favorite movies since it's a perfect mix of gothic and ghostly and mysterious and romantic—and everything a girl could want! It also is the perfect facsimile of a decaying mansion.

"The decor is nice, but where are the jump scares?" I ask, looking around for an asylum patient, zombie, or ghoul to jump out from behind one of the frayed tapestries or faded portraits of a white man who's a touch too pretty (which lets you know something was seriously wrong with the good Dr. Maynard; pretty boys are *trouble*).

"Just wait," Khy whispers, as we move through the entry parlor and toward the grand staircase. "The ground floor is used to set the mood and reel you in. Make you nice and comfy so you relax your guard. Then..." His eyes travel up the stairs. "I won't spoil it," he says, with a thankfully less high-wattage grin.

"It's okay," I reply, eagerly. "You can tell me now. I like spoilers. Love them, in fact! They make the experience all the better knowing what's coming."

He makes a choking sound. "You what? See, that's unholy."

I shrug. "To each their own."

He shakes his head, still looking at me like my confession is making the Ancestors turn over in their graves. His expression is so funny that I burst out laughing. He does, too.

"I don't think we're supposed to be laughing. We are terrible haunted house–goers," I whisper-cackle.

He clutches his stomach, laughing harder. "You right. You right."

As soon as our feet touch the second floor, an ear-shattering scream rips through the air, causing me to jump.

"Told you it gets good," Khy chuckles.

I raise my chin. I'm better than this. I've walked through the creepiest of haunts without losing it. "That reaction was only because I didn't expect it."

His mouth twitches, and he claps my shoulder. "I didn't stop jumping at all the spooks on this floor until my tenth time visiting."

The second story no longer looks like an old mansion. There's no worn tapestries or portraits. The floor beneath our feet is yellow tile, the walls are dingy white, and cracked, buzzing, fluorescent lights hang from the ceiling. Bloody handprints blot the ugly walls and more blood (or what is meant to look like blood) is smeared across the hideous floor. This landing looks like we've stepped onto a ward of an abandoned asylum—an asylum where some serious stuff went down. The lights overhead wink out and plunge us into darkness. I blink rapidly, and my eyes take an extended moment to adjust. When I can pseudo see, the hallway is only an inky outline of shadows. Then, the chilling screams kick up a notch.

BOOM!

I jump again. The sound comes from my left. Ghostly moaning swirls around us, and I cheese hard. "Okay. This is getting good."

A small light flickers on to illuminate a corridor to our left with a rickety sign that says "PATIENT ROOMS 1–24" above an archway with peeling, yellow paint. I start in that direction. Obviously, it's the route we're supposed to take through the manor since it's the only one visible.

"What happens next?" I ask Khy.

He purses his lips together and mimes locking them with a key.

I roll my eyes. Then, for added measure, gently elbow him in the side. "You suck."

"Really? I think I'm pretty awesome."

"You would," I mutter, "most boys like you do."

His eyebrows do that thing where they wrinkle together again, and I'm certain he's about to say something in defense of himself. But then loud knocking floods the space around us. The new hallway we're on has doors running the length of it, spaced about three feet apart. We come to one door marked "Room 13." It swings open on its own.

Khy offers me his arm. "Would you like to hold on for this part?" he teases.

He gets served a scathing side-eye. "You are *so* unserious right now. Does that line really work on the girls you bring here?"

I shoot a pointed, faux-irritated look to his raised arm and scoff. "I don't need it." I enter the room, leaving him in the hallway.

I hear the amused chuckle behind me, and then he's standing at my side where I stop a few feet inside the door.

In the room, there's a man strapped to a bed. He's screaming as a second man in doctor's scrubs stands over him. The doctor has a roaring chainsaw poised over the patient's abdomen. He lowers the tool toward the screaming man, but then he pauses an inch away from the chainsaw shredding the man's intestines. The doctor turns our way. He cocks his head in an inhuman fashion. A demonic grin crawls onto his face. A fresh delicious chill skitters down my spine. I almost shiver, but at the last second, I lock my muscles tight. I will not give Khy's smug self the satisfaction. The good doctor, Dr. Maynard, I assume, takes a gleeful stride toward us. "I enjoy newcomers," he says in a voice that sounds like Pennywise. This time, I do shudder because I *hate* that movie. Evil clowns are unnatural and terrifying.

Khy leans into me. "Still don't want the arm?" he says, being a smartass.

I decide not to deign to respond.

Dr. Maynard takes one step and then two and then a third toward us, repeating the same chilling phrase over and over. "I enjoy newcomers. I enjoy newcomers. I enjoy newcomers." He keeps walking until he's standing an inch away. My heart thuds in my chest.

"I enjoy newcomers," he repeats while staring dead at me. Then he lunges for me.

I scream. I grab Khy's arm, clinging to him with a death grip. My face is buried in his shoulder before I truly process my actions. My waist tingles where his arm is slung around it, holding me tightly. "You okay?" Khy asks.

Full awareness that I've practically plastered myself to his side slams into me. If it wasn't for his voice ringing with genuine concern, instead of sounding mocking, I'd try my hardest to burn a hole into the floor with my magic and plunge right into the center of the Earth. I disentangle myself from Khy, collect my pride, and say calmly, "Yup. Totally cool."

"I enjoy newcomers." I stiffen when the nightmarish doctor utters that god-awful phrase once more. Thank the freaking Ancestors, it's for the last time. Afterward, Dr. Maynard stalks back to his victim strapped to the bed.

I walk out of the room, quickly, and return to the safety of the hall.

The rest of the rooms we walk through paint scenes as eerie as the first. They each have their own version of a Dr. Maynard, talking in that hellish Pennywise voice. I manage not to turn Khy into a human plushie again. But only barely.

✦

"Okay, I'm high-key obsessed with haunts," I say as we walk out of Maynard Manor, "but this one is a no for me. I will not be returning."

"Told you it wouldn't disappoint," Khy says with a laugh in his voice.

I point back at the house I never want to enter again. "It was cool, but the clown from *It* voice that all the Dr. Maynards spoke in? *Helllll* no."

Khy shivers. "Yeah, that is pretty scary."

"I hate clowns," I admit. "I watched the original *It* movie with my cousin when we were eight. That was the worst mistake of my life. I fell asleep and dreamed about a clown sitting in the rocking chair in the corner of my room watching me with these soulless eyes and freaky smile." I suck in a sharp breath through my nose. "I swear I still have that damn dream sometimes."

Khy's lips twist like he's trying not to burst out laughing.

I swat his arm. "It's not funny. Don't laugh at my trauma."

"I'm not laughing. Though it's *soooo* hard not to."

I scowl.

"If it makes you feel better," he says, "I'm terrified of butterflies because of a childhood movie debacle."

My mouth drops open. "Butterflies?"

Okay, now it's my turn to try hard not to laugh. Unlike him, I lose the battle. I giggle hysterically.

"Hey!" he says. "I at least tried with your confession."

"I tried," I say, still dying with laughter. "But I'm sorry. That is just so ridiculous and bizarre. For real, you're scared of butterflies?"

"Yes." The boy is dead serious. "I watched this wild movie with my brother when I was little: *Attack of the Killer Zombie Butterflies from Outer Space*. The creatures started off looking like regular, cutesy, tiny butterflies. But when they got hungry, they morphed into ginormous, man-eating monsters that looked deadass like orcs with wings. They'd swoop down from the sky and tear off human heads in one bite." As he gulps, his Adam's apple bobs. "Ever since that movie, I do not fuck with butterflies."

By the end of the story, I'm cracking up to the point of crying. "I'm terrible for laughing," I wheeze through the few breaths I catch. "But oh my God. That is too hilarious."

He clutches his heart like he did outside the rescue. "See, now you've wounded me a second time. I'm crushed. You gotta make it up somehow."

I roll my eyes. "This is where you ask me to kiss you and make it better?" I ask, then immediately regret it. Why am I bringing up kissing right now?!

His forehead wrinkles. "No. That mess sounds corny.

Also, I'm not into emotional manipulation to get girls to kiss me. That'd make me a loser and an asshole."

I nod, impressed, and he triples in hotness. "It would." *Please let him keep being one of the rare decent rich boys*, I shamelessly pray to the Ancestors. Not that they'd take a vested interest in a teen's love affairs—I mean, *flings*. Doesn't hurt to toss the want out there to increase the odds, however.

"Look at that," Khy says, tilting his head at a car creeping to the top of a nearby wooden coaster on the Pier 21 Boardwalk. I catch the mischievous glint in his eyes and nail exactly why he calls my attention to it. He's trying to see if I'm game to ride. Is he pitching me his own test? I stand up taller, insulted if he's guessing my answer might be anything other than yes.

Amused, I study him. His hands are shoved in the pockets of his blue cargo shorts, and he's doing a good job of displaying nonpushy indifference to my answer. Until the coaster reaches the top. A breath later, it plunges to the earth, and Khy's eyes light up like a little kid's during Christmas or Yule, witches' winter holiday. (In my house, we celebrate both.)

I call him on it. "You like roller coasters."

"Yup," he admits, studying me back. "Do you? You seem like the type." Like with the haunted house, there's an appreciative note in his voice.

"I'm not any *type*," I make clear. "But yes, I do."

He points at the coaster. It's called the Twisted Octopus. "You wanna take a spin?"

Much like haunted houses and sneakers, roller coasters

are my kryptonite. That goes quadruple for ones with the heart-in-your-throat drop I just witnessed and the four loops on the track. So I say, "Absolutely," and decide that Khy isn't *near perfect*, he *is* perfect.

It should set off all types of alarm bells. But me having any good, sensible judgment right now is shot to crap.

Chapter Five

We ride the Twisted Octopus seven times. It more than lives up to the hype, and Khy is the perfect person to ride with. Not afraid to keep his arms up the whole time, not afraid to whoop and scream. So when Khy asks if I want to grab food after, I say yes, and we end up at Laveau's Gumbo House. I swear he must be psychic or something because he's nailing all my favorites—haunted houses, coasters, *and* seafood! Seriously, though, how do we both love so many of the same things?

As the hostess walks us to a table set for two overlooking the ocean, I ask Khy suspiciously, "Did you get a message from someone named Mercedes recently?" It's the precise sort of thing that Mercedes—who swears I've got it bad for Khy, can never mind her own business, and likes to prove a point—would do.

"Uh, no? Who's Mercedes?" Khy's forehead wrinkles, which I'm learning is a (really adorable) trademark expression whenever he's confused.

"I—uhhh . . ."

"Hi! I'm Kami!" says a chipper, pretty white girl who walks up to our table in a mermaid costume. I turn to her, infinitely grateful that her presence derails having to explain yet another embarrassing, *wrong* assumption I've jumped to. How does this boy have me so off kilter? "Welcome to Laveau's Gumbo House!" continues the merwoman. All the waitstaff are dressed as supernatural creatures. In addition to merpeople, there are werewolves, vampires, and ghouls servicing tables.

"What appetizers and drinks can I start you off with?" Kami asks. She's talking to both of us, but her eyes are solely on Khy. Of course. Regardless of the fact that she appears about five years too old for him. The boy is gorgeous. Kami can see it. *I* can see it. Heck, *anything* with eyes could see it. I do a happy jiggle on the inside that he's turning out to be more than decent.

"What would you like?" Khy asks me. That's when I notice the quizzical, amused way he's looking at me with one eyebrow half-cocked. His expression makes me realize that I was for sure staring at him. Like *thirsty open staring*, as opposed to drinking in casual, brief glances. Gah!

I scowl, trying to cobble together a scrap of self-respect. "I'd like the crab cakes and a frozen virgin hurricane, please,"

I say to our waitress. "Water, too," I add. My throat has gone super dry while ogling Khy.

Kami genially nods and punches the request into the tablet she's holding. "And for you?" Her voice definitely drops to a flirty octave when she asks Khy what he wants. *He's a teenage boy!* I want to yell at her. Honestly, I really don't know why I'm so annoyed by the fact that she doesn't seem to realize it—and that she probably wouldn't care if she did. She'd likely still be checking him out.

Like you're doing, a voice that sounds suspiciously like Mercedes pipes up.

I'm his age, I snark back. *It's not creepy coming from me.*

Khy must notice the way she's checking him out because he shifts uncomfortably in his seat. And then I go from annoyed to pissed. "He's seventeen," I tell Kami, and okay, I could be a bit less bitchy when I do, but also, she needs to get her life— and her eyes—together.

Her cheeks flush red. "Oh ... umm ... sorry," she says, fumbling with the tablet. "But I ... I swear that's not why I was staring. He just ..." she turns from me to Khy. "You look really familiar. Like famous and on-TV familiar? I can't place it, though."

Khy clears his throat. He turns so uncomfortable at the table that he becomes the embodiment of the expression *I want to turn to vapor right here in my chair.*

Then, I feel bad because shoot, did my mind being in the gutter make me misread the situation? Maybe I projected?

My cheeks warm, and I'm infinitely glad my skin is dark brown so the furious blush doesn't show. Did I accuse this poor woman of being sketchy when that's not what was going on at all?

"No, I'm so sorry," I say to our waitress, mortified. I'm going to have to leave her a gigantic tip just in case. If I have been crappy, it won't make up for things, but it'll still be a nice thing I can do.

What the hell is wrong with you? I berate myself. Was it jealousy? I don't even know Khy like that, *and* I have no claim to him. It's not like he's my boyfriend. Or I ever intend for him to be.

"Can I please get the calamari and a root beer float?" Khy asks the waitress, and I don't miss it as the evasion tactic it is. He didn't bother answering her question. Previous misjudgments aside, I have an impeccable bullshit meter when an actual lie—or lie by omission—is uttered. *Is* he famous? I eye him, curiosity piqued, wracking my brain for if I've seen him somewhere on TV or social media before. But he can't be TV/movie/music-star famous because there's no way we would've made it through an entire day together with this being the first time somebody noticed him. But he could be more low-key, social media famous.

The waitress types his order into her tablet, tells us she'll be back with the drinks and appetizers, and makes a getaway.

I look after her, then back at Khy. He's looking decidedly aghast, and I get extra suspicious. I narrow my eyes at him. "The waitress is right, isn't she?"

His rueful look reeks of guilt.

"I don't like being lied to," I say stiffly.

He grimaces and fixes his mouth to respond. But then he snaps it shut. Consternation creases his forehead. He rubs a hand over his eyes and then gives me a tight smile. I can tell he's grappling with something, but I don't let him worm off the hook. I cross my arms over my chest and wait for a truthful answer.

"I'm nobody, really," he finally mumbles. "But my mother is sort of, well, the United States' Witch Regent and works with the US President and Senate as witchkind's voice with the federal government. And my father sits on Texas's Witch Council, doing the same with politicians at the state level. And my grandmother is one of the Matriarchs who lead the Greater Houston Coven." He rubs the back of his head. "I'm uhhh . . . a witch. My family lines on both sides are supposedly big deals, but it's whatever. Our waitress probably just recognizes me from a photo op or interview or tabloid gossip or something. We're in the media a lot."

My jaw drops. It's thoroughly unattractive and rude, but I don't give a crap. The world literally comes to a screeching halt. Or at least it tries to. But it's like being behind the wheel of a car when you don't hit the brakes fast enough and crash into another car anyway. I grab my stomach under the table, sipping in air that doesn't ease the guilt stabbing into me. *Oh no. No. No. No.* I retreat behind denial. *This isn't happening. This can't be happening.*

Even though I didn't know Khy was a freaking Coven

witch, sitting across from him in the restaurant, laughing my head off on the coaster, loving the haunted house, the dozens of flirty texts we exchanged over the previous days—all of it is the worst betrayal to Mom and Dad. It's a slap in the face to everything they stand for, every value they've taught me, and all the sacrifices they made to be together. And if they knew I was associating with someone like him, oh God. They'd be so hurt. It'd reopen old wounds.

I *knew* something was off with Khy. My bullshit radar, while unhelpfully unclear, is functioning perfectly. Earlier when he'd been talking about all the water sports he does, he had been, without question, about to say he had a *Connection* with water—*because he's a damn member of a Coven House!*

Worse, he's not *only* a Coven Boy. He's a freaking *Royal Boy*. His mom is basically the queen of all USA witches, his dad is the Coven world's equivalent of a state senator, and his grandmother is a Coven leader. His family members being big deals is an understatement. Like extreme, colossal understatement. I manage to hold in a raspy laugh. I am so irked at myself for letting this date get this far and not figuring out why my internal alarms kept blaring.

My face must show everything I'm feeling about the revelation, because Khy drags in a heavy breath. "Well, that's one of the reactions I always get when people find out." He laughs, trying to make it light and unbothered, but there's a bitter quality to it. "Either I'm hated for who my family is or loved way too much and way too phony-like for it."

Something about that last part he tacks on chips away at

the irritation and hardened exterior I've been building up. My heart squeezes at the solemn way he says it, and it makes me want to reply with something not as scathing as I'd planned. I fumble for words that won't be too harsh and hurt his feelings more. I don't actually owe him an explanation or any niceties. But he has been really decent today, and he hasn't done anything remotely jerkish in nature, and he was sweet with Hades at the rescue, and *sigh*, I really don't enjoy dumping on people unless they prove they deserve it. I scrounge together the ability to speak, along with a smidgen of grace, and try to explain. "It's not you that I hate," I say, gently. "You seem great. At the moment. But, I'm a witch, too," I admit my own secret. For some mystifying reason I take it a step further, laying out my family wounds. "So is my mom. But my dad isn't. And when she fell in love with him and decided to marry him back before I was born, her Coven reacted..."

"Shitty as hell?" Khy finishes for me.

I'm a little surprised (pleasantly, I hate to admit) he'd say that, but continue on. "Well, yes. I've got major issues with it all. Her Coven tried to force her to choose between it and my dad. She chose my dad and was excommunicated from her Coven and her family. Coven Houses and the entire system can kiss my ass."

I've met a few Coven kids before, and we had this exact conversation when I finally decided to tell them I was a witch, too. They tried to defend the Coven system and argue for its traditions. We immediately stopped associating. It's why I don't date Coven boys or befriend any Coven kids anymore. They're usually all the same. Except...

Khy doesn't try to justify the supposedly great and esteemed Coven House system that he belongs to. Instead, he regards me pissed. "That's such bullshit. I'm sorry you and your parents have to deal with that foolery."

"Huh?" It's the only word my brain manages to formulate at first. "I've never heard that from a Coven kid before."

Khy grimaces again. "I'm sure. We're..."

"Stuck up, brainwashed, bougie, elitist, judgy, cliquey?"

He huffs a good-natured laugh. "All of that." He massages his chest. "That's the third time, girl. Damn."

At his repeated mimicking of being wounded by me, I laugh, too. "Sorry," I say, and I realize that I genuinely, surprisingly am. "It's the truth, though."

"You right."

Kami comes back with our appetizers and drinks, then asks about our orders.

Khy gazes at me, hopeful despite everything. Is he for real? I want to snap at him to show his jerk side already so I can feel less bad about what I'm about to say. Ugh! That hopeful expression remains in place while he graciously, and respectfully, and sweetly waits for me to be the one to decide if dinner continues.

"Sorry," I tell him. "I should go. I told you about my family's issues with Coven folk, and I have a strict policy about y'all because of it. I do not do friendships, relationships, or even *casualships* with Coven kids. I can't have anything to do with a Coven or people that belong to one." I fish my debit card out of my purse and hand it to Kami. "I'd like to pay for my half of the bill, please?" She glances at Khy sympathetically, takes my card, and speed walks away.

"I was going to pay for dinner," Khy mutters.

"I can pay for my own food," I mutter back.

"Can we—"

"Yo! Khy!" A white boy with blond hair shouts his way from across the restaurant. He's standing in front of the hostess stand with three other boys and two girls. The group steps around the stand and walks up to our table. "Dude, are you for real on a date? You didn't tell us! Who even is she?" Okay, I don't at all like the way the white boy says *who even is she*, like I'm, in fact, nobody. I'm already on edge, and I've got the time today.

"I'm Cayden," I say. He can get all the business if he's about to roll up being rude.

Khy looks between me and the group, helpless. "These are my friends," he says, tightly. He points to the out-of-pocket white boy. "This is Jordan." Next, he points to the Black boy with a short, curly Afro standing beside him. He doesn't come off as any more genial. "That's Darius." He points to the last guy, a tall Latino boy with brown hair, and the girls (one is Black with long, straight hair, and the other is Asian with short, dark hair cut into a bob) and names them each in turn. "That's Geo, Naomi, and Becca."

Only the Asian girl, Becca, gives me a warm smile and says, "Hello." Though she also looks me up and down suspiciously.

"Where'd she come from?" Naomi asks, like I'm not sitting at the table.

I read exactly what Khy's friends are about. "Other Coven kids?" I ask him. I turn to the group. "Let me guess, you've all come to rescue your friend from looking bad because he's stooped so low as to go on a date with someone who isn't an acceptable and respectable Coven girl?" It's how Mom's parents, extended relatives, and friends reacted when she started dating Dad.

Khy casts me an apologetic look.

"Yes, we're crashing your date," Geo asserts.

"Call it a rescue mission," Jordan says.

Naomi pats Khy's shoulder, and the way she does it is so ludicrous. It's that pitying, light pat that people give out at funerals—I'm immediately more insulted. Is that how she sees his date with me? "This is for your own good," Naomi says. She turns to me with a wince, finally deciding I'm worth acknowledging. "Yours too, sweetie. He's a mess for this."

Darius pulls up a chair from an empty table and plops down in it like he was invited. "Bruh, if people get wind of this, it's going to be a catastrophe," he says to Khy. To me, he says, "It'll be one for you, too. Cayden, was it?"

Well, at least the butthole remembered my name.

"Y'all are doing the most," Khy grits out. He throws them—and me—that helpless look again, and I roll my eyes because seriously, is that all he's got?

Jordan shrugs. "Rashaud told us you were out on a date with . . ." he slides a glance to me. "Some random girl." He shakes his head. "Nah, dude. It's going to blow up in your face. This isn't how to do things. Let's get out of here."

"This was a *terrible* idea," Naomi hisses.

"Don't worry, I was just leaving," I say.

Right then, Kami comes back with my debit card and receipt, and her timing couldn't be more perfect because I'm about to either punch somebody or bawl—either one is equally likely and equally, colossally, awful. I'm pissed and mortified, and Khy and his friends have managed to make me feel teeny, tiny, small. Now *I* sit in my seat like I want to sink into the floor. I hastily scribble my signature and Kami's tip on the receipt, blinking back tears. Afterward, I drop my debit card in my purse and stand. "Have a good night," I say to Khy. I hate myself for letting my voice quiver. *At least his ugly side popped out, confirming its presence.* His friends were jerks simply because I'm an outsider, proving why I don't associate with Coven kids in the first place. And doubly proving why, Khy failed to check them for coming at me sideways. That pisses me off the most—and it hurts. It shouldn't because I barely know him, but it does.

As I leave, I unlock my phone and delete his stupid name and number. It makes me feel marginally better as I march out of the restaurant.

My phone rings when I get to my car in the nearby garage. A number pops up without a name. I recognize the area code as a part of Khy's number. I reject the call and block the number so he can't call or try to text again with some loser apology or excuse.

✦

"How was the haunted house?" Dad asks when I get home. I'm glad his eyes are glued to the TV, because he doesn't catch the wince. Neither does Mom. The pair of them are snuggled up on the living room couch engrossed in the latest *Annabelle* remake. Watching horror movies together as quality time has been their thing for as long as I can remember. When I was little, I'd plop myself between them with a big bowl of popcorn and insist the film wasn't scary. The only reason I don't do the same tonight is because of the guilt gnawing at me.

"Maynard Manor was fun," I say enthusiastically. Technically, that part *is* true. As far as the rest . . . I shut that line of thinking down hard before Dad's own bullshit radar goes off. He's where I inherited mine from, and I might've (*I definitely*) only told my parents I was meeting up with some friends. I didn't dive into specifics, inform them that my *friends* consisted of a singular person, or mention it was the kid from the rescue Mom already met. Summer hookups don't need nosy fathers insisting on meeting the guy who's taking me out and interrogating him.

I barely hold back the grimace. If my parents had insisted Khy needed to come over to the house before our date so they could get to know him better, him being a Coven witch might've come out then, and it would've completely blindsided them. I stare at my parents hugged up and completely in love on the couch and think about how much they sacrificed to be together and build a family. Mom gave up her entire Coven, her own parents included. And Dad endured the brutal vitriol and hurt that comes from being told you aren't "good enough" simply because you don't have the right social standing. Thinking of the mess Mom and Dad have always been open about makes the guilt sink its fangs in deeper. As inconspicuously as possible, I draw in a quiet, calming breath through my nose.

You're never seeing him again. Ever. It's a statement that's 100 percent true. I use the certainty to help myself not feel as awful about enjoying hanging out with Royal Coven Boy at first. *Yooo,* am I glad he exposed the other side of himself before the night was over. I dodged a flaming dumpster fire in so many ways.

Chapter Six

I've got an idea," Mercedes says as I check our family email for any messages regarding the cookout we're organizing. It's only been two days, but me, Mercedes, Dad, and even Mom have dived right into pulling together the cookout. Mom is setting up an adoption event to hold at the cookout to help draw additional folks in and cast a wider appeal for media coverage. Ideally, we want as many outlets covering the cookout as possible, and the ones that an anti-gentrification rally won't reel in, a feel-good story about rescue pups finding good homes should do the trick! We *need* the cookout to be spectacular and the talk of all of Houston. In fact, we need it to be so hugely popular that other regional news outlets, maybe even national ones, catch wind of it and possibly run the story. If that can happen, then Cayden's Confections, which is officially sponsoring the cookout, will immediately get massive, nationwide publicity. Hopefully, it'll lead to a major upswing in local business and out-of-town orders.

I quickly scan past an email about my AP Lit Summer Reading List to what's important in the inbox: Dad's STU frat alumni chapter has agreed to donate BBQ plates, and Mom's sorority is going to buy tons of gift cards to local businesses and raffle them off at the cookout. Hell yes! My parents' friends are showing out. I scan the rest of the emails—mostly spam messages—and bite my cheek. One of the duties Mercedes and I took was publicity management. We've sent dozens of emails to newspapers, news networks, radio stations, and local podcasters over the last couple of days. I don't see a single response from anyone yet. We *need* this piece of the plan to come together, too, and in a big way. The whole success of the cookout hinges on news coverage, dang it.

A green sparkly nail snaps an inch away from my face. Mercedes smacks her teeth. "Dang, Sis. I'm over here planning murder on your behalf, and you're just gonna ignore me? See, being a ride-or-die gets no appreciation."

"Huh?" Clearly, I missed something. "I have no idea what you're talking about."

"Focus, girl." Mercedes draws out each syllable as she claps. "This is important, so we do it clean and avoid jail. As I was saying, the junk Coven Boy and his little friends pulled last night cannot go unanswered. We find where he stays, stuff him in your trunk, drive to a river, put the car in neutral, and push it into the water. *Pow!* Retaliation is coming for ol' boy. When are we striking? It has to be sometime at night so we aren't easily identified. And we need to wear all black. I'll coordinate our outfits; they'll be cute. And find ski masks."

"Hold up!" It takes my mind a few seconds to fully shift from worrying about the bakery to worrying over my cousin legit sounding like a mafia boss—albeit one weirdly concerned with retaining fashionista status while murking somebody. "You've been watching too many gangster movies," I finally say. "We can't murder K—" I mush my lips together because just beginning to speak his name is enough to make me perhaps not want to rein in my cousin from going all *Godfather*. I swear my blood pressure spikes as I envision a car with him in it casually rolling into a lake. I draw in a breath. "We can't drown *Khy*," I tell Mercedes, forcing out his name calmly. I can say it. He isn't Thanos, and what happened wasn't the big snap. Though it sure as heck hurt like it was. However, he's nobody. I don't need to treat what happened as a breakup. It wasn't. Just a dumb outing with a dumb, rich boy that I should've known would be terrible because he's a cringe-y rich boy. "Besides, with a Connection to water and being an athletic swimmer, Khy'd likely survive anyway," I grumble.

"Fine. We light his bedroom on fire with him inside. Can he conjure water from thin air to douse it?"

"I don't know. Maybe? It depends on the strength of his Connection. He—" Why am I entertaining this? "Forget about him. Our energy is better spent on solving our bakery problem." I pointedly wave the iPad I'm holding.

Mercedes rolls her eyes. "I know how to multitask. We can tackle both."

The bakery's bell chimes while I'm deciding whether to rub my eyes or cackle at my cousin's dedication for turning us into murderers. Mr. Charles walks in and orders his usual coffee and slice of pecan pie after he hands me the mail. We do the usual dance. He tries to hand me money. I refuse to take it. He tells me to tell Dad to stop being bullheaded.

"I got the pie," Mercedes says. She stoops to grab it while I walk to the coffee machine, pour Mr. Charles his usual night-black cup, and push enough extra heat into it so that it's the perfect temp when I hand it over.

Mrs. Morris stops by a bit later, coming for her cheesecake brownie a little earlier than usual, but other than her, it's dead. The excruciating lack of customers doesn't help my anxiety over news orgs not reaching out. I refresh my email seven billion times, willing at least one response to appear. Of course, zilch appears.

Later in the morning, a teen guy comes in. He orders a mocha latte and sticky bun. I take his order and grab the sticky bun while Mercedes makes the latte. I place his goods on the counter, and he snaps a pic of his order. The angle of his phone makes it obvious that he catches me in the background. I scowl as he uploads the picture to his Insta page. It's rude. He frowns when he looks up and catches my stank face. I smooth out my expression; he *is* the first nonregular customer we've had today. The thought makes me paste on a smile. It's probably best to serve up any and all new customers a five-star experience. "Make sure you tag *Cayden's Confections*," I exclaim brightly. Might as well take advantage of the free publicity, no matter how small. Every little bit counts.

"Sure thing," the guy says almost sheepishly. Can't help the smirk. *So now he wants to be shy?*

Shortly after he leaves, more and more customers start trickling in. All brand-new ones. All people around my age, like the first guy. Eventually, the influx of people grows so massive that the tables and booths fill up and a line we can barely keep up with spills out the door and snakes around the block.

"What the hell?" Mercedes says as we service the latest teen patron.

Dad is busy today making cakes for three weddings and a seventy-fifth birthday Vegas-themed party, so she and I have to manage and hold things down. Still, Dad can't help himself. He stops working every fifteen minutes or so to poke his head into the shop front and stare in wonder.

I wave a twenty-dollar bill at him the next time he peeks in on things before sliding it into the open register. "If we have more days like this, it'll be Slow Sales who? I don't know her. She doesn't go here." Cookout or no cookout, Dad and Mom won't have to worry about the rent surge in two places.

Dad nods, grinning wide, and there's so much joy on his face that I fight back ridiculously happy tears. He worked so hard to start a pastry catering business and bakery from scratch back when he and Mom were both fresh out of college. Mom was headed to vet school, and they had meager funds that grew even slimmer after Mom's terrible parents cut her off when she chose to leave their Coven House and marry Dad. I might be biased because he's my dad, but Dad deserves booming business. He deserves a city-famous—scratch that—a *world-famous* bakery.

"Maybe that guy who posted was a big food blogger on Insta or something?" I say to Mercedes as Dad literally shimmies back into the kitchen. Whatever he is, *THANK YOU JESUS!* I do a jiggle myself and praise the Ancestors. I guess my green candle and the aventurine stone I tucked in the register are working.

"*Dannnng*, that'd be so legit!" Mercedes exclaims. "I'm about to see who ya boy is!" She whips out her phone as I'm taking the next order to quickly do some sleuthing. "What the hell?" Mercedes croaks a couple seconds later.

"What'd you find?" I ask excitedly. But then I realize Mercedes looks more weirded out and confused than ecstatic. "What is it?" I ask again, nervous this time, when she doesn't say anything.

Eyes as wide as tea cakes, Mercedes turns her phone so it faces me. "That guy didn't post about food. He posted about *you*."

"Huh?" It's all I can get out at first, and I momentarily forget I'm supposed to be grabbing someone's order. "What you mean? Why would somebody do that? What about me?" Behind the string of jumbled questions, I lean forward to get a better look at the words scrawled above my head in the Insta story. She's super nice and a cutie!!!

I blink. I mean, he isn't wrong. But... ain't no way. "Why is some stranger talking about me on the internet?" I say, confused, to my cousin. *That's not creepy at all.*

Her eyes take on a hard, protective glint. "I'm gonna find out," she nearly snarls.

"Please do," I say. "I've got the line." I'm unable to shake how rattled the whole bizarre instance leaves me as I try to focus on servicing customers.

A couple minutes later, Mercedes shrieks. "Oh my freaking God!"

When I swivel her way, I swear she's paled a few shades. My forever well-moisturized cousin looks *ashy*. "What's the matter?" I ask it, yet I'm not sure I really want to know.

She winces, and I go on higher alert. "Umm, so you're gonna lose it, and... maybe we should throw up a *Be Back in Ten* sign so we can talk about this. And so you can be sitting down."

I lean forward to get a better peek at her phone, my mind spinning with what the hell she could be talking about.

But she clutches the phone to her chest, blocking my view. "I think this needs to be handled delicately," she tells me, and she sounds like she's giving the eulogy at somebody's funeral.

"You're scaring me," I say. Then I flap my arms at the never-ending line. "Whatever it is, just hurry up and tell me now. We can't afford to go on break." The bakery hasn't had this much business *ever;* I don't want to shove people away or keep them waiting too long.

Mercedes smiles weakly. "It's about your almost-witch-boo whose guts we hate."

"Huh? Khy? What do you mean?" I reach for the phone, more confused than ever. I have to give it a hard tug for Mercedes to let go.

I glance down at the screen. The first thing I see is THE SCOOP in big, red block letters. My eyes travel to the black print below the site's name. **America's Witch Royal Rebounds Quickly with Mystery Girl After Rough Breakup with European Counterpart!**

My brain begins to dimly understand that the headline is about Khy. And below the headline is a photo. Of Khy. And me. At Laveau's Gumbo House. Our menus sit in front of us. He's leaned partially over the table, angled toward me. I'm sort of leaning a bit over the table, too. We look cozy. It's clear we're on a date. My heart slams against my chest. I blink several times. That's when frantic denial sets in. I can't be seeing what my eyes are seeing. That headline cannot be blasting what I think it is. Suddenly woozy, I scan the mini article that's below our pic.

> America's Witch Royal, Mekhi Carter, the youngest son of Witch Regent Allison Carter, was seen on a date with a mystery girl after a very public, recent breakup with ex-girlfriend, Giselle "Gigi" Bernard, fellow Royal and daughter of France's Witch Regent. Gigi is rumored

to have broken up with Mekhi to date the Ghanaian young Royal heartthrob, Tano Osei. It seems Mekhi has moved on, too. But his new relationship isn't with a Royal—an occurrence that leaves millions of young women wondering who is Mystery Girl? In fact, an insider source told THE SCOOP that Mystery Girl isn't a witch—a juicy bit of information that will for sure steal the hearts of Mekhi's many non-witch admirers and leave them hoping they might have a chance with America's handsome young witch Royal, too, if current Mystery Girl doesn't work out. Mekhi dating her sets a new precedent and is the first time a Witch Royal anywhere has been linked to someone who doesn't belong to a Coven House.

My eyes bulge at the article. Khy has an ex? Who is this freaking witch princess? And my picture is in THE SCOOP? For anybody, *and they mama,* to see.

I drop the phone in Mercedes's hand like it's a toxic potion hissing flesh-eating vapors. Finding out Khy was a Coven witch mid-date is one thing. This . . . nah, this is too wild. I've lived my whole seventeen years of life being ordinary and low-key and avoiding messiness with Coven folk, exactly how I like things, but now my pic is on a gossip site, and I've been given some absurd moniker and become tangled up with the breakup drama of Witch Royals. I laugh, and it sounds more like a croak. I glower at the phone. "I'm on board. He can get got," I tell Mercedes. *What type of arrogant, narcissistic, thoughtless person goes on a date without telling the other person,* "Hey. I'm Coven Royalty, by the way. AND IT WILL BLOW UP YOUR LIFE IF WE'RE SPOTTED TOGETHER!" I manage to remember we've got a shop full of people who can hear me, but it still takes everything in me not to scream that last bit out loud and look unprofessional.

Mercedes steps closer to my side and rubs my back as I damn near hyperventilate. *So much for professionalism.* "Breathe, Cayden. I know you're freaking out," she whispers low enough to try to keep it between the two of us. "But Uncle Jason and Auntie Eva don't read gossip sites. Neither do my moms or Grams. Yes, this is awkward, but not terrible. Your parents still never have to find out about the date."

"Awkward is an understatement," I hiss.

"Everything all right?" asks the girl standing in front of the register. She's white with blond hair and looks between me and Mercedes with genuine concern—and a load of awe and curiosity. And now I completely understand why.

"Yes," Mercedes says quickly. "Give us one more second, though, please."

"Yeah," I lie, pulling it together and sounding miraculously calm. I step away from Mercedes and return to my post at the register. "Sorry about the delay," I tell the girl. "What can I get you?"

As the girl gives her order, I drag in a breath to make my coolness stick. *It seriously is fine,* I stress to myself. *My name isn't in THE SCOOP. They're only calling me Mystery Girl, at least for now. And I'm never talking to or seeing Khy again.*

That means there'll be no more stories about us. He and this particular Mystery Girl will be forgotten about, and I'm sure that asinine gossip site will then move on to stalking Khy and whatever new girl he ends up with, since it seems so concerned with his love life. My mom and dad really won't ever find out I consorted with the enemy.

Chapter Seven

Boy, am I wrong with the assumptions I make. As I'm handing the girl her s'mores cookie, Khy walks into the bakery. He's wearing navy cargo shorts, an electric orange polo (to my infinite irritation, the bright color looks gorgeous against his dark skin), and a pair of fresh, ice-white Jordan Retro 13s with baby blue soles. My brain has a moment where it forgets he's a Coven jerk and does that thing where it short-circuits around him. While it's scrambled, I can't decide which is more breathtaking—Khy or the shoes. Then, I remember his rude friends and his silence at Laveau's and damn near snarl.

My hands clench into fists, and I want to punch something. I blink away angry, insulted tears all over again. As if there isn't a line, he walks right up to me at the counter. Every head in the bakery is turned his way as he does. The kids at the front of the line don't even gripe when he says, "Excuse me," and steps in front of them. Looking at him in a completely ridiculous, starstruck manner, they simply step to the side.

I gawk at the exchange. Seriously. Who is this boy? I mean, I know who he is, but everything I just witnessed is *absurd*, absurd. Like to the twelve-hundredth-power absurd.

"What do you want?" I say, not bothering to be nice despite the audience we have. Phones are out and pics are being snapped, and I'm sure videos are being recorded, too. There's incessant loud whispers and chatters about who he is.

"I told you we might see him if we came here! I said he might come visit his new girlfriend!" A girl in line who looks a few years younger than me gushes to her three friends.

I shake my head, sure I've slipped into some *Black Mirror* alternate universe. *Please, please, please don't let Dad pop up while he's here.*

"I came to apologize for . . . everything," Khy says, bringing my attention squarely back to him.

I scowl. "You're going to have to be more specific because the irritations are piling up," I say frankly.

"Right." He nods and drags his hand along the gleaming waves atop his head, in the way some boys do when they're nervous or anxious. He sweeps a hand out at the crowded bakery. "Is there a private place we can talk? Would you mind that? If you don't want to, it's fine. I'll just—"

"Stop speaking. Now." I jab a finger at the sea of phones that I remember are recording everything. I shoot from behind the counter, seize his hand, and drag him to a storage room off to the side. In hindsight, it's a terrible idea to avoid further attention.

I clench my teeth as the door closes behind us. I just handed THE SCOOP a new headline.

Royal Boy and Mystery Girl Get Cozy in Bakery Closet!

I drop Khy's hand and spin on him. "Leave. Now. Before things get worse. And tell your adoring fans and media circus we're not dating on the way out!"

He winces. "Okay. I deserved that. And I will. Can I at least say sorry, in earnest, before I go? I feel like I owe you at least that much."

I fold my arms over my chest, Petty Cayden making an appearance. "You're right. But saying sorry won't make you less of an asshole."

He drags his hand along his waves again. "Give me five minutes, then I'll get lost?"

"You've got three."

Everything he says next comes out in a rush. "The situation outside is inexcusable. I should've figured something like this might happen when I asked you out, but," he scratches the back of his head, another nervous tell. "I sometimes forget how out of control the media and other people can get about . . . people like me."

People like me. He's competing with Mercedes for Understatement of the Year.

I stare at him, not exactly sure what he wants me to say. He fidgets with the slim, gold chain at his neck that he's wearing today. "I...um...also came to apologize for how our date ended."

"You left out ruining seafood for me, which is the most important offense."

He does that thing where his forehead wrinkles in confusion. "Huh?"

"Never mind. I don't feel like explaining it."

He gives me the half smile, and I swear there should be a law that requires him to register the thing as a deadly weapon. *Thou will not go wobbly*, I command my knees. *Thou shall not turn into Simone Biles*, I command my stomach. *And thou shall not erupt in the thirst that landed you in this mess to begin with*, I command every other part of me. *Thou shall also keep up with the damn time because I'm pretty sure his three minutes are almost up.* And yet, my mouth doesn't inform Khy of that.

Instead, for some reason, I let him continue with the trifling junk he came to say. "It's not an excuse for their behavior..." He clears his throat when I give him a *no shit* smirk. But he takes it in stride and keeps going. "My friends crashed the date because they guessed the circus that would happen. I realize that them showing up and acting how they did must've felt really terrible for you, so I want to apologize for that, too. I tried calling you after to explain and say sorry then, but I'm guessing you blocked me."

He releases an awkward laugh. "Usually, I would respect the fact that you said you didn't want to see me again. But when THE SCOOP article got released and all these pics started circulating on socials of you and random people tagging this bakery with your name, I figured I could find you here." He rubs the back of his neck. "I know this all makes me sound like a stalker. I promise I'm not. I'm just here to check on you since so much chaos is happening. I'm so sorry you got dragged into all this and that these people are cluttering your bakery. I already have my family's PR team reaching out to the media to do damage control and scrub the pictures of us together so your life doesn't blow up more. I can't do anything about Cayden's Confections trending, but hopefully that will die down soon and then everyone will forget about your bakery and stop harassing you here. It doesn't look like there's even any space for your normal customers. I'm so sorry. Again. I can try to tell everybody to clear out?"

"No! Don't do that!" I yell. The boy went way past his three-minute limit, but his offer to tell everyone to leave is what I latch on to first. "They're buying things, so they're cool. I appreciate the extra customers," I say, lowering my voice to normal levels. Then, my thoughts work through the tangle of everything else. "Your friends ... the other night ... you're saying they were trying to rescue you from an outrageous press story?"

Right then Mercedes pops her head into the storage room. "For real?"

"Aren't you supposed to be ringing up customers?" I ask my eavesdropping cousin.

She hitches a thumb behind her. "Nobody's buying

anything right now. They were all trying to crowd the door to overhear what y'all were saying—or doing. I valiantly risked my life, placed myself between the mob and the door, and told everybody to step back. So you should really be saying: *thank you, oh great and wonderful cousin.*

"Just to be clear," she says with a scheming, Cheshire cat smile to Khy, "your friends didn't crash y'all's date to give you a hard time about Cayden not belonging to a Coven House?" Her tone is way too gleeful about the revelation.

Khy looks appalled. "No. I wouldn't hang out with people like that."

Mercedes grins like a fiend. I give her a *don't start* look. In turn, she gives me an innocent smile. "Glad to hear it," she tells Khy. "Because that's what my cousin thought and that's why she cut out on the date and blocked you. But since that was all a mix-up, you should know she was *really* feeling the date before all that."

I swear my cousin is about to make herself the victim of a murder. Aunt Nikki and Aunt Vesha will be crushed, but they'll have to understand and get over the bloody death of their bigmouthed daughter.

Khy looks between me and Mercedes, gobsmacked. The surprise and embarrassment seem genuine. "I'm so sorry about that," he says, apologizing more profusely than before. "That wasn't it at all. After what you told me about your parents, I see how you thought it, though." He curses and drags a hand along the top of his hair. "I feel like I should make it up to you some way. Can I? I feel horrible."

"You absolutely should and can make it up to my girl," Mercedes says, still not finding herself some business and staying all up in mine. "Seems like a do-over date is a good idea!"

I serve her the look that statement deserves, and she knows why she gets it.

"What Uncle and Auntie don't know won't hurt them when Oh Boy is *that* fine," she shoots, looking Khy up and down. "Girl, if you don't lock him down, I will. Y'all talk it over. Schedule out a time and place. I'll continue holding off your witch boo's admirers." She gives us a thumbs up before closing the door shut behind her.

We are going to throw hands. Like legit square up. Is she insane? A do-over date is a terrible idea for all the reasons I had for not wanting to go out with Khy in the first place *and* for a bunch of new ones! Right now, I'm Mystery Girl. But if we go out, more pictures of us will end up in THE SCOOP, and likely other places, too. Then, the madness with the bakery and all the people popping into it today will only be the tip of the—LIGHT BULB. "You *can* make it up to me with a do-over date," I inform Khy.

Then, because I'm not manipulative and I don't like misleading people, especially when possible feelings are involved, I add straight, "But it won't be about *us*. Not that there is an *us*. Or will be an *us*." I strive to make myself glass clear. "Like you said, I told you about my family's drama with Coven folks. Sorry, but you're one of them. Also, while I did have a good time yesterday at first, I was never planning on something heavy between us popping off when I agreed to hang out." Had we gotten to the kissing part of the date, I would've expressed that before the kisses for us both to be on the same page, but I don't need to say all that right now. "But," I continue getting to the essential part that Mercedes is right about (Mom and Dad never need to know if it helps them). "The press from our date has kicked up good business for my dad's bakery, and honestly, we seriously need it. So can we hang out again? As just friends? More press could mean more business. Did I mention we really need more business?"

I just spent the morning agonizing over snagging media interest to boost the bakery's visibility during the cookout and rally. But we won't even need that anymore if I can keep social media and gossip sites obsessed with me and Khy supposedly dating. I realize how ridiculous my proposal is, and there's no reason for him to ever agree. What would he have to gain? Typically, Coven witches don't look out for anybody outside their precious circle. I'm prepared for him to say no, but he does the complete opposite.

"Sure. Just name the time and place," he says, dead serious.

I barely believe it. "Really?" I nearly squee, but I've got more swag than that. "You're willing to do that?"

He shrugs. "I pay my debts, and even if it was a misunderstanding, my friends acted messed up toward you. If hanging out a second time is what you want to make it cool, then all right. Let's do it." He grins the half grin.

"Why are you going along with things so easily?" I ask, ever suspicious.

His rich brown complexion is only a shade lighter than mine, so when he blushes, his cheeks only smolder with a red tint that's barely visible. "The truth is embarrassing to say out loud," he mumbles. "I just got dumped for another guy, as I'm sure you read about. And I'd really, really, *really* like to seem like I'm not a sad, lonely, pathetic loser who's still crushed over Gigi. That's sort of why I asked you out. I mean I was vibing with you, a lot, too," he quickly says when I cut my eyes at him. "So that was just as much of the reason. But I also wanted to not be wallowing over my ex while all of the world watches me do it."

"So, I was your Rebound Girl?" I scowl. Yet, I can't decide if I'm truly insulted. I mean, on one hand, I get it. What he did is something I've done a few times myself. But also, I don't like being on the Rebound Person end of that equation.

"It sounds really bad when you put it like that," Khy says, the reddish tint lingering on his cheeks. I hate how cute it makes him look.

"There's no way not to make it sound bad," I reply. "It's also something I've totally done before. I understand and it's whatever," I confess to Khy. "We can hang, as friends, and help each other out. Deal?" I hold my hand out. A handshake seems like a nice, friendly, professional way to seal a mutually beneficial arrangement.

Khy shakes his head. Then laughs. "This is bananas." *That's the third Understatement of the Year.*

"It is," I agree. "But if hanging together helps make it look like you're not sweating this Gigi girl and brings more of your admirers into the bakery, then it seems worth it to me." Especially if the droves of people also realize how delicious Dad's sweets are and keep coming back. It could really be a permanent fix for Dad's struggles. Cayden's Confections might become a big thing, like Crave Cupcakes or House of Pies, off social media clout alone.

Khy's hand slides into mine. "Deal," he says, and I try not to notice how his touch sends goosebumps up my arms.

Chapter Eight

Three days later, I can't help but feel like I've willingly dived headfirst into deep crap. Only, the swoony butterflies in my belly from when Khy showed up at the bakery aren't what's plaguing me. Nah. They've been replaced by a swarm of insects that carry stingers and wings protruding talons. I clutch my stomach that's spasming painfully as I look up at the huge house—*mansion*— situated along Clear Lake. The opulent structure absurdly rises four stories high with a terrace that wraps around the entire top floor and a fountain out front that looks like something called baroque that we studied in my art elective last year. Then, there's the freaking valet I handed my car keys to and the dozens of luxury sports cars, sedans, and SUVs cluttering the wrap-around driveway. *Ancestors help me.* Even the outside of the lake house reeks of Coven snobbery.

Why are you here again? A voice that's ready to jet asks me.

Because Dad and the bakery need me to be here, I remind the jitters. I wince behind the thought. Is this really the only way?

Yes! I hiss to the part of me that's searching desperately for reasons to back out. None of the media outlets we've reached out to about the cookout have gotten back to us. I don't have a choice. *So put your big girl pants on, suck it up, and go mingle with Khy at this Coven party.*

I've never been one to wimp out of stuff, and I've already agreed for this to be me and Khy's next date-that's-not-really-a-date, so I place one foot in front of the other and trek toward the mansion's entrance.

"I have an idea for our next hangout that'll help us both," Khy had said before leaving the bakery. The tentative way he'd spoken should've been my first red flag.

But, giddy off the bakery being saved by such a simple thing, I'd been eager to hear his suggestion. Then, he'd dropped the bomb—he'd suggested I be his date to a lake party in celebration of Midsummer that the Houston Coven was hosting.

Naturally, I'd laughed, responded that I'd rather be subjected to water torture than attend a Coven function. But Khy swore the Midsummer party was a big fancy affair, where all the Texas Covens would be gathering to fellowship and honor the solstice, and thus, there'd be tons of press. The first two things did not convince me any further. However, his last point . . .

Well, that's why I'm standing outside of an enormous glass

door with a party of witches behind it. I raise my hand—and promptly drop it to my side. Do I knock? Ring the door bell? Simply walk inside? When Mom and Dad, or Grams, or Auntie Vesha and Auntie Nikki have big parties, they leave the door unlocked and most guests know to just come right in. But none of them are Coven-snooty, and I have no idea how arriving at these kinds of parties work. And ... why am I stressing over this so much like I actually care?

Because you're stalling. BIG TIME.

I sigh; I really am. I settle for ringing the doorbell like I'd do if I was going to a party at anybody's house that I didn't know well. A tall, handsome Black man wearing a dark suit opens the door. He holds an iPad in one hand, and the only greeting he extends is to ask for my name. I can't decide if he's supposed to be a butler or security because he's built like a pro bodybuilder but dressed like Geoffrey from *The Fresh Prince of Bel-Air*.

"I'm ... Cayden Jackson," I say twisting the strap of my purse, suddenly more nervous. "I'm here as Khy's ..." I refuse to say *date* out loud (because I am *not* truly that). I settle for, "I'm Khy's friend who he invited."

The man nods and gazes down at the iPad. I assume he's checking a guest list. He taps the screen, then waves me inside wordlessly.

"Umm ... thank you." I say awkwardly, unnerved by how little he's spoken.

Then, my attention—and every ounce of breath in my body—is stolen by the inside of the house. It is somehow decked out in more splendor than the outside. Last summer, I took a student trip to France with my school's Art History Club, when I was trying to figure out if I maybe wanted to major in something arty when I get to college. I figured out spending my days in museums and cultural exhibits wasn't for me, but I was fascinated when we visited the Palace of Versailles. The interior was as gorgeous as the outside architecture. And the gold and white decor of the lake house is seriously giving Versailles a run for its money. My jaw drops. For a minute, I don't notice any of the people milling around the expansive living room and spilling out onto a back terrace. I'm completely enraptured by all the shiny and sparkling things.

My marveling is cut short when I notice a tall boy with dark copper skin, a fresh haircut, and dimples for days is grinning at me and cutting across the living room to where I stand. Him, I notice above the beauty of the house—because I don't think I'd ever not notice Khy when he's in my vicinity. The boy is mad fine, but it's also more than that. It's like this magnetic pull exists between us, a sizzle of electricity that zaps through me on the spot and shoots directly his way. Khy frowns as he approaches me, and I realize that I'm scowling at that thought. I fix my face and manage a polite smile by the time he reaches me.

"Everything okay?" he asks in genuine concern. "Did you have trouble clearing security?"

I shake my head, mute for a second. Then, I get myself together and remember how to actually speak words. "No.

The guy at the door wasn't rude or anything, if that's what you mean."

Khy visibly relaxes, beams wider. "Good. I'm glad. I left your name at the door as my... ummm... my friend that would be coming. I also asked Roland to let me know as soon as you arrived so I could come meet you up front."

So Silent Guy's name is Roland. It certainly sounds like one of those names that carry a certain toughness and power. "Is Roland a butler or a bouncer?" I ask curiously.

Khy does the thing where he gets shy and rubs his hand down the front of his head. "He's a part of my mom's personal security detail. You know, because, she's—"

"The freaking Regent of North American Witches," I say, still not believing that's who his mother is and that I'm attending a Coven party with a kid who is witch royalty.

Khy rubs his head again. "It's really not that big of a deal. I mean *she's* not really that big of a deal. It's not like my mom is the monarch of England, or the president of the United States or something."

I give him a look. "Riiight. She only just helps govern all witchkind in the US and Canada while simultaneously acting as a revered ceremonial figurehead. That's nothing like England's monarch or America's president at all."

"Okay, you're right," Khy says, chuckling.

His laughter is like a sugary-sweet, gooey, rich brownie-bottom cheesecake fresh out of the oven. It causes my own lips to tug up into a smile and before I know it, I'm laughing right along with him. The thing about Khy is that, regardless of how big of a deal his mom is, you'd never know it based on the way he acts. Khy is so chill and lacks any traces of conceit so far. It's probably why I vibe so hard with him—even if I wish I didn't.

"I'm glad you came," he says, gazing at me in this super intense—and unnerving—way when we manage to rein in the laughter. "I was a little afraid you'd back out."

Ignoring the fact that he's right and I'd seriously considered turning around multiple times, I tell Khy, "It *is* a lot, but I've never been to a lake party before, and now I can cross it off my bucket list."

He eyes me quizzically. "You've got a bucket list? Now, I wanna know what else is on it."

"It isn't a *list* list," I answer. "There's not like specific experiences on it that I want to check off. It's just a general goal to see and do and enjoy as many different things as possible."

"I like that," Khy says. "In fact, I might steal it."

"I'm gonna need to charge you to license the usage," I deadpan.

"Cash App or Zelle?" he shoots back, not missing a beat.

I giggle; I can't help it. "Nice house, by the way." I have no clue why I feel the need to point out the obvious. I think my nerves make me start rambling to avoid us descending into awkward silence. "Is it yours?"

The slight darkening of Khy's cheeks tells me the answer. "It's one of our vacation houses we use to get away from the city," he mutters.

One of his *vacation* houses. I'm not surprised. Royal Boy probably has about a dozen, scattered across the globe. Khy must read at least part of what I'm thinking on my face, because he stiffens as if awaiting my judgment.

But we're supposed to be friendly now, and me throwing shade at him won't make our hangouts very fun. So, I only nudge his shoulder with mine. Tell him with clearly playful teasing, "It is pretty damn bougie to have a mansion you consider a backup house. But now I know I can tack on a few extra zeroes to the Cash App request I'm sending for jacking my philosophy."

He relaxes at my light tone. "Did I say this was *my* house? That was cap. It's somebody else's." He's grinning again, and I'm not sure why *my* insides warm at seeing *his* mood lifted. Maybe it's his dimples on full display? I swear those damn, impossibly deep dimples are unfair to wield against people. "The house is open to chill in, but the main party and the press are outside around the lake," Khy says and holds out his arm for me to take, like we're in an episode of *Bridgerton*. I roll my eyes and can't help snorting at the stuffy gesture.

"I know it's corny," Khy says. "But the press will eat it up, us walking outside this way."

The boy makes a good point. And I tell myself it is the *sole* reason that I loop my arm through his. Well, that and the near certainty Mom and Dad will never lay eyes on any viral photos. They don't do gossip sites, but I needed backup protection to minimize my anxiety, all the same. So I blocked any web pages that contain my name, Khy's name, or *Mystery Girl* from loading on their phones and any devices connected to our house's internet before leaving for the party.

A flurry of pictures get snapped as soon as Khy and I step onto the terrace. A lush, green backyard sprawls out around the terrace, and beyond the humongous back lawn sits Clear Lake. There's a dock at the edge of the yard with the kind of sleek speedboat that Dad literally just rented two days ago; he cops one every Juneteenth to take us out on Lake Houston.

It's only after all the camera flashes die down that I decide to grow self-conscious about how I'll look in the myriad photos beside Khy. I cut a glance at Royal Boy who, of course, is fly as heck. It's mid-June in Houston, which means every time you step outside, day or night, it feels like standing in the center of a volcano. It's likely why the attire for today that Khy passed along is semiformal and not all-out-sadiddy-formal. Yet the distinction doesn't change the fact that Khy looks, once again, like he's stepped off a Paris Fashion Week runway, rocking a fit by some posh but edgy high fashion designer. He's wearing a sky blue linen suit that I'm positive costs a fortune. Its bottoms are starched shorts instead of pants. And instead of loafers, he has on a pair of University Blue Jordan 4 Retros. They're not my favorite model of Retro Js, but they look killer with his fit. (I'm convinced no clothing could actually look bad on this boy.) "Nice kicks," I say to fill the silence that's probably gone on too long.

"Thanks," he says as I do a sweep down at my own fit to make sure I won't look like a slob next to Khy when the pics turn up on THE SCOOP; my ego won't stand for it. I reassure myself that the short yellow sundress I swiped from Mercedes is gorgeous and chic, without requiring a ludicrous designer price tag to make it stunning. And Khy isn't showing me up in the footwear department either. *Thank the Ancestors*, I stood my ground and didn't let Mercedes pester me into swapping out the ice-white Nike Dunks I'm wearing for the strappy gold sandals she (wrongly) swore looked better with the dress.

Khy bobs his head down at my Dunks. "I might need to hunt down a pair of those." He grins, slick. "I'm surprised you wore them to a lake party with how distressed you were about my Starry Nights getting dirty."

"Very funny," I drawl. "I've perfected keeping my sneakers clean when I wear them out the house down to an art form," I let him know. "I've owned these masterpieces for three years, and they still look brand new."

Khy snorts but gives me my props for the feat. (As he should.) We remain on the terrace for a while, standing near a lavish charcuterie table, and slip into an easy convo about our favorite special edition sneaker releases. As we talk, a picture gets snapped every so often. Usually, it's when Khy does something like lean in closer to hear me over the party chatter and live jazz band playing on the other side of the terrace. It's only after we've been talking for Ancestors know how long, when I realize our arms remain linked—and have been linked the whole time. I'm not sure how I feel about it, because us holding on to each other is the opposite of what *just friends* would do. But I'm sure it made for juicy photos and Khy's fans will eat it up.

I decide to let good sense prevail and gently extricate myself from Khy; how comfortable and oblivious I was to our former position has all sorts of alarms ringing. "I think we can stop hanging on to each other now," I tell Khy. "The press have gotten enough pics of us looking cozy already. And it's hot. I don't want to sweat on you. That's gross." *And I'm rambling. And flustered—which I never get around any boy. Ugh! Why does this one knock me off my dang game so much?*

As soon as I pitch the question out to the universe, I shut down that line of thinking hard. I'm not trying to have an inner voice (or the Ancestors) answer back with a fact I'm trying to intentionally have ostrich-syndrome about.

Khy's lips twitch knowingly. Thankfully, before he can comment on my rambling, his friends—all five of them—swarm us. The Black girl, Naomi, smacks Khy's arm. "We decided that we gave you a solid half hour alone with her, and that's all you get."

Khy scowls.

Naomi pops glossy mauve lips that match her knee-length tea dress. "Get over yourself," she says. "Honestly, you've launched this scheme to make yourself look like you are not sweating Gigi, so this other girl is going to be around a lot for a time, right? That means we'll be hanging out with her, too."

"I have a name," I say, still holding a grudge, even though Khy claims it wasn't like that. "It's Cayden, remember?"

Naomi swings my way. The look she gives me is ice cold. "I thought they weren't snobbish jerks," I mutter to Khy.

"We're not," Naomi snaps. "Khy told us what you thought in Galveston. Just because you misread the situation doesn't mean we like you any better. We don't know you, and Khy is like the modern version of Romeo, always pining over some girl that's gonna smash his heart. Like Gigi." She slides that last part at Khy, and it is the only reason I don't tell her about herself. If what she says is true, then she's being bitchy because she's protective of her friend. I can halfway respect that.

"Chill," the Asian girl, whose name I recall as Becca, says. "Do you have to call him out like that? Especially here?"

"Yeah, Nae," the Black boy from the restaurant, Darius, speaks up. "That's not why we came over here. We came to be supportive. Make it so Khy doesn't feel awkward and to . . ." he looks at me. "To apologize."

Naomi crosses her arms over her chest. Says nothing.

I roll my eyes, but Becca steps up to me. "I'm sorry about before. All of us are. We were terrible and are ashamed of how we acted."

She offers me a genuinely warm smile, and I smile back because I appreciate the gesture. "That's cool of you," I say and mean it.

"Let's start over," Becca says. She puts her hand out. "I'm Becca. It's super nice to meet you, Cayden."

I shake her hand, letting go of what happened before—at least with her. "Same," I say.

The guys follow her lead and reintroduce themselves, too. They're as pleasant as Becca this time around, if not still distant, and I squash whatever lingering bitterness I have toward them.

The crew turns to Naomi afterward. Stares her down. I decide that if this version of them is real, then I could maybe like Khy's friend group. (Minus Naomi.)

After a long, absurd second, Naomi huffs. "This is stupid and juvenile," she grouches but sticks her hand out to me. "I'm Naomi. Welcome. We'll be good as long as you aren't foul."

Becca elbows her in the side. "That is not what you were supposed to say."

Naomi pops her lips again, wholly unapologetic.

"It's fine," I tell them all. I decide to be the bigger person and shake Naomi's hand. Okay, maybe I am only slightly the bigger person, because I still pettily return, "I don't make a habit of being foul unless somebody's stank attitude makes me go there. Then, I absolutely will be shady right back."

Jordan, the white boy, snickers. "Okay, I think I like her."

Naomi quickly shakes my hand, then drops it.

Becca slings an arm around my shoulders. "Come on," she says. "We're hanging at a table out on the lawn that Khy was trying to avoid bringing you to."

Khy groans. He tells his friends that he and I are good where we are. But Becca refuses to be deterred. Still holding on to me, she leads me to one of the standing tables decorated with a blush covering and gold runner in the middle of the lawn. Khy and the rest of his friends follow.

"So, you're a witch, too? Just not a part of a Coven?" The Latino boy, Geo, asks once we reach where their crew has posted up at. He doesn't say it disparagingly. Only genuinely curious, so I decide to answer.

"Yes. My mom used to belong to Dallas's Coven until she married my dad who isn't a witch." I get that out in the open, state it unconcerned and unbothered myself—with steel behind it—so they know I'm not the one to play with.

Geo bobs his head. "Mama sounds like a boss."

Okay. That isn't a rebuttal I've ever gotten when I've told Coven kids about my parents before. I'm used to pity cast my way—like I'm broken or drowning in misery because I'm Covenless. Or straight-up disdain, like I'm inferior.

"She is," I tell Geo proudly.

"So your grandparents are still a part of the Dallas Coven?" Darius asks.

"Yes," I answer wearily.

"Are they here?" He gazes around at the mass of people on the lawn as if he might spot a pair of witches who look similar to me.

Crap. I hadn't thought of that. If this party is for all Texas witches, then maybe Mom's parents are here. "I actually don't know," I say, shifting from one foot to the other. "We don't speak at all."

"Sorry. That's crappy," he says.

I shrug. "Can't feel some type of way about people you've never met, right?"

"So what's your Connection?" Becca asks me, clearly changing the subject.

I throw her a grateful look. "It's not that interesting. My Connection is to forms of energy," I answer. "I can borrow energy from one source and transfer it to something else."

Darius's eyes sharpen on me. "Sis, how is that not interesting? You're like a walking motor, conductor, and generator all in one! I bet you're a beast in science labs. Oh! Are you taking an AP Chem or AP Bio class next year?! I am. We should compare notes. Too bad you don't go to Gramercy Prep with us. We could be lab partners. I—"

Becca slaps a hand over his mouth. "Excuse him," she says over Darius's muffled words. "He gets too excited about nerdy shit and gets carried away. Don't overwhelm her or make us look weird," she hisses to her friend. "Find some chill, okay?" She waits for him to nod before she removes her hand from his mouth.

"My bad," he says sheepishly. "I promise we aren't weirdos."

"Are you sure about that?" Khy mutters. "All of y'all are making a good, repeated case."

I laugh at how mortified he looks by his friends. Maybe I truly did misjudge them because they are nothing like I expected so far. Except Naomi. She can kick rocks.

"Sorry to be a letdown, but me and STEM don't mix too

well," I tell Darius. "I suck at math, and all of the upper sciences involve a migraine-inducing amount of math."

Poor Darius looks crestfallen.

Becca snickers. "I think you almost got your fake girlfriend stolen, Khy."

She placed fake in front of the word but my cheeks grow hot at her calling me Khy's girlfriend in any capacity. "We're friends hanging out," I correct her.

"Riiight," Becca says. "You're strictly friends and THE SCOOP can conclude what they want from how cozy you two looked clinging to each other on the terrace. Understood."

"Ummm, speaking of that, it looked real to me," Jordan says.

Khy's jaw clenches. He looks like he wants to turn to vapor and float away.

Naomi throws up her hands. "But I'm the bad guy for insisting this is a terrible idea for him! We all know how you get," she tells Khy.

"We're seriously just friends," I say hurriedly to help him out. *I'd never actually date a boy like Khy for real.* It's on the tip of my tongue but would likely hurt his feelings, so I don't voice my particular reason for being 100 percent positive nothing about Khy and me is real and it will never be real.

"What Cayden says is right," Khy speaks up. I ignore the disappointment in his voice—and how it tugs at something I refuse to closely examine.

"Can I see your Connection? Like can you demonstrate it?" Darius says exuberantly, still apparently hung up on it.

I'm actually grateful for him geeking out because it brings another change of subject right on time.

"Sure," I say. I swipe a rose-shaped tea light candle floating in a glass votive off the table. I focus on transferring heat energy from the burning wick to the surrounding water. A second later, the flame winks and the water starts to boil. I sit the votive down quickly so my fingers aren't scorched and force the water to hotter temps until there's solid roiling action going on. I keep pushing energy into the votive's liquid until it boils at the vigorous level you'd see with water in a pot that's been resting on a burner turned up to high for a good bit of time. Hey, I might not think my Connection is cool, but if I've been asked to show it off, then I'm gonna at least attempt to wow observers.

"Duuuude! Look!" Darius exclaims. "I'm so jealous!"

"Impressive," Jordan adds. "I haven't met anybody with this kind of Connection before."

"It is pretty cool," says Becca.

Naomi only looks on.

"What's y'all's Connections?" I ask, unable to curb the curiosity. And since they're being nosy, I can, too.

Geo claps. "Oh, hell yeah! We get to have like a mini talent show!"

Jordan punches him in the shoulder. "You're a dork. I don't know who's worse: you or Darius."

Geo returns the lick, smacking his back. "But you're gonna participate with us dorks anyway." He gives an exaggerated bow. "Matter of fact, the person presently being a jerkface should go first."

Jordan grumbles something about it being corny but obliges. He snaps his fingers—clearly just to be a showy wiseass because you don't need to actually do anything physical to manifest your Connection— and a small patch of grass beside him catches fire. It's a slow, controlled burn that doesn't spread any further. "You aren't the only one that can bring the heat," Jordan tells me, smirking.

I roll my eyes. "Okay. What you just said—that is corny," I let him know.

"Nah, I'm dope as hell," he says, full of cockiness, like he's certain it's the truth.

"Put the fire out already," Darius huffs. He gazes at Jordan's flames like they're wreaking havoc. "You're unnecessarily burning the grass, you tool."

"Ancestors forbid we burn one insignificant blade of something green and precious," Jordan drawls. But the fire disappears immediately. "Happy?"

"Yes," Darius says. "Thank you."

"Your turn," Jordan tells Darius. "Wow, Khy's girl with your juice."

"I'm not his girl," I insert at the same time Khy expresses the same thing.

"Whatever, dude," Jordan says. "Like Nae pointed out, we all know how you roll. Cayden wouldn't be here, attending Coven stuff, mingling with your friends and family if you didn't have it bad—the hell, dude?! Seriously?" Jordan sputters, shaking water from his medium-length blond hair. One minute he was talking shit, the next everything from his chest up was drenched. "Real mature," he snaps to Khy.

Khy shrugs unapologetically. "You should shut up sometimes. Most times, actually. And you can easily dry yourself."

Jordan has already done just that by the time Khy finishes. "Not the point," he says irked. I don't bother to swallow my chuckle. The boy deserved what he got.

"That's my demo," Khy says, glossing right over why he dumped the equivalent of a magical bucket of water on his friend's head. "Darius, you're up."

Clearly Darius assists Becca with being the peacemaker of the group because he swoops right in and does as Khy asks. "Watch and be dazzled," Darius declares, grinning and pointing to the patch of grass Jordan scorched. Fresh, verdant green blades pop up where there was only a round circle of dirt left before. And he doesn't stop there. In the middle of the new grass, a thick green stem sprouts, grows about a foot tall, and then a dark pink flower tipped in yellow erupts at the end of the stem. Darius reaches down and plucks the flower he's conjured from the earth. He bows gallantly, handing it to me. "It matches your outfit," he says with a wink.

I take the flower and stare at it, mouth hanging open. One: I've seen the wildflower I'm holding countless times along the side of the road and none of them are ever as gigantic as my fist. They're usually small splotches of color among grass. Two, no flowers, whatsoever, covered the ground before—or any of the backyard. "How'd you grow it?" I ask Darius. He wasn't flexin' before; I really *am* awestruck. "Can you just make whatever you want that's a plant appear in whatever space you want it to?"

Darius shakes his head. "I wish! But, sadly, that's a no. Working material has to already be present. Khy's backyard would naturally be covered with wildflowers if the lawn wasn't always mowed. The root system for the firewheel you're holding was in the soil. I only forced it to grow."

"Still pretty stunning," I say, waving the flower. "And thank you. It's gorgeous."

"It is," Khy says, deftly taking it from me. He stares at me funny for a sec—and for the same passing second my breaths come quicker. While I'm fussing at myself to get it together, he leans in and tucks the flower behind my ear. "Darius is right," he says. "It goes perfect with the dress and kicks."

Naomi pops her lips. "See, this is what I mean—"

"My turn," Becca says, cutting her off. Without the fanfare Darius or Jordan presented their Connections with, a soft breeze kicks up around us. It lightly rustles my hair that I've left down in corkscrew coils, which I created by washing my hair and letting it dry in Bantu knots before taking them down.

"Cool!" I say to Becca. "Can we play airball?"

She looks at me, face twisted in confusion. "Huh? What's that? You mean air hockey?"

Surprisingly, it's Naomi who gets my *Avatar: The Last Airbender* reference. She giggles. Then abruptly squashes it.

(Ancestors forbid she doesn't think I'm gonna destroy Khy and wreck his heart for half a second and actually show she's warming up to me.)

"Khy's ... friend was talking about a TV show," she tells Becca. "ATLA."

Recognition lights up Becca's face. "Oh. You mean the one you made me watch with the annoying little kid and the girl who gets shipped with him when she should've obviously gotten with the fire boy?"

I chuckle. I can't help it. "You have good shipping taste," I say to Becca.

"That I do," she says, flipping her sleek, black hair. "And it's scary spot on. In fact, I'm pretty dang sure I have a secondary Connection as some kind of matchmaker, like in old-school days. I can always tell when two people are right for each other or not." She hikes a thumb toward Darius. "I'm the reason this one found the love of his life. If you're around at the end of the summer, you'll meet him when he gets back from his summer program at Oxford. I also told Khy that his ex, Gigi, was—" She slams her mouth shut. "Never mind. Sorry," she says to Khy.

"It's all good," he replies, voice surprisingly even. "We can't *not* talk about her when the press keeps harping on our breakup. *And* she'll be in town for Cotillion soon."

All right. Whoa. That revelation is loaded in so many ways, my head spins. Cotillion is a big deal in the South in general, but it's a huge deal across the world for witches. It's one of the few things from Mom's past that she talks about fondly. I can see why Khy would be nervous about his ex being there. He tries to laugh it off, but the bruise the topic leaves is clear by the way he's so obviously working hard to look unaffected.

I do not touch any of that, however. It is not my business. Not one single dang bit.

"Geo can't show you his Connection unless one of us punches the other in the face or something," Khy says, barreling right past the subject of his ex. "But he can heal injuries."

"Not sicknesses, though," Geo adds quickly.

Good to know. If I end up having to punch Naomi in the face, it won't be a big deal. I behave myself and don't snark the comment.

Speaking of Naomi, I turn her way, making it plain I'm not intimidated by her. "What about you? What's your Connection?" I ask it exuberantly, like her attitude doesn't ruffle me one ounce.

Naomi gives me a flat look. "You don't want me to demonstrate mine."

"Naomi can speak to the dead," Becca says soberly. "It's . . . kind of creepy."

I swallow. Okay. Didn't guess at that. "You mean like . . . you can commune directly with the Ancestors?" I ask, trying to put it in noncreepy perspective. "That's not bad. Don't we all try to catch impressions of advice and guidance from them anyway? That means you've just got a more direct and stronger line, right?"

"What it means," Naomi says, "since you're all up in mine, is that I can communicate with anybody who has died, not just witch Ancestors. And I see the dead, too. A lot."

A chill races down my spine; I suck in a breath. If that's her Connection, no wonder she's all Wednesday Adams moody—albeit a super prissy, posh version of Wednesday in a pink sundress.

"All right, gang. This was fun," Khy says with exaggerated exuberance. He steps closer to me. Holds out his hand. "Do you need some space from my *extra* friends?"

"Hey! I resent that," Jordan quips.

"Me too," Darius says. "I've been nice!"

Khy ignores them and nods to the lake beyond the edge of the yard. A mischievous smile spreads. It's a new look that I haven't seen on him before. And it has my knees going wobbly again. I lock them. Steel myself against yet another facet of Khy that's too damn fine for my own good. "We can take the boat out if you're down for it. The press will eat it up," Khy says. "Our boat excursion will be the pics from today that make headlines, rack in a ton of fawning. *Mekhi Carter Takes His Mystery Girl for a Cozy Boat Ride to Steal Alone Time Amidst a Posh Coven Party!* And it won't even be untrue." Okay. I've dated enough to know when a boy is flirting with me, and Khy has shifted to laying it on thick. It's an abrupt change, but not one I'm necessarily complaining about.

He slides his hand into mine, mischievous grin still in place. My mouth goes dry at the trinity of him smiling that way, asking me for alone time, and his electric touch. My brain screams *helllll no*, because his suggestion certainly feels like blurring the line between pretend and reality. But my hormones win an ensuing battle of wills. "I'm down," I say. My mind offers up a vivid image of Khy and me kissing when we're out on the lake alone. I force Thirsty Cayden to calm the heck down. Like Khy mentioned, the boat ride will make for splashy pics, killer headlines, and hopefully a trending hashtag—and all of that will rack in a fresh round of customers for the bakery. So, I walk beside Khy toward the boat. I do it for the cause—*for the bakery*. Not because I'm letting my thirst lure me into some mess.

Chapter Nine

I adamantly stick with that excuse when I end up sitting on the deck of Khy's speedboat in a picture-perfect pose between Khy's legs. His arms are wrapped around my waist and my back is pressed against his chest as we float in the middle of the lake. The position was my idea—only to really sell some powerful ship-us-together-hardcore vibes, of course. Nothing more.

That *is* the truth. And yet... as I gaze out at ripples in the water shimmering from the sun overhead, a sense of complete (and wholly unnerving) bliss settles over me. It's undeniable that being in Khy's arms feels just right. Then, there's the damn muscles that make up the parts of his body I'm smushed against. Those are seriously hard to disregard, too. In fact, I clench my hands into fists, so I don't do something supremely stupid like snuggle back into his broad chest more enthusiastically and run my hands along the smooth dark brown skin of his arms. It's exposed from when he shed his jacket and rolled the sleeves of his dress shirt up to his elbows—ack! I swear this boy knows what he's doing and is well and truly trying to orchestrate my downfall. The logical part of my brain screeches the danger warning that keeps going off around him. But the self-indulgent half of my brain conjures up images of me acting on the impulse. My mind nosedives deep into the gutter, and I think about my initial mission with Khy—summer fun that consisted of lots of kissing.

What if you just had a teeny, tiny sample? A reckless voice asks. *Wouldn't a pic of a kiss make the internet go crazy?*

I shut that insane line of thinking down. *Absolutely not*, I tell my thirst, working extremely hard to decide that I mean it.

"Umm... are you good?" Khy's question drops me into a cavern of embarrassment. The only thing that makes me feel marginally better is that Khy's voice definitely betrays he's as affected by our proximity. His question comes out in a hoarse pitch that's several octaves deeper than his usual voice.

"I'm terrific." I make sure my voice comes out normal when I answer. "I think we've stayed this way long enough for plenty of photos to get snapped." It's time to haul myself out of perilous territory.

Khy immediately drops his arms from around me, sucks in a breath as if it physically hurt him to do so, and scoots from behind me. When he repositions himself directly beside me, our legs touch. I should move over a fraction. No parts of us need to be touching. Him being so near keeps short-circuiting my brain. But the same electric warmth as before shoots through me at our reestablished connection, and I stay where I am. Clearly, my self-control is trash where Khy is concerned. It's another red flag that I pointedly ignore.

A silence settles between us as the boat continues to waft under the late afternoon sun. I think about how I'm sweltering and how I'd much rather be in a swimsuit while out on the lake. Of course, that is the wrong thought to have. Because next I think about Khy shirtless and in swim trunks. I cough. Several times. End up choking on my spit.

An alarmed Khy scrambles to his feet. He grabs a water bottle out of a cooler nearby and hands it out to me as he sits back down. "Are you sure you're okay?"

I swipe the water bottle and nod. Gulp several swallows down. I grip the bottle in my hand, clutch it tight to my chest like it's Cap's shield and I'm using it to place a much-needed barrier between Khy and me. Khy glances down at the bottle quizzically, yet says nothing.

Get a grip, girl!

I reach for small talk. "So, water—how much command do you have over it? What all can you do?" I ask Khy.

If Khy knows what I'm trying to do, he doesn't let on. He only says, "Watch the lake," while sweeping a hand out at the water all around us. The ripples in the water become more vigorous, bubbling up like the fountains back at his lake house. Then the water rises into a dozen swirling columns surrounding the boat that seem to stretch to the sky. While the rest hold their position, the column directly in front of us spreads out into a wave shape and careens forward. My heart shoots into my throat as I watch, sure we're about to get drenched. But the wave stops an inch from the boat and plunges back into the lake Khy summoned it from. Our boat barely rocks from side to side and not a drop gets on us.

"Wow! That's incredible—and slightly terrifying," I say, breathless. "I was right when my cousin was scheming to drown you for what went down in Galveston. I told her it wouldn't work," I jokingly say.

Khy clutches his chest. "Damn! Ouch! *Again*. How do you keep skewering me every time we meet up?!"

I pop my lips, falling into the banter. "It's a gift. Maybe my secondary Connection is that I excel at keeping cute rich boys humble so they won't plague the world with big-ass heads."

Khy's laughter is a rich, booming sound that curls around me as tightly as his arms formerly did. "Listen, I don't even mind the shade since you called me cute. I'll take it."

I snigger. "Is me mentioning you're cute really all you're gonna focus on? Of course, we both know you're fine. I have eyes, and you have eyes. So, it's a given—and not that deep. Lots of boys are hot." Ha! That should keep Royal Boy extra humble and from reading too much into my admission.

Khy sagely nods like he's been listening to a super important lecture and learning volumes. "What I'm hearing is: my good looks and stunning water tricks aren't enough.

If I really want to impress you, I've gotta come harder. Got it. I told you I'm an athlete, right?" He says smugly. "We tend to be competitive. Which means I'm bringing my A game whenever we hang from now on."

The intense way he declares it makes it feel like all the oxygen gets sucked out of the air around us. I bite my lip, stealing a minute to shake off the disorienting effect. At least, that's what I aim to do. But the equally intense way Khy stares at me makes it impossible. "Why—" I clear my throat that's suddenly dry. "Why do you care so much about what I think? The entire world already adores you." I try for a teasing tone, but I fail at it, too. Because I find myself truly wanting to know. Why *is* my opinion of him so important? I'm just one random person, who he just met. Plus, I'm not one of his Coven folk. Even if he isn't the level of uppity I thought, he's still a part of a Coven and that will always mean he values his own people's judgment of him above anybody else's. It's just how Coven folk operate.

"Because . . ." Khy starts to answer my question but then trails off, his voice low. His brow furrows like he's deep in thought. "Because . . . I think you're terrific. Your energy is fly, and you're smart and funny and cool. And you don't take crap from folks, and I like all of that about you. Plus, because of who I am, I'm used to a lot of phoniness. Most folks automatically pretend to like me regardless of how they really feel about me. But you didn't. You were authentic. That makes me want to prove to you I'm nothing like the person you judged me to be up front."

"Oh." One word. Two letters. That's all I can manage. I think of how his friends gave him a hard time earlier about possibly liking me for real. His answer for sure makes it seem like he does. And I am such a traitor to my parents and everything *I* stand for because I think I like him back. A lot. "Having to always deal with fake friends sounds tough. I'm sorry; you don't deserve that." At first, I start saying it to keep the silence from stretching into awkward territory. But I realize how much I mean it and how much I want to make Khy feel better. And how irritated I am on his behalf. All of those are reasons I keep going and say comfortingly, "If it means anything, I can't see how anybody wouldn't like you for who you are just off the strength of how dope *your* energy is. I can't see why anybody would need to fake seeing that."

By the time I finish, we're both now gazing at each other super intensely. And have we somehow scooted closer to one another? Our legs don't only touch now. Our arms and shoulders do, too. We're near melded to each others' sides. And it doesn't rattle me into placing greater distance between us this time. I let myself enjoy the pleasant warmth buzzing through me.

"I'll also admit that after today, I have another reason to convince you to keep thinking I'm pretty damn dope," says Khy, with a hint of the mischief his voice held when he asked me to take the boat ride.

"Really. What's that?" I'm pretty sure I know, but I still ask because I shamelessly decide I want to hear him say it.

Khy grins. "I figure then I can convince you to let me take you out on a real do-over date, eventually."

A real date won't happen. Ever. It's not something I'll change my mind about. It's the firm answer I should give him. Except, in this moment, the inflexible *no* that I reach for is nonexistent. "I think maybe I'd like that, too, at some point," I say. And I can't even try to squash my humongous smile.

Chapter Ten

Despite adding content blocks to our internet settings, I'm hella paranoid for a few days after the Midsummer party that my parents will see the many pics of Khy and me that went viral. Using the lake party to increase the buzz around folks shipping us worked a little too well. One pic in particular, where his arms were around me while we were sitting on his boat, garnered *millions* of likes after Khy posted it to his own Insta page. But Cayden's Confections is staying booked and busy. So, I simply send a prayer to the Ancestors that my content blocks will be enough to keep my parents from discovering what's up and keep rolling with fanning the mutually beneficial hype over our ship. That's how I find myself surrounded by Coven witches again, less than a week after the lake party.

This time, I stand just inside the black iron gates that

encircle Magic Row. Though Magic *Rows* would be more accurate. A few years ago, several city blocks near University of Houston-Downtown were bought up by witches, and what used to be all warehouses and skyscrapers were knocked down to make room for a chic open-air, members-only market for witches. I've never been to Magic Row before, since I buy my spellwork materials online. I admit my curiosity is piqued while I wait for Khy to show up for our next fake date. He suggested the place because apparently paparazzi hang around here a lot since this is where the who's who of witches shop.

My eyes travel to the vendor tent a few feet to my left. Lots of bracelets, bangles, and earrings are arranged in neat rows atop a table, and a middle-aged white woman stands behind it. I catch the iridescent glint of a rainbow moonstone and know immediately the jewelry is embedded with stones for spellwork. I work with simple spells that require loose stones, like the aventurine I placed inside the register. But some complex spells are cast with wearable talismans, like an amulet that wards against evil, a ring that gives you a prolonged energy boost, or a choker that fortifies your immune system during cold and flu season. Wearable talismans are crazy expensive, though—like walking into a Tiffany's store and buying a signature charm bracelet expensive—so I've never bothered to even look into getting one. Staring at them now, curiosity gets the better of me and I wander over to the tent while I wait for Khy.

"Hello, welcome." The older woman greets me in an accent that sounds like she might be from New Jersey. She's dressed in a pair of posh black slacks, a shiny silver blouse, and silver sandals. Her hair—auburn red—is pulled back into a low ponytail. Around her neck is a rose quartz pendant (for romantic spells, friendship spells, or self-love rituals) hanging from a gold chain.

I give her a small smile in return and then turn my attention back to the talismans. I run my fingers over the ones closest to me, and I swear I can feel the magic coming from each of them. "Did you make these?" I ask.

She dips her head proudly. "I sure did. My Connection is within the range of metal weaving, and I assure you my craftsmanship is impeccable. If you went to St. Josephine's in the Spell Shoppe for one of their hastily made talismans, you'd pay triple for a subpar result. I also fill custom orders," she informs me.

I smile, admiring the shade she just threw at bigger and obnoxious witch corporations. "Sorry. I can't afford anything here. I wish I could, though," I say after glancing at the price tag on a tiger's eye silver bangle, seeing that it's marked at two grand. "To be honest, I've never been to Magic Row, and your stall has gorgeous talismans, so I just wanted to look around."

I brace for the Coven witch to express disdain. Maybe even demand I move along and stop wasting her time and taking up space in front of her tent. But the older woman smiles at me. "Look your fill. If you change your mind, I'll be right here." She motions to a velvet-topped stool in the back left corner of the tent and then strides to take a seat.

My phone dings as I'm gazing back at the tiger's eye bracelet and seriously wishing I did have the money for it. It's giving what it needs to give, would be cute as hell on me, and I could wear it as a daily accessory to ward off bad energy messing up my own mood. I tear my eyes away from the bangle and look down at my phone. The message from Dad to the family group chat makes me cheese hard.

> I don't know what's made things change but if these kinds of crowds keep up then you might get off the hook from working this summer Cayden 😊

I grin bigger because I can practically hear Dad's excitement. *Hell yes! The fake dating is working better than I could've imagined!* Even so, I text Dad back that I still want to work. That way, he can keep operating costs down, just in case.

"Cayden!" Khy calls my name about a second after I hit send. I look up to see him jogging toward me while waving. Hades trots at his side. *Great.* The Demon Dog returns.

Khy reaches me, and I have to tell my knees to stay strong when he smiles at me. "Hey, sorry I'm a little late. I hope you weren't waiting long," he says.

I wave him off. "Nah, you're good."

A low growl vibrates in the space between us.

I stiffen and glance down at Hades. "Hey to you, too, Archnemesis," I grumble.

He tilts his head, gives me his doggy side-eye. He doesn't growl again, per se, but his lips pull back from his teeth.

I roll my eyes. "Glad to see you still hate me for no good reason." I take a hefty step back from Hades before he decides to engage in his favorite hobby and bludgeon my leg with his massive tail.

Khy's eyebrows shoot up as he stares down at Hades. "Bud! What's wrong with you?!"

I smirk at the Warden of Hell. "Oh, ya boy was on his best behavior when you adopted him. But he hates me down to the depths of his petty soul," I inform Khy. "Always has." And now that I'm on the subject . . . I serve Hades my own side-eye because I have a bone to pick with His Majesty. (Pun definitely intended.) "What gives, bruh?" I hitch a thumb at Khy. "Your new bestie's a witch, too. So, why *we* got beef?" Obviously, Larissa's theory that Hades doesn't like witches was incorrect because he's now pleasantly resting his head against Khy's shorts, doing his best impression of a scolded toddler trying to get back into his parent's good graces.

"C'mon, boy, don't be like that," Khy says. He stoops down so he's eye level with Hades. The demon dog flashes me teeth over Khy's shoulder. *So* over his ridiculousness, I smack my teeth to let Hades know that *I know* he's nothing but a big, goofy, hyperactive teddy bear who would never hurt a fly. Khy scratches behind Hades's ear. "I like Cayden, a lot. But regardless, you should be nice to *everyone*. Don't be a butt. Okay, dude?"

Hades leans into Khy's hand but does that bougie sniff-the-air thing he likes to do, as if he hears you but doesn't deign to actually listen. Then, good ol' Hades keeps the stank-face dialed all the way up for dear ol' me. Khy sighs.

Clearly, Khy hasn't gotten to know his pup's stubborn-as-shit side. And today he's getting a front row seat. Khy helplessly looks between me and Hades when Hades doesn't thaw toward me. "I'm sorry. I didn't know you and my dog had beef! I can take him home if it's a problem?"

"No, it's okay," I answer truthfully. "Hades and I have been nemeses for forever. He and I know how to stay in our respective spaces to avoid cataclysm." I look at Hades. Take a few steps back. "Is this amount of distance suitable for you, Your Majesty?"

Hades finally relaxes. I almost roll my eyes, but I'm brokering peace.

Poor Khy remains bewildered. His forehead wrinkles intensely like he's thinking hard about something. A few seconds later, he holds out his hand, palm up, in front of Hades's face. I'm a witch who has grown up with my own magic and have seen Mom work her juju on animal patients, yet I still gasp when a sphere of rapidly spinning water about the size of a tennis ball appears in the center of Khy's hand. Hades yips, tail wagging frenziedly. "I knew that would make your attitude better," Khy chuckles. He pats Hades's head. "Let's make a deal. You be nice and *friendly* to Cayden, and we'll play your favorite fetch game later. But if you keep being mean, then no Water Ball today." The liquid sphere vanishes from Khy's palm as quickly as it appeared.

Hades whines and nudges Khy's hand with his nose. "I meant what I said," Khy responds firmly but gently.

Hades gazes at Khy's empty palm longingly. "Go give Cayden a fist bump," says Khy, then he points directly at me.

I wait for Hades's doggy side-eye. But, miraculously, the humongous chocolate poodle trots to stand right in front of me. He sits back on his hind legs and raises his front right paw in the air.

"He'll be nice now, I promise. Pound his paw back and see," Khy says when I just stare, gobsmacked, at Hades.

Khy stands and strides to my side. "It's okay," he says encouragingly to me, as if he needs to soothe me to accept this new arrangement as much as he had to do with Hades. Honestly, I think he does.

I'm skeptical as hell. (Hades might be playing me, getting me to let my guard down so he can get one good thwack in with his tail.) But I am not about to let the demon dog look like the more mature, levelheaded, reasonable one. I fist bump Hades's paw. He, miraculously, allows me to make contact. I execute it quickly, though; it's best not to press my luck.

"That's a good boy!" Khy grins, ruffling the (admittedly adorable) curly fur atop Hades's head.

I can't stop myself from smiling at the two of them all sappy.

My mind floats back to how good it felt to sit in Khy's arms on the boat at the lake party. How he made sure I was comfortable around his friends after my misunderstanding and then even tried to pitch me a save when he thought they were maybe getting to be too much to handle. And now here he is with Hades, showing infinite patience for his high-maintenance antics. Khy is *really* nice. And kind. And *good. Decent.* Matter of fact, those words might not even adequately capture him. He's not just a ten. He's a surreal twelve. I think it right as Khy looks at me, and I find myself stuck, unable to do anything except stare into the warm brown of his eyes for a second. He's a good bit taller than me, so while I do it, he looks down at me through those unfairly thick, dark lashes that cast shadows on his upper cheekbones. I lower my eyes before things turn awkward, but they land on his lips.

I recognize the peril at once. Khy's kissable lips are the last part of his body I need to be looking at. Then, I'll start envisioning what it'll be like to kiss him. And no. That ain't it. Things need to stay friendly and simply mutually beneficial between me and Royal Boy for now. They unequivocally do not need to turn all cozy and complicated before I've properly thought about if I really want to go there and invite a potential hurricane into my life. I won't be able to keep a whole Coven boyfriend from my parents! They *will* feel some type of way about that! Yet, for all of how certain I am, I haven't stopped gazing at Khy's lips, and my mind conjures a vivid image of—

Shoes! Yes, let's see what shoes he's rocking today. That'll firmly ensnare my attention on safer parts of Royal Boy.

"Nice ones today; I'm surprised you went with a subtle pair," I say about his all black, suede Nike SB Dunk Highs. There's nothing super eye-catching about them, and the ordinary person would dismiss them as basic. But the bottom soles are a shiny gold, the inside is lined with gold satin, and a mere twenty-five were released into the world last year. And zero retail stores got them. They were auctioned at a charity event held during the NBA's All-Star Weekend in Houston. "I'm not gonna even ask how much you dropped on those," I tell Khy. I already know they're worth a small chest of gold.

He just chuckles and says, "It was for a good cause. It benefited—"

"Libraries in underfunded Houston schools, I know," I finish for him. I know because I followed the hell out of that sneaker release and the media coverage of the auction during All-Star Weekend. Hell no, I could never ever afford to actually score a pair, but it still didn't stop me from ogling every sneak peek that sneaker blogs managed to get their hands on. "Your globs of money *did* go to something really good," I concede to Khy. I smile teasingly. He smiles back, and I get stuck on it for the umpteenth time—*and damn it; I did not stick to my plan to keep my eyes fastened to his shoes.* Not that it was a sensical, or even doable, plan to begin with. Clearly, I can't spend the whole night with my eyes glued to Khy's sneakers and not have him become highly disturbed. "So...yeah...one day I'm gonna come visit heaven, which I'm positive your closet is the equivalent of, and drink in all the crazy shoes you've scored, okay?" I say it to Khy while trying to dampen the potent spell he keeps casting. Seriously, what in the hell? Even if I were looking for a serious boyfriend, it's much too soon to be catching serious feelings for somebody I've known for so little time.

Khy grins wider, which has the opposite effect of what I need to achieve. "You can roll through whenever you want, but the invitation better go both ways." He nods down at the Air Max 90s with cheetah print and a neon pink Nike checkmark that I'm wearing. I love me some 90s because their shape is cute, they're technically running shoes and comfy, and they are criminally underrated by most sneakerheads so I can snag killer editions that don't run my pockets.

"They're gorgeous, right?" I stick my right foot out and strike a pose with my hand on my hip like I'm modeling the shoe. I use my best Riley from *The Boondocks* voice. "Now before you get mad, be honest. Ain't I fly, though?" I keep a straight face when I deliver the near-quote from my all-time favorite show.

Khy doesn't miss a beat. He twists his lips, snickering. He gets major brownie points for getting the reference. He gets more points when he says, "I love that show. I rewatch all the seasons at least a couple times a year."

"Me too!" I exclaim.

"That means we need to link up and watch it together. You down?"

I know that this is where I should remind him that our

arrangement needs us to meet up in highly visible places, and watching TV on one of our couches isn't that. But a giddy thrill zips through me at his proposal, and all I really want to do is squeal: *Let's do it!*

"Excuse me? Can I get a picture?" Thankfully, the teen girl who walks up saves me from having to choose which response to ultimately give Khy.

He turns to her, all manners and humility. "Sure!"

I step to the side and offer to the girl, "I can take one of you and him?"

"I meant a picture of you both," she says. "I mean, if you don't mind? I think you two are so adorable together! I saw the picture of y'all cuddling on the boat. It was so romantic! Y'all are my new favorite OTP!" She informs us excitedly as if we're some epic fictional couple. "Like, for real. I hated Gigi for you," she tells Khy. "You're too chill and too nice. She's so extra and such a diva. I knew as soon as y'all started dating last year that you and her didn't fit," the girl goes on like she and Khy are longtime besties. "And, oh my God, I just know all of her charity projects she pushes are totally for clout, right? Like there's no way somebody that sketch is an actual good person. I was crushed for you when she cheated. I can't believe her; you deserve better!" All right. This chick is way too comfortable with sharing how obsessed she is with the details of a stranger's personal life. Hell, I'm uncomfortable for Khy at this point. Poor Khy looks like he wants to melt through the grass.

I pitch him a save and interrupt the girl's ceaseless

talking, since he's too gracious to do it. "I'm sorry, but we've got to leave soon," I tell her amicably. "Do you want to go ahead and snap the pic?"

"Oh. My bad. Yes! Please!" She's already got her phone out and waves it excitedly. "My friends are gonna be so jealous I met y'all. As soon as THE SCOOP posted y'all had been spotted together here, I raced over from UHD. Is it too much to ask for you two to hug or something? My friends will lose it."

She's the one who's lost something—her damn mind. Does Khy really have to endure occurrences like this all the time?

"We don't have to do that if you don't want to," Khy says low to me.

I consider saying no off principal alone. Asking for a picture is one thing. Requesting a specific pose is quite the audacity. But racking up positive social media buzz is the whole point of Khy and me hanging out. Which is the only reason I don't let his fan know about herself. "It's fine," I tell Khy with a smile. I step into his side and wrap my arm around his waist. He does the same, following my lead. Like on the boat, an electric buzz instantly shoots through me when we touch. I take in the yummy fragrance of his cologne—citrus, sandalwood, and fresh rain—and inwardly sigh at it all. I bite my tongue so the mortifying sound does not escape. *Please hurry up and take the picture!* I think at the girl. She's now standing beside Khy so she'll be in the shot too, and she has her phone raised in the air. As soon as she gets a pic, I put some distance between me and Khy. Breathe in air not suffused with his scent.

"Thanks so much! Have a good day," the girl says and walks off.

I stare after her. Shake my head. "Does that happen to you a lot?"

"Not all the time. But enough," answers Khy ruefully.

I shouldn't pick at the issue of his ex. I'm certain I should mind my business. But I can't help asking, "What that girl said about your ex, if Gigi's actually that awful, why'd you date her?" I'm not quite sure why I care, or why I'm suddenly hung up on hearing his answer.

"I know you heard the girl say that she thinks Gigi is only into doing charity stuff for clout. But I swear, it's really not performative crap with her—at least, I didn't think it was while we dated. It's what made me dig her. She isn't super generous about everything, admittedly, and she can be self-absorbed a lot of the time, but for the stuff she believes in and decides is important, she goes hard. So, we had that in common, and it made me fall for her, I guess." He laughs in the self-deprecating way you do when you're trying to make something embarrassing sting less. "Guess I was wrong about she and I."

"Unless you have a Connection that's linked to mind reading or forecasting the future, you couldn't possibly have known she'd cheat on you," I say. "And what she did, you don't gotta be embarrassed about it. *She* should be embarrassed that she's trifling and that the whole world witnessed it."

"Most of the time," Khy says, "I remember that. But there have been times since our breakup where I've wanted to crawl under a rock until everybody forgets I got played and dumped." He pivots to face the jewelry tent brusquely enough that I peep he's downplaying how much the whole mess bothers him. "Did you see something you liked over here?" he asks, doing that thing he does where he blatantly switches topics when he doesn't want to dwell on something.

I roll with it, feeling sort of bad for him—I can't imagine what it'd be like to live my life under a literal camera lens. "This tiger's eye bangle is pretty," I say, fingering it. "But not all of us are as rich as Tony Stark, so it's out of my budget," I say teasingly. "And even if it wasn't . . . I'd drop that kind of spending money on kicks before jewelry."

Khy snorts. "That means your priorities are in A-plus shape."

We laugh—a thing that comes so easy with Khy. It makes me feel the exact same goofy bliss I do every time I inhale a fresh pan of Dad's brownie-bottom cheesecake. My stomach syncs up with my thoughts and embarrassingly growls; I remember that I've only eaten the single bear claw I shoved into my mouth that morning right before I flipped the bakery's sign to open and the day's rush began, not ending until closing time. Khy arches an eyebrow. "You hungry?"

"Starving," I admit.

He grabs my hand. "Come on. I remember you mentioning something about me ruining seafood for you, and I need to make it up to you."

Chapter Eleven

We end up standing in line at The Cajun Cat. It's one of a dozen food trucks parked along a side gate of Magic Row. I inhale, letting delicious aromas like the smell of fried breading seasoned with Cajun spices, lightly sweet hush puppies, and gumbo entrance me like a love spell. Dad's the pastry chef, but I'm the true foodie. And my love of good food that feeds the soul and sparks joy isn't restricted to sugary goodness.

"You know what you're gonna get?" Khy asks.

"The fried shrimp and hush puppies with a side of red beans and rice," I tell Khy. I spied the option on The Cajun Cat's menu as soon as we got in line. "Oh, and a bag of beignets. What about you?"

"Gumbo, voodoo fries, and catfish," he spouts off like he's

been here millions of times. His next statement confirms the guess. "You've gotta try my voodoo fries. They're fire."

I'm sure they are. I can already taste the blissful combo of Cajun seasoning, ranch dressing, and cheese sauce atop fresh-cut fries. "I peeped those," I admit to Khy. "But I was trying not to go overboard."

He knocks his shoulder against mine lightly. "See, that was me with the beignets. But I guess that just means we're sharing both."

"Definitely," I decide.

"This gonna sound corny but Cajun cuisine is literally my soul food," Khy says as we step up to the ordering window with Hades in tow. "It's like..." He struggles to find the words.

"Like it wraps you up in your happy place, like a warm hug," I finish for him.

He looks at me surprised. "Yeah!"

"I feel the same," I say.

We order, wait on our food to be made, and then grab a spot on the grass free of vendor tents that stretches out in front of the food trucks. Khy picks the spot, and I don't complain about it at all because I actually love laying out on the grass. But I do glance at the scattering of tables and benches nearby, curious about his reason for skipping them.

While scratching behind Hades's ear, he follows my gaze. "I thought this would give us the vibe of a picnic, sort of," he says. "I...umm...I like those joints."

He says it almost bashfully—and adorably. He opens up his container of voodoo fries and scoops up three. "Taste 'em." He holds them up to my mouth. And I eat them right from his hands.

Oh Lord! I just let this boy feed *me; that is* not *casual friends' territory.* It doesn't hit me until after I'm letting out a sigh at how good the gooey fries are. And yet, I still open up my white paper bag and hold a fluffy beignet out to Khy, the powdered sugar dusting my fingers. "Your turn." I try very hard to not stare at his lips like a creeper and am, amazingly, successful. Then, he's angling his head downward as I'm lifting the beignet upward. The pastry smashes into his nose.

"I'm so sorry!" I squeak and snatch it back. My whole face burns as I fix my stare on my hands and wipe the powdered sugar that coats them onto the grass.

I am drowning in mortification when Khy softly calls my name. I look up as he pokes out his tongue and tries to lick the powdered sugar off his nose. "Dang," he sighs when he can't quite reach his nose. "I really thought that was gonna work. Hold up. Let me get a do-over." He makes a show of repeating the attempt.

I melt into laughter. "Bro, what are you doing?" I manage through the fits of giggles.

He erupts into laughter along with me. When our laughter dies, he says, "I didn't want you to be embarrassed, so I figured I'd embarrass myself. You don't gotta be perfect around me, Cayden," he adds. "I like you for *you*."

I choke on air. The amount of tries it takes to clear my throat would be hella awkward if it didn't buy me precious minutes to come up with a response. "We're just hanging as friends," I say finally. Neither of us needs to forget it.

Khy automatically looks sheepish. "I meant as a friend. You're a really terrific person to hang with. As a friend."

"Okay..." I pick at a blade of grass. Without consciously meaning to I think about how, before meeting Khy, never in a million years would I expect to hear a Coven witch tell me that they like half-witch, half-human, totally Covenless Cayden exactly for who she is. But everything about Khy keeps shattering my initial perceptions, and before I went and made stuff sort of weird, I'd found myself so completely at ease around Khy. *As a friend.* And now, well, now I can't return to my former relaxed state, because the way he emphatically uttered he likes me *for* me reminds me of what he said about some people being phony with him and how much it bothers him.

"I like you for *you*, too, Khy. A lot," I tell him. I want Khy to know it's 100 percent true, so there's no hurtful doubts that creep up. "I'm not like those folks you mentioned on the boat. I'm not gonna put you through that and just be chilling with you because of your celebrity status." I groan as soon as I say it. "I'm sorry. That sounds stupid. I am literally doing exactly that with this fake dating arrangement. But, if we hadn't launched this scheme and I got to know you, I'd still want to hang as friends. You're cool people." *And I am rambling so much at this point; I should really shut up.*

"I know you're not one of those people. That's the opposite of the energy you give." Like at the lake party, Khy stares at me in this super intense way.

I swallow and hold the beignet in the air between us. "Shall we try this again? I don't think my crash landing made for the best photo op." I drawl, trying for sassiness to lessen the unnerving potency of what runs between Khy and me.

He twists his lips, going with the pace I set as usual. "Yeah. Let's."

I raise the beignet and he takes a big bite. I eat the rest. It might be one of the best I've ever had. "Yoooo, this is *chef's kiss*, right?"

"Fa' sho," Khy says, picking up a handful of voodoo fries and eating them. I place two beignets beside the pile of fries inside his carton and he pushes the carton so it rests equidistantly away from us both. I place the bag with the rest of the beignets beside it. We eat those two items first and then start in on the rest of our food. By the time the food is gone, I'm stuffed and I can't do anything except lie back in the grass, looking up at the cloudless sky. Khy lies beside me, and Hades plops down on his other side. For a second, I have this insane urge to reach out and grab Khy's hand. But that'd make this feel so much closer to a real date, and the lines with Khy are already blurring. So I keep my hands to myself.

The embargo I place on touching Khy doesn't make the butterflies in my stomach less insufferable, though. Nor does it diminish how hyperaware every inch of me seems to be of how close Khy and I are. Literally, if I turned to the side, and he turned on his side, and I leaned over a tad more, our lips could touch. A vision crashes over me of the two of us kissing. The world wobbles more. My lips tingle like we've actually just kissed. I blink. Shoot up to a sitting position. Khy stays lazily sprawled on the grass. His hands are folded behind his head, making the hem of his shirt ride up to reveal smooth dark brown skin. I snap my eyes to his face.

Luckily his phone beeps, and it keeps me from having to fumble for something to say. He sits up and slides his phone from his pocket. "That didn't take long," he says. He turns the phone screen so I can see the new pics of us that THE SCOOP has posted. There's the shot the girl who goes to UHD took with us hugging, one of me and Khy standing at the jewelry tent that captured our side profiles, another of him feeding me voodoo fries. My cheeks heat at that last one because things *look* as cozy as they'd felt between us.

"Well, we definitely appear to be boo'd up," I say, nodding toward the pics. "Hopefully, all the trending pics are salvaging your rep after the stuff with your ex." It's the first time I've brought up his ex-girlfriend, and I keep my tone light and casual. It's not like I care about if he's still hung up on her. I'm only being nosy.

Khy pushes out a breath, and I want to take back what I said immediately. His upbeat energy dims in a way I hate.

"Sorry for bringing it up," I say.

"Nah. You're good," he mutters. "It actually is helping me

feel better about being played in front of the whole world. Plus, Cotillion is coming up, which means Gigi's rolling into town soon. And our pics will send a strong message to her—and the world—that I'm not stressing her or Tano or their relationship when she gets here."

"Sounds like you kind of are, though," I hazard. *That's not your business*, a cautioning voice pipes up. *And pressing him about it definitely blurs lines more.* But he's clearly feeling some type of way about his ex, and for a reason I don't examine too closely, I decide I don't want to drop it. "Do you still have a thing for her?" *Not that I care on any deep level.* I'm only asking so I fully know what I've gotten into with this fake dating scheme.

Khy vigorously shakes his head. "Hell nah. She cheated on me and then dumped me. I'm so good on her. But my friends, and the world, and my family, and probably Gigi herself, has been thinking I'm all twisted up since it happened. I'm so sick of being *that poor guy*. You coming along means everybody is finally believing what I've been telling them." He waves the phone. "I guess the Gigi stuff was just the first time that I got hella media attention that wasn't positive. *That* did leave me twisted for a minute. It's not like they made me the bad guy or anything, but being seen as the *sad* guy didn't feel great either. I just gotta deal and try to make sure I'm portrayed in the light I want to be. That's the exhausting part—always worrying about being inaccurately represented or made to look like something I'm not."

"I get that," I say, scooting into his side. "It would suck to always need to think about your image, or whatever."

Khy smiles ruefully. "Ugh!" He smacks his forehead. "I probably sound like a spoiled movie star. *Please* tell me I don't?"

I hold up my thumb and index finger with a teensy space between them. "Only like this much."

He laughs, genuinely laughs. His whole face lights up and the funk lifts from him. "That's one of the things I like about you," he says. "You always keep it one hundred—even if it means coming for my neck."

I shrug. "I don't do phony, bruh."

"All right then. Can I ask you something?" he says. "I know you're cool with the publicity because of your bakery, but what about your parents? How do they feel about you being so much in the public eye over dating some boy who's a Coven witch? I've been wondering because I know . . . I know you told me about the bad history with them and Covens."

I wince. This isn't a conversation I expected to have with Khy, but he's been open and honest with me, so I guess it's about time I do the same. "The truth? They don't know anything about this. They'd definitely take it pretty brutally for exactly the reason you said, and they would murder me if they knew it was some bogus scheme to help out the bakery." Seriously, I'm near shuddering just thinking about that one. "They'd tell me that wasn't my burden to take on, especially not in this way."

"They wouldn't be wrong," Khy responds quietly.

I stiffen, and Khy holds up his hands. "I'm not telling you what to do. You can make your own decisions. I'm just saying—"

"You don't need to. I'm aware I don't *have* to do this, but I am seeing it through," I let Khy know. Then I ease up a little. "Thank you, though," I say. "It's sweet that you care."

"When it comes to you, I couldn't *not* care, Cayden," Khy says.

The butterflies in my stomach quadruple. And there's this intense sensation in my chest that leaves me rattled enough that I say, "I should get going." Enough splashy pics have been taken, they've already made their way onto the internet, and I've been in Khy's orbit for way too long today. I swear this boy is like the sun. Glossy and brilliant and stunning and surreal—and potentially all-consuming and blinding. Like in a way that could make me lose sight of what I care about most—my parents. Not hurting them. The reminder of that is all I need to find the motivation to hop to my feet.

Khy stands with me, Hades following. "Where'd you park? I'll walk you to your car," he offers like some freaking perfect Prince Charming straight out of a modernized Disney fairy tale.

"Don't worry about it," I say, attempting to place some distance between us. I need breathing room, so I can mentally shake myself free of the spell Khy keeps casting on me. "I don't want you to go out of your way," I tell him politely.

"Bye!" I turn away hurriedly and start across the grass toward the exit before he can object.

But Khy is right at my side, towing Hades along. "Did you park in the UHD garage right across the street? I did, too, so we'll be going to the same spot anyway."

I did not. I should lie. Walk in the opposite direction, meander around downtown until Khy has likely gotten to his car, and then go to mine in the UHD garage. "I did," is what comes out. And the traitorous butterflies execute thrilled backflips at stealing a few more minutes with Khy.

We pass a tent with magicked flowers on the way out of the market. There are bunches of roses, lilies, and tulips whose petals repeatedly snap closed and then unfurl in a dramatic fashion. It's pretty neat. Hades must think so, too, because he plunges headfirst into one of his hyperexcited shenanigans. He barks raucously and starts darting around Khy and me, his leash wrapping loosely around our legs.

"Hades, cut that out," Khy says, trying and failing to untangle us as Hades gets more and more excited.

Then all of a sudden, Hades bounds for the flowers and his leash causes my feet to fly out from under me. I yell. Khy yelps. Then we're crashing to the grass in a tangle of limbs. Khy lands on top of me—and the universe is really messing with me, because I am vertical in the grass with this boy again and his lips are literally an inch from my face.

Khy gazes down at me like *I'm* the sun that *he's* blinded by for a second. He blinks. His face morphs into a stricken expression, and he quickly scrambles off of me. "Sorry," he says, reaching a hand down to help me stand, too.

"Hades has always been a goofball." I laugh to lessen the hella awkward moment. Which . . . I am really racking them up today.

Hades yips. We hear a deep male voice bellow at him to get away. Khy and I both turn to see his dog munching on yellow mums.

Khy curses, and we run to Hades. He swallows Hades up in a hug, pulling him back from the flowers. "He won't get sick, will he?" Khy asks me frantically. "Mums aren't like some flower that's poisonous to dogs, right?" He curses again. "I should've read up on that already. I should know this!"

I touch his shoulder. "Calm down; Hades is fine. Mums are harmless to dogs."

Khy nods, hugging Hades tighter. I just about melt at how damn adorable he is with the demon dog. Hades snuggles into Khy's chest like he's an angel who has done nothing wrong.

I smirk Hades's way. "He might have a tummy ache, but that's it." I tell Khy to watch out for lilies, tulips, hyacinths, and azaleas—plants that are typically common enough in yards and homes that can be nasty for dogs if ingested. Larissa made a list and has a massive, can't-miss poster tacked on a wall at the rescue for when volunteers take our furbabies for exercise.

Khy apologies to the flower shop owner and covers the cost of the damaged flowers, and then some.

"You're lucky you're cute," he mutters to Hades as we hurry away. Hades only burps in reply. I giggle, and Khy looks over to me. "Thanks for helping me calm down back there. I didn't know being a dog dad would be this stressful."

I laugh again. "Happy to help. I may not have my mom's Connection to animals, but I've picked up a few things at the rescue."

Now in the parking lot, I can see my car up ahead. I point it out to Khy, and he walks me over. When we reach it, he gets a thoughtful look on his face.

"Hey, can I ask one more question about a touchy subject?" Khy asks.

"We've already had one sharing circle. Go for it," I say while digging for my keys.

"I was thinking about the stuff we talked about at the lake party, and I was wondering . . . Have you ever, like, met your mom's parents at all?"

I trip over my next step. My hand tightens around the key remote. "I haven't," I say as coolly as possible.

Khy shakes his head like he can't wrap it around such a fact. "I mean, I know families can have rifts, but that's crazy that they haven't tried to meet their own granddaughter, ever."

"Yeah, well, that's their loss," I snap, although it isn't directed at Khy.

He seems to get that because next he says, "I'd be majorly pissed about it, too. But I'm sure it's also brutal, right?"

Normally, I'd pull on my usual tough-girl exterior and toss out some wiseass crack. But the way Khy says it—like he's personally pissed off and gutted *for me* makes the truth pour out. "Yeah, it hurts. Family means so much to me—it means *everything* to me. My dad, my mom, my aunties, and cousins. And knowing how super close I am with my grandparents on my dad's side, too ... I'm not sure what kind of people miss out on their grandchild's whole life."

"Me neither," Khy says. "I'm close with my family, too. Everybody on both my mom's and dad's sides. I can't imagine any of them being strangers to me."

I smile without mirth. "No shade, but I imagine it's easy for Coven witches to play happy, perfect family when everybody belongs to a Coven and is *suitable*."

He winces. As he should. "I deserved that."

"You did," I say, opening my door. "But you're good. You were trying to come from a good place, even if it came out hella insensitive."

He clutches his heart—a running gag, apparently. "You. Are. Vicious."

I do an exaggerated curtsy, grinning to let him know everything is still cool between us. "You're welcome, my guy. So let me ask you, then: What do *your* parents think about our trending relationship?" I ask, growing curious. Unlike mine, I'm sure they're exceedingly tuned into media stories about themselves and other witches. At the very least, I'm betting Allison Carter, North America's great Witch Regent, has people who stay up on what's being said about her and her family in the media.

"They usually don't pay outlets like THE SCOOP any attention," Khy responds. "They hate gossipy news and the paparazzi."

"Got it," I say, not missing that he didn't actually answer my question. Of course his parents know, and of course they've given him shit about it. I'm a witch, but I'm a Covenless witch—and I'm certainly not witch royalty like them or his ex. I hold back a scowl and don't give Khy a hard time about it. Truly, it doesn't matter. And it actually does me a sorely needed favor. It reminds me precisely how snobby Coven witches are and that Khy is an anomaly. Most importantly, it emphasizes why Khy and I would never work for real, even if I am, admittedly, into him a lot.

Later that night, I get a text from Khy. I steel myself against the butterflies that are *so* unserious, they've already forgotten the timely reminder in the parking garage for why they need to vanish. But when I open Khy's text, I read something besides a flirty comment or a suggestion for our next fake date.

> Before you put me in my place again . . . I know it's not about me . . . it's about you. I can't stop feeling bad and thinking about the stuff you said earlier though. I promise all of us aren't like that. And I grabbed these for you in case you want to know something about your grandparents. They're profile pages from a Coven app.

Below Khy's text are two screenshots. Fury and guilt twist through me all at once. I've never seen nor talked to nor met my mom's parents, and I don't have this burning desire to do so. I wasn't lying to Khy about that. But, with their member profiles right in my face, I can't deny I'm curious about *who* they are. About who mom came from. About who I'd call Grandma and Granddad under different circumstances. I almost give in and click on one of the screenshots. But then that would be giving terrible, soulless people too much power. It would be admitting I kind of, maybe, do care. Worst of all, it'd be a slap in the face to Mom and Dad after everything they've gone through and sacrificed. And that's not something I'm willing to do.

Chapter Twelve

Dad's bakery has always been the family gathering spot. Ever since I was little, me, Mom, Dad, Mercedes, Auntie Nikki, Auntie Vesha, Grams, and Grandpop would get together in the bakery after closing time to do stuff like plan family vacations, celebrate milestone birthdays, or just munch on the day's leftover pastries and hang out.

The entire gang is crowded into Cayden's Confections again today, this time organizing the fundraiser. We're spread out between two booths, grinding away on the tasks I assigned everybody to help pull off the cookout. Dad's making calls, trying to find a business willing to donate folding chairs and tables. Mom, seated beside him at the booth in front of mine, is doing the same for rental AV equipment. Auntie Vesha and Grandpop each have laptops in front of them, taking notes via a shared Google doc about who commits to donating what and how we'll get the materials when it's time. Mercedes, Grams, and Auntie Nikki are in my booth. While I return the emails of several news orgs eager to cover the cookout and "hopefully be granted an exclusive interview with me and Khy" (that information does *not* get added to the shared doc), Mercedes sends invites to local influencers, Auntie Nikki works on a letter to solicit monetary donations, and Grams designs the menu for the BBQ plates Dad's frat is contributing.

Dad has placed baskets of cinnamon rolls, doughnut holes, and tea cakes on the tables along with pitchers of sweet tea. We chow down while we work, joking and laughing with each other between phone calls. While Auntie Nikki tells an animated story about two kids she teaches at her ballet studio—capturing the family's attention in the way only she, a woman who's wowed the stage for almost all of her life, can—I listen and soak up how much I love it when the whole gang gets together like this. I don't mean for my thoughts to go where they do next. They just do. And it leaves me unable to shake the mental image of Mom's parents' profiles sitting on my phone. I catch myself and smooth out my face before it can betray the bitterness that creeps over me.

"Yo, are you all right?" Mercedes asks in a low tone beside me.

I grimace. Of course she picked up on my change in mood. "I'm good," I tell her. "Just getting tired." I try really hard to make it true. To actually *not* be twisted up over a pair of people that have never bothered to get to know me or reach out. But the bitter feeling lingers. And just like that—thanks to Royal Boy and his prying question—I've apparently gone from happily feeling nothing at all about my estranged grandparents to this tart resentment. I grow angry with myself because those people do not deserve *any* emotion from me.

Mom's annoyed groan hauls me out of the funky headspace. I glance her way and see her face pinched tight. She stabs a finger at her iPad. "See, this right here is why we need a fundraiser in the first place!" she says angrily.

"Eva, girl, what's the matter?" Auntie Vesha asks.

Mom shakes her head. "Apparently, The Spell Shoppes aren't enough. I just came across an ad for a new day spa exclusively for witches opening off McGowan next winter!"

Auntie Vesha scowls. "How much of the neighborhood are they going to hijack?!" she exclaims fiercely. Unlike Dad and Auntie Nikki, Auntie Vesha didn't grow up in Third Ward. But she did attend STU, and now she, Auntie Nikki, and Mercedes live near the university.

Grumbles about Coven witches and how they care for nobody except themselves ripple between both my aunties and parents. Guilt eats at me because I've been chillin' with the very people they're rightfully criticizing. *But it's to help out*, I stress to make myself feel less like a traitor. *You're not hanging around Coven witches because you* like *what they're about.*

The logic helps, but only so much.

Grandpop's booming laughter rumbles through the room. He's laughing so hard that his broad shoulders shake uncontrollably.

Auntie Vesha, who's sitting beside him, pats his arm, her mood lifting. "What are you cracking up over, Pops?" She peeks at his phone to see for herself. Amusement lights up her hazel gaze. "Really? You're going on like that over Tik-Tok? I swear you're as bad as one of the youngins."

Grandpop huffs. "Oh, what, you thought I was an old head? I *am* one of the young folks."

"Not if you're talking like that, Dontae," Grams quips from my table.

Mom kisses Grandpop's temple, then says, "Ignore them both, Pops. If you say you're young, then you're young. Period. We're only ever as old as how we feel, ain't we?"

Dad snorts. "Eva, stop lying to that *old* man. He out here at sixty-eight trying to be twenty-eight. I bet you're watching another one of them dance videos, huh?"

Grandpop scowls. "Mind ya business, son. And remember you ain't never too old to catch ya daddy's hands, a'ight?"

"Dang, I forget you a gangsta sometimes, Grandpop," Mercedes says. "Uncle Jason, I think you about to get a beat down for real today."

Auntie Nikki kisses her teeth. "*Please*. Pops is a teddy bear. He's the definition of all bark and no bite."

"Because I love my pain in the ass kids too much to really

go upside your heads," Grandpop grumbles. He pins Daddy with a look. "But you grown, now. So keep talking slick."

The whole table bursts out in laughter, including me, because we all know Grandpop isn't serious. He and Dad like to go back and forth and good-naturedly clown each other; it's their love language.

"Let me see the vid, though?" Mercedes asks when our laughter dies.

"I wanna see, too, Pops," Auntie Nikki says. "I wanna know if it's one of the new ones the kids at the studio be doing."

Grandpop grumbles again. And this time, he informs the whole family that we're nosy. But he also passes his phone around so everybody can see.

Mercedes giggles when the phone gets to her. "It's the way I need you to finally make a dance vid yourself, since you stay watching them," she informs Grandpop.

"Your grandfather has no rhythm," Grams exclaims.

"He really don't," Dad chimes in.

"Neither do you," Grandpop reminds Dad.

"Lord, they about to start it up again," Grams mutters.

But before either can, Mercedes stands from her seat, walks to Grandpop, and tugs at his arm. "Come one, *young man*. Get up and let's get to filming," she says. She waves his phone. "I'll teach you the moves to this one. It's easy!"

Auntie Nikki hops to her feet. "I already know this one. Let's go!"

Auntie Vesha tosses herself into the fun and stands next. "I don't usually dance, but I'll participate for Pops. Teach me, too."

Mom, Grams, and Dad all end up standing and ready to partake in Mercedes's shenanigans.

This freshest display of our extreme closeness should be wrapping around me like a bear hug. I should be hopping up excitedly to do something so goofy yet feel-good with my family. But it steers my thoughts back toward the set of grandparents who are strangers to me, and then I am annoyingly thinking about what it would be like if Mom's parents weren't total snobs or strangers. Would they be in the bakery with us right now? Would Mom and one of her parents have their own special love language that I immediately recognize because I've soaked it up my entire life?

"I'm gonna run to the bathroom," I say, hauling myself out of my seat. I just need a second, a little bit of space to get myself together.

But when I'm alone in the restroom, I do the opposite of that. In fact, I do something that leaves me annoyed as hell with myself for a second time. I grab my phone from my pocket and click on one of the screenshots Khy sent. The name at the top says CAROLYN HILLIARD. That's Mom's mother's name. I know that much about the woman. Carolyn's picture is smack-dab at the top. Her dark brown hair is styled into a flawless body wave that frames her face and falls past her shoulders. She's got pearls in her ears and a strand around her neck. She's dressed in a cream pantsuit and nude heels. She's seated in a leather armchair, legs daintily crossed at the ankles, hands primly folded atop her knees. I scowl. "She looks like the queen of bougie," I mutter pettily. This woman is *over-the-top* extra. And while I don't truly *want* to learn a thing further about her, one thing I do suddenly want to know is how someone like Carolyn birthed a woman so down to earth and chill as my mom. So, I let my eyes dip below the photo and skim what's printed. I find out that Carolyn was born on February 3, 1960, in Dallas, Texas. She's an equestrian (obviously); she attended college at Yale University (because of course she did); she's served as the fundraising chair for a slew of charities since graduating (meaning she's always been wildly rich with the time and privilege to be a full-time philanthropist); and she's currently the Social Affairs President for Dallas's Coven (imagine that).

I close the screenshot, not having gained any insight into how it's possible Mom came from that level of hyper snooty. I'm driven to click on the second screenshot, the one labeled ROBERT HILLIARD III, to see if Mom's father is any better. Judging by the man's picture, the answer is *hellllll no*. Robert's photo is one of him in a severe gray suit, standing beside a fireplace with hands in his pockets. The dark brown–skinned man is angled partially to the side so it's an artsy pseudo-profile shot of him cutting a lofty figure. My maternal grandfather appears as stuffy as his wife.

And his bio confirms it. He was born two months before Carolyn (December 12, 1959), attended Yale, too, and returned home to Dallas after college to take over Hilliard Ranch—which breeds Longhorn cattle and elite horses. Apparently, his Connection is one that's broadly categorized as Magical Husbandry, and he's able to amplify the fertility, number of healthy pregnancies, and healthy births among livestock animals. Admittedly, that last detail is fascinating. I can't even front; it's a really cool Connection. I guess I found something Mom has in common with her parents after all—her dad's giftedness with animals is similar to the magic Mom can work.

Khy's name pops up on my phone requesting a FaceTime call. I rest my phone atop the sink's faucet and prop it against the mirror. Then, I threaten my resident butterflies with decapitation if they stir.

"Hey! Have you seen that we're still going strong as a trending hashtag?" I ask, all business.

At least I intend to do that. The butterflies don't give a crap about my threat. They take flight when Khy's dimples flash. He's slouched in a hanging egg chair; I catch a glimpse of Hades curled up on the floor at his bare feet. And then Thirsty Cayden notices how fine he looks in the casual gray sweatpants and sleeveless maroon *Saint Vincent's Row Team* T-shirt. His bare arms are certainly giving what they need to give. I blink and then get it together.

I focus on Khy's face and *only* his face as he says, "Yeah, it's dope. But ummm... I was actually calling to ask... if you'd maybe... decided to look at those screenshots I sent?

No pressure, and feel free to tell me to mind my business," he quickly adds.

Ironically, I'm grateful that Khy brings up my grandparents. It swiftly severs any and all thirst. *Good.* But then the guilt hits. It's like the butterflies vanish and moldy cake replaces them, making my stomach queasy. "I was just looking at them," I admit. "Is that terrible? Is it awful that I weirdly wanted to know *something* about that side of my family?"

Khy vehemently shakes his head. "No. Not at all. It's normal. Anybody else in your situation would want to have some clue about their grandparents."

I fidget with a teal napkin I grab from beside the sink. "But I *have* a set of grandparents. Really terrific ones. Two people who have always been in my life and loved me and supported me and *known* me. That's enough." *Isn't it?* I chew my bottom lip. It should be. It always has been—right up until Khy sent those dang screenshots to my phone. Then, I just had to go and read Carolyn's and Robert's member pages. Now... Now, I don't even know how I feel if I'm keeping it one hundred. It still pisses me the hell off every time I think about how they treated my parents and *why* they aren't in my life. But then there's the other thing: *Anybody else in your situation would want to have some clue about their grandparents.* Khy isn't wrong. *I've* simply never felt that way until now.

"It's okay if it isn't enough," Khy says quietly.

I shake my head. "It *is*, though." I decide right then and

there. "Thank you for what you were trying to do and thank you for listening," I say to Khy. "I think I needed to just talk about it all for a sec. I'm good now. I don't need to dig up more info or give any more energy over to those people."

Khy regards me intently for a moment as if he isn't convinced. But he throws me a small smile and says, "Anytime."

There's a bark and then Hades leaps into Khy's lap. Khy's phone jostles, and he drops it. I hear Hades bark again and Khy saying, "All right, bud. You can have cuddles." A moment later, Khy picks up the phone and holds it up and out of the way of His Majesty who is snuggled up in Khy's lap as if he's a toy poodle instead of a massive standard poodle. "Sorry about that," says Khy.

Hades turns toward the phone, and I swear he smirks, letting me know he is swiping Khy's attention away.

"When do you wanna hang out next?" Khy asks. "I was thinking maybe we can plan something for this weekend?"

Yes! It's on the tip of my tongue and a little too eagerly. Fortunately, I have to say, "I won't have much time to go out over the next couple of weeks."

"Oh," Khy says. His forehead wrinkles. "Is this your way of letting me down easy? If you've gotten what you need already out of our deal, that's honestly cool. You don't need to feel like you have to make up excuses or anything." He smiles weakly. "If you aren't vibing with our arrangement anymore, I can post about the bakery on my social accounts instead, so people still swarm it."

I don't realize how fast my heart is beating as he talks

about us ending our scheme until he falls silent. Then, my pulse wooshes so loud in my ears it's deafening. But that reaction is absurd. We don't truly mean anything to each other. And the out he offers isn't a bad deal. Maybe I should say yes and thank the Ancestors for helping me dodge a train wreck while the bakery still gets publicity.

"That's not the reason." The words sort of tumble out themselves. They're like an unstoppable force that I couldn't curb even if I tried. I belatedly realize how rushed and nervous they sound. I clear my throat to find some chill. "I wasn't making up excuses," I say more evenly. "My family is planning this cookout fundraiser to help the bakery and some of the other businesses nearby. The whole neighborhood's rent is skyrocketing because, no shade, bougie-ass witches want to move into the area and throw up their fancy-ass shopping plazas and condos, so this is really important. My cousin and I are kind of taking the lead to organize stuff, and I super don't want to let my dad, or the other businesses the cookout could benefit, down. But . . ."

I pause and give a shaky laugh, allowing myself not to display 100 percent confidence for a tiny bit. I've been keeping it one hundred with Khy about everything else during our convo. I might as well confess this truth, too. "I'm nervous as hell." I admit to Khy and myself finally. "It's a big deal. A huge deal. I've done stuff like prom committee at school. But I've never led organizing a whole-ass community fundraiser before. So yeah. I want to give the project 100 percent of my attention."

Khy grimaces. "I'm sorry. Gentrification is fucking terrible, and I hate how us witches are a big cause of it. Can I help with the cookout, or anything else, in any way?"

"Thanks," I say. "You're doing plenty with our dates." I laugh to keep my comment light, but Khy's tone makes it clear he'd do any and everything I asked to pitch in. I smile. *Hard.* Seriously, how can one person be so great? I can't believe he cares—like legitimately cares—about the cookout. It's something that doesn't affect him one dang bit, and yet he's willing to contribute to the cause. A lot of people would be too self-absorbed or shallow. Most *rich witches* certainly would. Khy keeps proving himself again and again, and it's getting harder and harder to remind myself this is all for show. "Maybe we can hang out sometime after I pull this cookout off?" I say. "I'll have more free time after." *And maybe we can go on a for-real date?* I bite my tongue. I'm so close to uttering it. No, I'm not looking for a serious boyfriend. But if I was, Khy is getting pretty freaking close to checking off all the right boxes.

"I get you," Khy says. "But can I make a suggestion about a date this weekend that might help you plan your fundraiser?"

I lean in closer to the phone's camera, curious. "I'm listening."

"The Coven does lots of charity events, and I usually volunteer on the planning committees. In fact, you're not the only one chairing your first fundraiser. I'm doing the same for one on Sunday afternoon. It's a charity golf tournament that I've been planning since last fall as part of Cotillion. Maybe you can swing by to see how one is run? Get an idea of the logistics? I can also give you some pointers about how to recruit and coordinate volunteer staff. We're also holding a silent auction during it. Those are usually a hit and can rack up a lot of donations from people attending the event. You can see how that's done, too, and maybe use it for the cookout."

"I'm in!" I say, immediately. *You can make time for another date if it's work related.* That's true, but I also use it to justify how excited I am about chillin' with Khy again.

"Bet. I'll text you the details." Khy grins as hard as I do.

"Sounds good. This Cotillion, by the way," I say, curious, "it's a huge deal for teen witches, right?" Mom has told me about hers from when she was seventeen. It's a yearly event that brings together witches from all over the world. Mom's was held in Abuja, Nigeria.

"Huge ain't the word," Khy chuckles. "Think about the biggest, fanciest, bougiest ball you could imagine—and then double whatever image is in your head." He smiles sheepishly. "It's wild and over-the-top, but it's a rite of passage for Coven teens and we look forward to it—more than prom, even. And Houston's Coven is the host for this year's Cotillion. The golf tournament I'm chairing is the first official Cotillion event, and us teens are working as volunteers as a new community service requirement this year. I pitched the idea to my mom, and she loved it. That's how I ended up organizing everything."

I whistle. "Damn. All right. I see you!"

Even with Hades weighing a ton and cozy in his lap, Khy manages to sit up straighter and super proudly.

And your ex will be in town for Cotillion, right? The question is at the tip of my tongue, but I do not stick my nose into business where it doesn't belong. Still, I can't help the pang of jealousy over Khy's ex. Things may not have ended well between them, but he loved her for real—not just for show. And I wish I didn't care the same couldn't be said for me.

Chapter Thirteen

On Sunday afternoon, I can't believe I'm actually standing outside The Spell Shoppes, of all freaking places. "Some powerful mind control juju must've been placed on me," I mutter. The most tragic part is I definitively know I haven't been brainwashed. I made the decision to come to this tacky, unholy place of my own free will. I might not be stepping foot inside The Spell Shoppes exactly, but the adjoining, shiny new golf course is just as bad. It's yet another ritzy development that's exclusively owned by and caters to witches. Seriously, they could've stuck the useless thing on their own turf inside one of their gated communities. Or somewhere nearby in the surrounding suburbs if land space is now limited. Or they could develop new living and leisure spaces for their snooty kind some place farther away from the metro Houston area. The country has a plethora of open land; there's a gazillion pastoral acres to choose from if you travel west, east, or north.

Dad's voice chimes inside my head: *The available land for agricultural use in rural spaces has become a limited resource, too, and continues to dwindle further.* It's a discussion-turned-economics lecture we've had before. (Dad truly might have a second calling as a professor; he'd kill it. He has this uncanny way of making ordinarily boring topics seem riveting.)

I continue to stare up at The Spell Shoppes—though glowering is probably a more apt descriptor. I get that there's no easy, or fair, solution for *any* community where the expanding "needs" of inconsiderate, self-absorbed witches are concerned. But, damn, did witchkind have to move in on my neighborhood first? They *do* have their own uber-posh master-planned communities. They *could* have stayed put. They could simply build upward to address overcrowding—like how New York City did back in the day. And witches have magic at their disposal to build structures more magnificent and innovative than what old school NYC architects accomplished. They could build a whole-ass futuristic tower that was a thousand floors and held their own closed city inside of it if they really put their minds to it. Okay, I'm not totally positive about the actual feasibility of all that. But still, they should look into it.

Ugh! How did I think meeting up with Khy at The Spell Shoppes, the very existence of which irks me down to my soul, could be anything other than a spectacularly bad idea?

I fix my churlish mood and stop looking at The Spell

Shoppes as if I can reduce them to rubble using my scowl alone. I *am* here for a good cause; I can stomach The Spell Shoppes for an afternoon if it helps Dad and other small business owners in my neighborhood.

After several inhales and exhales—and counting to ten twice— I'm able to achieve a (mostly) serene, chilled disposition. As ready as I'm ever gonna be to attend this Coven event, I march up to the gleaming black iron gate that wraps around the humongous *private* golf course dropped in the middle of Third Ward. I have to fight hard not to think about the number of homes and/or businesses that got bulldozed for it to be created, and the general waste of space and resources golf courses are.

Beside the gate, there's a cute Black boy with low-cut curly hair and a fresh fade. He must be one of the Cotillion kids Khy mentioned were volunteering. He's wearing an orange golf polo, khaki cargo shorts, and brown loafers. It's not a bad fit, but Khy would pair fly sneakers with the preppy outfit and make it look like he's modeling it for some high fashion ad. I swat that thought away as soon as it comes. I shouldn't be thinking about Khy and how much I'm into his swag.

"Hi," I say to Loafers Boy. "I'm Cayden Jackson. I should ... ummm ... be on the guest list." The words come out clunky; saying such phrases will never get *un*awkward, no matter how many times Khy and I hang out before our arrangement is over.

Loafers Boy grins wide. "Oh, I know who you are. You're my brother's new girl."

My mouth hangs open. I'm not sure what leaves it dang near touching the pavement—the fact that I'm meeting somebody from Khy's family or the fact that Khy's brother just called me his *new girl*.

"We're just chilling as friends," I say.

Humor lightens his dark eyes. He smushes his lips together tightly, and I get the feeling he's trying to hold in laughter. What the hell is so funny?

I find out when he drawls, "Riiiight. My brother couldn't do casual to save his life."

I bite the inside of my lip at that slick statement. It's near the same thing Khy's friends said at the lake party.

"I'm Rashaud, by the way." Khy's brother grins wider as he holds out his hand. The two of them could be mistaken for twins. They share the same bone structure. The same classically handsome square jaw. The same deep dimples. The same smile. And they're both unfairly tall. But it's the smile I go back to and focus on. Since Rashaud's is identical to Khy's, you'd think it would completely bespell me like Khy's does every time I see it. But I don't get stuck on Rashaud's smile. It's handsome, yet utterly mundane. *This boy's smile doesn't make jittery butterflies erupt in my stomach.* The observation is highly unnerving.

I swallow, mouth dry. Shake Rashaud's hand. "Cayden," I say. And I need to slap myself because we've already covered that. He knew my name several minutes ago. "Why are you out here working the gate if you're Khy's big brother?" I ask

Rashaud. "I thought only this year's Cotillion class was on volunteer duty." Why's he standing out here blocking riff-raff from wandering in?

Rashaud's lips twitch.

In my mind, rattling off the questions was going to reverse how goofy I made myself look by shifting attention away from me. But I didn't consider that strategy well. I don't know this boy, and the nosy questions place me all up in his business.

"*Riffraff* is an interesting word," Rashaud quips. "I'm playing bouncer because the kid that was stationed here is pretending to be sick to get out of community service, and I'm doing my little brother a solid by filling in." He readily offers the explanation. Behind it, he winks and cracks his knuckles, fully (and extremely dramatically) embodying the whole *bouncer* act. Which, honestly, that could be an accurate description of Rashaud if this was a club. His upper body is broader than Khy's; he's got more muscles, too. Whereas Khy has the sleek build of the swimmer he is, Rashaud resembles a running back. The boy is also much more arrogant than his younger brother. While I'm sizing him up, he purposely flexes the biceps left on display by his short shirt sleeve.

I roll my eyes. "Are you expecting me to swoon? Tell me you didn't think that corny junk was gonna have any effect?"

He folds his arms across his huge chest and huffs a laugh. "No. Yes. Maybe? It worked on Gigi, which is why I told baby bro: *she ain't it.*"

I'm about to inform him that the details of whatever went down between Khy and Gigi is Khy's business, but then I realize something. I never said *riffraff* out loud. Rashaud responded to a *thought* I had.

I serve Khy's brother a severe side-eye. (Or the equivalent of a side-eye when you're staring somebody down head on.) "So you're conceited *and* rude? Reading minds is shitty."

He has enough of a conscience to at least look shamefaced at getting caught. "You're right. I suck. But I couldn't pass up the chance to size up the *Mystery Girl* my brother and THE SCOOP are so into. I wanted to see what you had that's been making Khy act like Gigi didn't take a hammer to his heart when she cheated on him."

I clench my hands into fists. I'm irked *only* about the breach of privacy, not the multiple mentions of Gigi, or Rashaud saying Khy's ex had the power to smash his heart.

"Don't lift my thoughts again," I snap at Khy's brother.

He holds up his hands. "My curiosity is satisfied; I won't. For what it's worth: I like the vibe you give off, Cayden, and I'm pretty confident you won't mess over my brother."

I get it now. Rashaud is like Naomi: another overprotective person in Khy's life trying to look out for him but going about it in a butthole way.

As I march past him, I think it loud and clear, halfway hoping he hasn't stuck to his word.

I spot Darius before Khy. He's standing near the entrance creating a breathtaking array of topiary animals that sprout from the grass. He's forged a bear, lion, deer, flamingo, swan, and horse so far. A spotless, emerald-green giraffe springs up next. "'Sup!" he says, waving to me and leaning against the giraffe.

I make my way over to him, clapping. "I see you! Why is this so gorgeous, though?!"

Darius's complexion is a light enough brown that I can see a visible blush. He grins, then bows. "Thank you." He points to the right after he straightens. "Khy is over there finishing up some last-minute decorating, too, if you want to head over."

I look in the direction and see Khy a good distance away—I blink. He's making a fresh lake. In the middle of the course. Water dramatically sprays upward from the center and then plunges downward, creating the illusion of a waterfall floating above Khy's lake. I marvel at the waterfall for a few seconds (*not* at its maker), and then I go over and say hey.

"Hey!" he says back, sliding his hands in his pockets.

"Hey," I say again. Khy is wearing a similar outfit to Rashaud: white cargo shorts, a golf polo a shade of bright red that makes the rich brown of his skin *glow*, and a stunning pair of Air Jordan Retro 11s in cherry and white. I'm still so annoyed with his brother that I can barely appreciate how I was right earlier when I guessed Khy would be able to make the outfit look *way* better than Rashaud. "I met your brother coming in."

The lingering irritation must be all over my face because Khy winces at the mention of his brother. "What did Rashaud do?"

"He demonstrated his Connection without me asking."

Khy curses. "He read your mind?" He looks shocked, mortified, and pissed.

"I told him off. It's fine now," I say, reaching for the serenity I found before running into Rashaud at the gates. "Fair warning though: if he does it again, I'm gonna punch your bro in the throat." Some chill is slightly more difficult to achieve this time.

Khy's jaw tightens. A muscle along the bottom left edge ticks. This is the first time I'm seeing Khy mad about something, and his supermodel-sharp jaw flexing like that is kind of hot. *Very* hot, if I'm keeping it one hundred.

"It isn't fine," Khy says. He pivots toward the entrance where Rashaud is stationed.

I grab his hand. "For real. *It is*," I say. "I can take care of myself, and I let him know he was a jerk for it. I'm over it."

"Are you sure?"

I'm not entirely, but I answer yes. Khy storming off to get in his brother's face about it might cause a scene. I've already spotted a few people with press badges around their necks milling around; they snapped some pics when I greeted Khy. More importantly, the idea of Khy defending my honor makes us feel more like something real instead of the fake, mutually beneficial arrangement we're supposed to be maintaining.

It takes Khy a few seconds longer to nod and, thankfully, turn away from where his brother is stationed at the front gate. He doesn't drop my hand when he does, though. He laces his fingers through mine and tells me, "Come on. I was going to set up the volunteer registration table next. I'll get you checked in and a name badge. Afterward, do you want to stick around it and help me do the same for everybody else?"

"Sure," I say. I inwardly scowl at how dang out of breath I sound. I ignore the zing that's going on between our clasped hands, too.

Khy and I work our post behind the registration table as the other Cotillion volunteers steadily arrive. I mark their names off Khy's volunteer list and give them preprinted name badges, and then Khy directs them to their duty stations. A sizable number of teens approach our table since the worldwide witch community holds one big annual Cotillion event, and debutantes from all over the world are checking in.

I can tell which ones are from the most prominent witch families by the number of press folks who decide it's worth capturing pics of the greetings they exchange with Khy. He and I sit side by side and work in a good, professional rhythm that's keeping the volunteer check-in line relatively short. I make mental notes about how efficiently organized Khy's process is so I can duplicate something like it for the cookout. Aware of the cameras, every now and again Khy or I do something swoon worthy. It's not a scheme we verbally plan out. We just wordlessly fall into sync and end up executing it. Once, he grabs my hand and squeezes it briefly. Another time, he brushes an invisible speck of something from my cheek. In turn, I do little cutesy things like lay my head on his shoulder for a sec as we work or brush my hand down the back of his fresh fade, as if appreciating his recent haircut, in the way I'd do if he were actually my boyfriend.

I almost forget none of it is real.

"If this tournament is for charity, what cause do the proceeds go to?" I ask Khy when there's a break in the stream of kids. For my own sanity, I've got to throw up a buffer between us. I turn to casual conversation like it's a Vibranium shield.

"Since Houston's Coven is sponsoring it, we got to select the recipients of all the charity events," Khy says proudly. "I convinced my grandmother to persuade the rest of our Coven's Matriarch Elders to use today's tournament to raise STU scholarship funds for students of color who want to attend an HBCU but can't afford a private school's tuition." I stare at him with an open mouth. "What?" he asks.

I should've asked a different question. Something harmless—like if he prefers summer or fall. Something that wouldn't make me like him even more. I snap my mouth shut. "Nothing. That's just ... really nice," I say. It'd be extraordinary regardless, but the fact that Khy's chosen cause benefits an HBCU that's right here in Third Ward ... I've gleaned enough about him to guess it isn't a coincidence. "You suggested it because of the gentrification happening, huh?"

Khy doesn't shy away from the question. He nods, guiltily. "I know there's folks on both sides who think gentrification can be a good thing economically for inner-city communities like Third Ward, but usually it just pushes existing residents and businesses out. So, I wanted us to do something *for* the existing residents. STU is really important to Third Ward. It does a lot for the area. I figured we could invest back into the community and its cultural institutions by making a crazy endowment to the HBCU that's here."

Khy is more than impressive. He's rare. Damn near surreal—on the level of spotting a striped, purple lion. He's at least *one* wealthy, absurdly privileged witch who is able to think beyond "needing" more personal luxuries. If anything were capable of making ya girl for real fall for a boy like Khy, that trait would absolutely be at the top of the list.

Khy brushes a hand along the waves of his hair—his nervous tell. And it's then that I realize why he's turned all awkward. How long have I been staring at him? And oh my God, what's been splashed all over my face as I have? *Please* don't let it have been any of my sappy thoughts about him.

Of course, while I'm trying to get it back together and appear normal, my mind chooses this moment to recall the few times Khy and I have been near enough to kiss—like when we lay beside each other in the grass at Magic Row or when we were cuddled up on his boat. Or when Hades pulled his usual antics and toppled Khy literally on top of me. Maybe it's because we're seated so close once again? Or because we keep just staring at each other with an unnerving intensity? Or because Khy really is everything I could want in a guy? I start thinking about what would happen if I kiss him right now. If I lean a little bit toward him, like he's started leaning toward me . . . we can finally, *actually* . . .

A throat clears. "Excuse me. I need to check-in."

We spring apart.

I gaze up at a girl that could give Mercedes a run for her coins in the glam department. She's got dark skin that is literally glowing and these dazzling brown eyes rimmed in mascara in a way that only accentuates their magnetism, her hair is in flawless butterfly locs, and she's wearing a strapless coral romper that shows off her long, smooth brown legs. Seriously, the romper is as casual as the white jean shorts and blue and pink floral crop top that I'm wearing, but something about her fit screams glitzy. Maybe it's the visibly soft fabric, or the gorgeous girl wearing it, or the fact that the romper is probably some designer piece that costs a fortune. Either way, I glance down at my own outfit, suddenly feeling *underdressed.*

The accent that tumbled out of the beautiful girl's mouth as she spoke certainly doesn't help me be any less self-conscious. She sounded French, and it suddenly hits me who she is. Khy confirms it when he makes this sound that's akin to the frenzied cough-grunt somebody emits when they've swallowed water down the wrong way. Then, there's the side-eye she serves me. It says *why are you all up on my man?* I do not hold back my answering eyeroll. Khy stopped being *her* anything when she cheated on and dumped him.

"Gigi, right?" I say serenely. "What's your last name? Let me check you in and get you a badge."

Khy's ex sweeps me over, and the *tired,* catty thoughts

are written all over her face. "Actually, it's Giselle," she says primly. "Only close friends get to call me Gigi."

So, you're close friends with THE SCOOP and every other media outlet? I'm on my best behavior today and refrain from snarking it. "What's your last name?" is all I return.

She smiles in this way where she smushes her face together and wrinkles her nose—I find extreme joy in the fact it makes her look sort of like a pug. My joy quadruples when she breezily tells me, "I'm sure you already know it. Everyone does. I am royalty, after all."

I have an impeccable memory. I recall immediately THE SCOOP referring to her as *Giselle "Gigi" Bernard.* "Sorry," I say. "I've got no clue who you are. I don't follow witch royals who have literally zero impact on my life." I keep my tone perfectly polite and professional, like I would with a customer at the bakery or shelter, even if they were on my last nerves. I *am* volunteering, and I always strive to put my best foot forward with all my work—even when I'm being subtly petty.

Gigi purses her lips. *Ha!* "It's Bernard." She says it slow enough that it's unquestionably meant to be a jab at my intelligence (which is all kinds of wrong and jerkish).

I ignore it, find her name tag, and hold it out to her. "Here you go," I say brightly. I refuse to let this girl think she has a scrap of power to get under my skin. Who even is she? Really?

The tips of her fingers grab the name tag, like she fears accidentally touching me will make my inferiority rub off on her. I clench my teeth because *Giselle* is the perfect example of the kind of Coven witches who irk my soul.

She peels her name tag off and sticks it to the front of her romper. She holds the paper backing out to me. "Would you toss this in the garbage, please?"

I point to the small trashcan that's at the end of the table. "You can do it yourself."

She blinks several times, like she isn't used to someone giving it back to her. Or hearing any variety of *no*. She swings away from me. Gives Khy this appraising look like *he* should be guilty about something. "So this is the rebound girl you've got all over THE SCOOP and social media? At least *I* gave you the courtesy of being linked with a fellow royal. It's making me look bad that you jumped from me to some *non-royal* random!"

Oh no the hell she didn't.

Khy beats me to checking her, because *I think the hell not*. "Don't be rude, Gigi. Her name is Cayden, and you being so ugly is the *real* bad look." He speaks plainly—never losing the easy charisma and spotless manners that ordinarily cloak him. And all right, I admit it's cool as hell that he readily has my back. Yes, I am tough and can handle myself. That doesn't mean it isn't nice when somebody shows they care enough to do it for you.

Gigi's eyes widen. Then immediately narrow. She slices a glare between me and Khy that I guess is supposed to intimidate me, since it embodies the phrase *if looks could kill*. But she just looks absurdly comical, and I have to hold in a laugh so I don't cause extra drama for no good reason.

"How's Tano, by the way?" Khy smoothly asks in Gigi's (blessed) suspended silence. "Super cool dude. Will he be in town to escort you to the Cotillion Ball? If so, tell him we should hang. It'll be good press and can show everyone there's no hard feelings after our breakup." Khy tosses out a winning smile—and I peep that behind the princely charm and faultless etiquette, Royal Boy can clap right back with somebody when the situation calls for it. Naomi and his brother don't need to be so overprotective—Khy can hold his own.

Gigi smiles back at Khy, plasticky and stiff. "Tano's stuck in England for the summer. He scored an Oxford law internship that most incoming prelaw undergrads never get selected for. But you know Tano. He's brilliant at everything!" I stifle a snort. She is so transparently trying to make Khy jealous. She's being a heifer, too, because she slides me a smirk and then has the nerve to ask Khy, "Maybe me and you can pair up and be each other's escort since Tano isn't coming? It'll be fun! We agreed to stay friends, didn't we? Friends can attend balls together."

Do not agree to her mess! I shout at Khy in my head, barely managing not to hiss it out loud. It isn't because I'm jealous or because I'd want to be his escort to some silly-ass ball (not that he's shown any interest in asking me). If Khy doesn't decline her garbage offer, I'm gonna be pissed *only* because he should have more self-respect. Hell, *I'm* insulted by Gigi's suggestion and this has squat to do with me.

"That's not a good idea," Khy says stiffly. "We *are* still friends. But I'm sure Tano, your *boyfriend,* won't vibe with your ex being your Cotillion date. It'd be shady. I'm not about that kind of stuff."

I gawk at Khy. Is he really this pure? Yes, he turned Gigi down. But I would've thrown her cheating in her damn face as my reason for telling her to kick rocks. Khy didn't so much as mention his own pride. Just simply stated why it'd be a terrible thing to do to somebody else.

"Yes. I remember how you are," Gigi snaps. "Mekhi Carter, the media's beloved Good Guy, obsessed with keeping the act going for the whole freaking world." She spits it at Khy like it's an insult.

Is she for real? Ain't no way.

"Do we know the same Khy? It's not an act. If you can't believe someone can be truly good and not just do it for show, that says a lot more about you than him." The words are out my mouth before I can stop them.

Gigi swivels her neck. There's a nasty comment written all over her glower.

"I've got you volunteering at the refreshments table," Khy says before she can let it fly. He walks from behind our table, and it's never been clearer that the boy was born into a family entrenched in politics. Diplomacy could be his middle name when he smiles cheerily at Gigi. "Let me show you to your work station," he offers.

I know he's only trying to diffuse the situation and not kick up more drama. That doesn't stop my stomach from sinking while I watch him walk away, shoulder to shoulder with Gigi.

"You pulling off an event on this scale and raising more money than any Cotillion fundraiser in the past is spectacular. You can give me tips for when Paris hosts next year," I hear Gigi say. When it's only her and Khy, her voice is free of snootiness. And she sounds like she really is impressed. My gut twists when I remember the reason Khy gave for liking Gigi in the first place, that they bonded over both being into charity projects.

How do you compete with a beautiful royal?

I don't know where in the hell the thought comes from. I'm not competing with Gigi—I'm just helping Khy make it clear to the world that he's over her. I quickly squash the thought to itty-bitty pieces. I shove those pieces in a box. Slap a combination lock on it. Spin the lock. Then banish them somewhere far, far, *far* away—to a different universe, in fact. One that will never overlap with my real one.

Chapter Fourteen

Khy and Gigi walk to a table where three people in navy and white catering uniforms are setting up bottles of water, ice buckets, chilled lemonade, sweet tea, and an assortment of finger foods. *Hors d'oeuvres* is what Khy's bougie witch clan probably calls them—like that isn't just an unnecessarily fancy name for small bites to eat. I should turn away from Khy and his royal ex. Look at everything else going on around the golf course. Scroll my Instagram feed. Get lost in the black hole that my For You page usually morphs into. I should do *anything* except sit behind the check-in table staring at Khy and the girl he used to date—and be in love with—who is a literal damn witch princess. But I can't turn away from how Gigi keeps finding excuses to touch Khy—a bump of her shoulder here, a brush against his arm there. At one point, she playfully flicks his ear.

Then I see Becca and Naomi march up to the pair, Naomi looking every bit as ice cold and fiercely protective of Khy as when she and I first met. Naomi and Becca sport tennis dresses. Naomi's is white and Becca's is sky blue. Gigi glares at Khy's friends like they've intruded on something. Becca shyly tucks a loose strand of raven black hair behind her ear, but Naomi is a Queen B, same as Gigi. She returns Gigi's side-eye at equal intensity. Gigi must say something wild, because Naomi cocks her head and whips a hand to her hip. I don't hear the words that leave her lips from where I am. But I feel the smackdown she gives Gigi in my soul. I never thought I'd be cheering for Naomi blasting her bitchiness around. But here we are. *Get her ass!* I silently gloat. Since Khy is too nice to do it on the level Gigi truly deserves, somebody has to.

Gigi spits something back that's directed to Naomi *and* Becca. Then, she utters something else to Khy. Khy turns to his friends; his face is oddly stiff in a way that reeks of annoyance projected at the wrong people. Whatever he expresses to Naomi and Becca makes Becca's eyes widen like she can't believe it. Naomi's fists clench at her sides. She directs heated words at Gigi, who issues a response that appears to be delivered as a cool and confident, smug-ass statement. Afterward, Khy's friends turn around, look straight at me, and start toward the check-in table.

"Khy says he's gonna stay and help Gigi with refreshments," Naomi says when she gets to me. "He told me and Becca to help you out here."

"I'm sorry? He said what?" I must blink a dozen times. *Oh no he didn't.* He wouldn't! Would he? Khy is too decent to play these types of games; he literally just told Gigi that himself when he turned down her trifling suggestion that they be each other's Cotillion escorts. But... Gigi *is* his gorgeous ex, and she's Coven royalty, and he's probably still in love with her. *She* crushed *his* heart, after all. It wasn't the other way around. So yeah, maybe Khy would turn shifty under these circumstances? Every inkling of resentment and hostility and distrust I have toward Coven witches rears its head.

Remember what happened in Galveston. This could be a misunderstanding. I try to assuage the wounded feelings that settle in my stomach like moldy cheesecake. Galveston *was* a misunderstanding, and I got pissed over something that wasn't what it seemed. The hope that this situation is similar is the only reason I don't get up from the table and leave right then and there, then forget Khy ever existed.

Tournament participants and spectators start arriving then, so Naomi, Becca, and I get them checked in with wristbands and direct them to the area where opening ceremonies will be held. When the tournament starts and the registration desk is meant to close, I look back over to where Khy is still (*still*) working alongside Gigi. The two of them smile and laugh like the old friends they are, and I hate how much it bothers me that Khy can't pull his eyes away from her.

"C'mon," Becca says, breaking me from my trance. "We should go to the greeter station."

We relocate to a chill-zone tent designed to look like an igloo that's been enchanted to be a cool reprieve from the summer heat. Becca conjures up a continuous breeze so cool air also swirls inside the tent while we act as greeters. We hand out water bottles and remind folks of the QR code posted on a wall of the tent that'll take them to an online silent auction running concurrently with the tournament. I position myself near the opening of the igloo so I can use my Connection to divert any heat that might raise the blissfully cool inside temp by even a few degrees.

"There's so many cool things to bid on," I say to a super pretty Latina woman who looks to be in her thirties and has two adorable little boys. "There are spa retreats, Disney World tickets, a signed baseball bat by this season's Astros roster, a Texans football signed by the Houston legend that is J. J. Watt, an old-school Cowboys football signed by Deion Sanders when he played for them, go-karts, gorgeous Yule wreaths for Winter Solstice..."

The woman's kids beg her to bid on the Disney World tickets, the baseball bat, and two go-karts. She bids on everything they request and a spa retreat for herself. My eyes pop out of my head when I do the mental math of how it'll run her pockets if she wins everything.

"Damn! You're good at this! She's like the sixth person you've gotten to bid globs of money." The comment, astonishingly, comes from Naomi.

If she can be nice today, so can I. "Thanks," I say. "You've been working magic on folks yourself!" She's gotten a grand total of ten people to participate in the silent auction.

Naomi grins, flashing the single dimple in her left cheek. "It's what I do best. Plus, I kind of love it. I'm gonna be a business major at Harvard when I go year after next. And after I graduate, I want to spearhead my own philanthropic foundation. Something that makes a real difference for all people across the globe, but especially the Black diaspora."

"That's really impressive," I say, because it is.

She beams brighter. "Thanks! What about you?" Wait. Have we slipped into a friendly convo? I glance upward to see if the sun has dropped out of the sky. Nope. I laugh. It's not because she's being uncharacteristically cool, but because I'm at a loss over how to answer her question. I'm not like her—somebody who has the path of her post–high school life mapped out. I don't shrink away from the question, though, since there's nothing wrong with not having everything figured out. "I plan to go to Howard University," I say. "I've got no clue what I want to major in, though, or what I want to do after college. There's a lot of things I find interesting, but none that I'm super passionate about yet." Having that feeling is important to me when I do eventually pick a career. Until then . . ."My plan is to just go with the flow," I tell Naomi. "I'm gonna enroll in college, enjoy the hell out of the experience, take classes in lots of areas, and see what comes out of it." When I finish, I wait for the snide comment or judgment.

"That makes sense," Naomi says, shocking me again.

"There's so much pressure to have everything figured out early. Not everyone our age does, which is totally fine."

I blink. "I didn't expect that response from someone like you." It's out of my mouth before I can snatch it back.

She shrugs. "That's fair. Especially with how I acted the last two times we met." She sounds genuinely apologetic. Ain't no way! And the surprises with her keep on coming today, because she adds, "Listen, I'm sorry, for real, about how I was when we crashed you and Khy's date and then at the lake party. You met Gigi earlier, right? She's terrible, and Khy knows she's terrible. At least, now he does. When they first started dating, she kept the awfulness on the low until he'd already fallen for Satan, and it was too late. Gigi truly thinks acts of service absolve her of being a massive bitch and careless as fuck with people's feelings. Literally, she said that delusional junk to me when I called her out. So, I just didn't want Khy to make the same mistake again. But that doesn't mean it was okay to be ugly to you. And . . . you seem cool and actually nice and nothing like Gigi." She pauses, tosses her glossy, straight brown hair over her shoulder. It's clear she's entirely uncomfortable and unused to giving apologies.

I appreciate the effort and understand where she was coming from, especially now that I've met Gigi. "I get it," I say. "Let's start over. I'm Cayden." I hold out my hand.

She smiles faintly, then shakes it. "I'm Naomi."

"Awww, I love this," Becca says. She swoops in beside us, slings an arm around our shoulders. "I was quiet before and letting y'all do your thing to sort stuff out, but let's all be besties now, please?" She squeezes my shoulder. "We need a third girl in the group. I'm so tired of the guys outnumbering us."

Naomi wrinkles her nose Becca's way. "Let's not get mushy." She looks to me. "The three of us *could* maybe hang out sometime without the boys, if you're up for it. We can have a girl's day, or whatever. If Becca has claimed you as a bestie, she'll be insufferable until we do," Naomi grumbles without any true heat.

I consider it. Becca has been dope since the lake party, and I've seen a different side of Naomi today. She could be cool people once you crack her exterior. Auntie Vesha is that way, and she's one of the most spectacular people ever. And, I guess, Khy has proved that not all Coven kids are snobs. Maybe I was wrong to write the lot of them off because of a handful of bad encounters? "Sure! Let's do it," I tell Naomi and Becca.

"How cute," drawls an airy, grating voice. We all turn to Gigi who's standing in the middle of the igloo's opening. She's got the door propped wide open, and a scorching blast of heat gets past my best efforts to keep it outside. Gigi's holding the handle of a rolling cart while sneering between the three of us.

"Close the door. You're messing up the point of this being a chill zone," I tell her.

"What do you want?" Naomi throws Gigi all of the attitude she exudes right back at her.

Gigi flicks a look at the cart like it's obvious. "Our station is out of water bottles and Khy wanted me to get some from here to restock."

Naomi smirks. "And how'd you end up coming to get the water instead of him? We all know Princess Gigi doesn't do manual labor." Naomi folds her arms, sweeping a pointed look down the length of Gigi. "Trying to make sure Khy and Cayden stay far apart, huh? You are *so tacky*, Gigi. You do remember you broke up with him, right? *And* cheated on him?"

Gigi pops her lips. "Just fetch the water and place it on my cart. We have parched attendees at our tent."

"I'm not your dog," Naomi snaps. "*Fetch it* your damn self."

Gigi looks to Becca, expectantly. "She's not getting it either!" Naomi fumes.

Gigi's eyes travel to me next. I snort. "Don't you remember the trash can?"

She huffs and drags the cart farther into the tent to where there are cases of ice-cold water bottles stacked beside a table. She hauls a case and then another onto her cart. I feel a twinge of guilt and sort of want to help her. But my petty side remembers she's rude as hell. Case in point, she still hasn't bothered to expend the energy to shut the door behind her when she leaves.

When Gigi strolls back to Khy, I shouldn't watch to see how he reacts when she rejoins him. But I do. And seeing him smile—the blinding one that could beat out the sun itself in brilliance—is like a dropkick to the gut.

Forget them. Ignore them. Turn away! I hiss at myself. And yet, I can't.

The two of them laugh about something Gigi says. He comes from around the table and hauls the cases of water off the rolling cart. Then they both go back to stand behind the table. Shoulder to shoulder. Real buddy-buddy like. Gigi starts up making excuses to touch him in small ways again, and Khy doesn't move away or tell her to stop. He's leaning into the little connections this time. Laughing. Grinning so big I see his dimples from a this far away.

Khy is definitely all-out flirting with her.

The vicious feeling in my stomach intensifies. I blink. Suck in a breath because it *really* shouldn't matter. Ugh! Why the heck are Khy and Gigi bothering *me* so much? Both are damn nonplayable characters as far as my life goes! Me and Khy's relationship is bogus—strictly for show. There's no way I'm catching real feelings for this dang boy, right? *Ancestors, please save me!*

"Are you all right, Cayden?" Becca's question cuts through the full crisis mode I'm about to descend into.

Standing beside Becca, Naomi scowls. "Don't let Gigi get to you, girl," she tells me. "I had my doubts before, but Khy is not checking for her with you in the picture."

"I don't care what he does," I mutter. I can't even make my voice sound convincing. Is she blind? Or just trying to make what's happening at Khy's and Gigi's tent less brutal for me? Anybody—and everybody—can see clear as glass that Khy *is* still in love with Gigi.

"Don't they look darling together? I hope the two make up." A stunning dark-skinned Black woman with pin-straight hair falling around her shoulders walks into the igloo, a man beside her. She's dressed to the nines in a lilac pantsuit and taupe heels. She exudes an elegance that rivals Wakanda's Queen Ramonda—she looks like she should be perched on a throne inside a palace, too, instead of slumming it on a golf course. The dark-skinned man she came in with has hair cut into a neat temp fade and looks like he belongs in the boardroom of a multibillion-dollar megacorporation, or on his private yacht soaking up the sun. He's wearing a pristine white linen suit that screams money.

I recognize the pair as soon as I see them. Khy and his mom share the same gorgeous deep copper complexion and the same shade of brown eyes. And Khy is near the spitting image of his dad—only a younger version. They share the same strong jaw, the same handsomely sharp bone structure, and the same unfairly long dark lashes.

"Perhaps they'll reconnect and smooth things over while she's in town for Cotillion," Khy's dad tells his mom.

They are talking about Khy and Gigi, of course.

Allison Carter, North America's reigning Witch Regent, nods. "Hello, dears," she says to Naomi and Becca, smiling warmly.

"Hello, Mrs. and Mr. Carter," Naomi and Becca both politely say back.

Clasping her husband's hand, Khy's mom walks to the water bottles we've got stored in a cooler I'm standing beside. She grabs one. Her husband does the same. The pair then meander around the igloo, looking at the items in the silent auction and bidding on some. I stiffen. Khy told me at Magic Row that his parents know about us and THE SCOOP's *many* stories at this point. So Mrs. and Mr. Carter both absolutely recognize who I am. Yet neither of them has spared me a glance. *Why would they bother, though, when Gigi is the one outside cuddling up with their son?* Bitterly, I remember how Khy dodged my question at Magic Row when I asked what his royal parents thought about our trending relationship. *I guess I've got my answer.* Clearly, I'm not even good enough to be afforded the decency of acknowledging that I—their son's supposed new girlfriend—am standing right in front of them. Their message is plain as day; I don't get the same warmness as Naomi and Becca, acceptable Coven teens and approved friends of their son, because I am none of that.

Instead of calling them on their rudeness and making myself look graceless and foolish (because that's how they'll spin it in their snooty heads), I decide simply to be done. With Khy. With attending dumb Coven events. With being his Rebound Girl. With giving this world *any* benefit of the doubt. And with our arrangement. We might only be friends and might only be hanging out for the press. But he doesn't get to be a jerk while it happens. And I refuse to let some irrelevant boy make me look goofy for any reason.

"I have to go," I say to Naomi and Becca. Then I jet. Quickly. Because if I don't get away from the golf course immediately,

I might do something that really makes me look graceless and foolish—like cry. Khy, Gigi, and his parents don't get to see that.

And you will not do it, regardless, I grind out to myself as I'm making my getaway.

Chapter Fifteen

"Shithead just DM'd you." Mercedes sucks her teeth, staring down at my iPad in her hands. She and I are sitting in Larissa's office at the shelter, waiting for Larissa to join us so we can all plan how to make pet adoptions a part of the cookout. Mercedes stabs the screen of my iPad with a neon green stiletto-shaped nail. Then, she gives it the middle finger. "He has some nerve!"

I might snarl. The annoyed sound I make comes pretty darn close. "Obviously, I'm gonna ignore it," I tell my cousin. I'm not sure why he thinks sliding into my DMs will achieve different results than his many texts all morning—I left him on read with those, too. Mercedes is right, though. I can't believe his trifling behind thinks we still have—or need—to say anything to each other. Does he think I'm that dumb? Or that pathetic? I cut Mercedes off when she starts to go in on Khy harder. "Can we just drop the subject of him?"

"The subject of who?" Larissa says as she comes into the office.

"Nobody," I answer quickly.

I try to beat Mercedes to dishing about Khy, but she's already started filling Larissa in on the golf tournament.

When Mercedes finishes, if heat vision were real, Larissa's glower would scorch everything in the room. "Oh no that fuckboy did not!"

"I'm over it," I say. It's a lie. I'm having a hella hard time not being majorly pissed—and I'm rattled as hell about how upset I am when it was supposed to be fake. But neither Larissa nor Mercedes needs to know all of that. It'll only make me have to talk about Khy more, which is the last thing I want to do. I'd love to forget about ever meeting Khy, agreeing to be some stank boy's rebound, and temporarily losing my mind. I *know* better.

Mercedes and Larissa both look at me like I'm not fooling anyone.

"So the doggy adoptions," I say, changing the subject. "Do we want to bring the pets out to the cookout or set up a QR code where interested Paws Parents can view our furbabies' profiles on the website?"

Larissa, thankfully, drops Khy. True to form, she gets right down to business. "Maybe we can do both," she says after thinking it over for a moment. "We can bring the furbabies who will do well in a crowd and set up QR codes for the ones that might have social anxiety. How do you feel about that?"

"I love it," I say.

"Me too." Mercedes chimes in as she takes notes on the iPad.

After the meeting, I squeeze some snuggly time in with the pups—because boy, do I need it. Mercedes hangs around the rescue and joins me, even though she isn't a huge dog person. I cuddle Neyo, our only pitbull puppy and youngest rescue, while I sit cross-legged in the middle of the grass in Lucky Paws' back courtyard. Mercedes sits beside me, reaching over to pat Neyo on the head every now and again.

"Hey, Cayden. You've got a visitor!" I look up to see Keenan, another volunteer, poking his head out the shelter's back door and grinning. He steps to the side and—*oh hell no!*

The Ancestors are really testing me today because the last person I want to see walks into the courtyard. Khy's hands are shoved into the pockets of a pair of gray joggers. He looks shamefaced, as he should.

I cross my arms. Shove my shock aside, so how pissed I am blasts across the courtyard loud and clear. "Why are you here?" I grind out. "Didn't you get the message from me ignoring you?" I look pointedly to door. "You can turn around and go."

Khy's face twists in anguish. *He is* so *unserious!* "I tried calling and DM'ing you," he says pathetically.

"And?" I snap. "I figured I'd return your courtesy from yesterday. Pretend like *you* don't exist. Matter of fact..." I turn to Mercedes. "Do you see somebody else standing here? Talking to me? Because I surely don't."

"Nope," Mercedes says, glaring at Khy from her place beside me. She pops her lips. "Must be the wind."

"I don't... I don't know what I did to make you mad," Khy says, and he must be a damn good actor because he really sounds perplexed.

The look Mercedes lobs him would incinerate him on the spot if she had a Connection to fire. As it is, I consider warming a pocket of air around him to make it feel like he's standing inside a smoldering heat dome. I smile inside at the image of Khy sweating profusely, no longer looking so obnoxiously fine in the simple joggers, maroon Air Jordan 1s, and white T-shirt he's wearing. But Mom and I have a strict agreed-upon rule about magic use: we never use it to hurt someone. Ever. In any way. This is the one time I wish Mom and Dad didn't raise me so well.

"For real, though, what are you doing here?" I ask Khy again. I curl my hands into fists. "Don't you have Cotillion things to do *with Gigi.*" I gnash my teeth after I involuntarily add the last bit. I shouldn't be making it seem like I'm jealous of his ex!

Khy's expression grows even more stricken if that's possible. His eyebrows furrow. "Why would I be concerned about Gigi? I'm here because I've been calling and texting and DM'ing you, and I got worried when you were just silent. So, I... umm... I figured I'd see if I could catch you at the bakery to check on you and make sure you were all right." He shifts awkwardly on his feet when he mutters the last part. But that's not what I pay attention to.

"You went to the bakery?!" I shriek. "Who did you talk to? Who did you see? Was it my dad?" My heart beats a mile a minute in my chest. If he talked to Dad and Dad grilled him—

"No." Khy's answers crashes into my panic, making it mostly scatter. "There were two kids about our age behind the counter. One of them told me to try the shelter."

Slowly, my pulse returns to normal. Khy is talking about Cayden's Confections' newest employees as of two days ago. They're the pair of part-time workers Dad is training today. He recently hired them on a short-term, summer-only basis since business has continued to boom and he felt bad about me and Mercedes working so many days.

"Are you high?" asks Mercedes. "Give me one good reason my cousin shouldn't be freezing you out. What you did with Gigi, in Cayden's face, was disrespectful as hell."

"I didn't do anything with Gigi," Khy snaps. His head swivels between me and Mercedes. His brow remains furrowed, and he clearly has an attitude.

"You are not serious right now," I tell him. "How do you have any right to be upset about anything?"

"I don't know what the hell you're talking about!" Khy exclaims.

"First of all, check your tone," Mercedes growls. "Second of all, don't gaslight my cousin." Neyo yips and starts squirming in Mercedes's arms. He wiggles out of them and then just stands halfway between her and me. The puppy gazes between Mercedes, Khy, and me anxiously. *Poor thing.*

I sigh and make myself calm down for Neyo's sake. When he came to us at the rescue, one of Dad's friends who works for the sheriff's department had taken him from a not-so-great home after his owner got arrested. Neyo gets super nervous around raised voices or even mildly angry energy.

I draw in a breath, make sure I really am good, and then reach out for Neyo. "I'm sorry, little dude," I tell the three-month-old puppy soothingly. I cradle him to my chest, hug him tightly so he feels safe and comforted and protected. "I need you to go," I tell Khy calmly. "Whatever games you're playing, I'm not with it, alright? I saw how you and Gigi were all over each other and flirting at the tournament. Whatever you want to do with your cheating ex—that's on you. But leave me out of it, okay?"

Khy blinks. First, greater shock colors his face. Then horror. Then understanding. Finally, he clenches his jaw. He groans. "I think I know what happened." He shakes his head. "I should've known she'd pull this crap. I swear you didn't see what you thought you saw. I wasn't flirting with Gigi. She complained about having to work her volunteer station alone since her assigned partner didn't show up. I felt responsible to pick up the slack because it was my event. So I stayed at the station to help her work it."

Mercedes snorts. "Be *so* for real."

"I *am* being straight up. Y'all have gotta believe me," he

says. There's a desperation to his voice that snags my attention. It's so strong that it would make him an Oscar-worthy actor if he was lying. This realization is the only reason I ease up—just a little.

"Explain how I didn't see you and Gigi flirting at your tent then, Khy. I'm listening."

He blows out a breath. "Gigi's Connection has to do with glamours. She can skew the way people perceive stuff. She can make folks see things happening that aren't really going on. I think, *I'm positive*, she messed with you because nothing I did with Gigi could've been interpreted as me flirting. I made sure of that." He grimaces. "The press behind it would've been uncontrollable, and I don't want to be attached to Gigi in any way ever again."

Nothing he says about Gigi's Connection is in the implausible realm as far as magical gifts go. And Gigi absolutely has the delightful personality of somebody who would pull such a grimy move.

If I wasn't so exhausted by just thinking about it, I'd laugh. *Oh, Khy's ex really is a piece of work.*

Not that knowing the truth changes anything. Fake-dating Khy was a colossally bad idea, and me hanging around Coven folk always had the extremely likely chance of blowing up in my face. It's better that I go ahead and maintain distance between me and Khy—and me and any danger of catching true feelings.

"Thank you for clarifying things," I say to Khy. "But I met your parents at the tournament, too. They ignored the hell out of me. Wouldn't even look my way. So yeah, they were about as mean as a pair of rattlesnakes." It's one of Grandpop's sayings, and it fits too well. Even if what happened with Gigi was a glamour, what happened with his parents certainly wasn't.

Khy frowns. "That doesn't sound like them. They're really nice with my friends. I'm sure the vibe was only off because Mom was in diplomat mode and trying not to give the rumor mill more fodder. She hates when the media pries into our private lives."

Mrs. Carter's wistful words about wanting Khy and Gigi to mend their rift worm their way into my head. *That, I certainly could not misunderstand. And it had nothing to do with diplomacy.* I catch my stank face before it forms. I remain outwardly serene and unruffled.

Right then, Keenan pokes his head back out the door. "Are y'all planning to stay hanging out here for a bit? Because I can bring a few more pups your way to get some yard time in, if that's okay?"

"Sure!" I answer. "There's nowhere else I need to be."

Khy looks from Keenan to me. "I'd love to stay, too," he says sheepishly. "I mean . . . if you don't still want me to kick rocks."

I consider it, but he needs to squirm a little more first, so it is crystal clear that I am not the one to play with. I turn to Mercedes and ask her, "What do you think?"

She smacks her teeth, immediately playing along. "I don't know. I still don't like his tone from before."

"My bad for real," says Khy.

She rakes him with a look.

I let him stand nervously, bearing the weight of her glare for a few seconds. Is it fair to him if he really didn't do anything wrong? No. Does it still make what Gigi pulled sting less? Absolutely. Besides, he should've let her stay at the volunteer station alone to begin with or found somebody else to pair her up with if it was that deep. I ignore the inner voice that quips I sound jealous. "You can hang out," I finally tell Khy. I do it for the fur-babies, so they can have another playmate. Yup. That's totally the only reason I ease up and don't kick him out.

Mercedes smirks between me and Khy. She stands. "I'm sure y'all can handle the dogs. I'm gonna give you some alone time now that you've made up," she says, slick.

My cousin is a traitor.

Mercedes leaves, and Khy helps Keenan bring out five additional dogs for play time.

At first, Khy and I individually play with the dogs without saying much to each other. He throws a baseball around for four of the older dogs to wrestle over. Whoever wins the lighthearted tussle bounds back to Khy with the ball in their mouth, the others right on their heels. I keep Neyo and a Doberman pup that's only a month older out of the fray and hold their attention at the doggy playground with hoops to jump through, tunnels to crawl in, and ramps to climb up.

"How is Hades doing?" I ask when the extended silence grows a tad awkward.

"Terrific!" Khy says. "If I'd known this is where I'd end up, I would've brought my boy with me. He might disown me when he smells all these guys on me when I get home."

I snort. "Or drench more than your shoes the next time he needs a bath."

Khy chuckles. I do, too. The lingering tension washes away. "I'm really sorry about Gigi," he says earnestly.

I wave it off. "We've already covered that. You don't need to apologize again."

"But it hurt your feelings, so I do," Khy states intently as he throws the baseball once again. Khy's insistence that the added apology is needed simply because I felt hurt makes a weird sensation ripple in my chest.

"It didn't feel great," I say as I help Roscoe, the Doberman pup, make it up a ramp that's a little steep for him. I shock myself by admitting I was even a fraction bothered. But I guess how comfortable and completely at ease I feel with Khy is what makes me not care about projecting anything except the truth. Now that the record has been set straight, I don't feel the need to be "tough." Like at Magic Row, it's easy to just be *Cayden* while I'm around Khy.

"Just so you know, yesterday made me *sure*, all the way, that I don't have feelings for Gigi anymore. I like spending time with you, not her. I like *you*. A lot," Khy says softly.

I clear my throat. But that doesn't lessen the wild way my heart beats. And it just barely holds back the response on the tip of my tongue, one that feels as natural as breathing.

"Thanks for clearing things up," I tell Khy. *Thanks for*

caring enough to expend all the extra effort. He could've dropped things—dropped me—when I tried to ghost him. Somebody else might've shrugged me off and went on about their business. Moved on to the next person. But Khy... Khy was worried about me when I went silent and he didn't know why. It's yet another time that I plainly see how much he cares, so much, about everything—about people's feelings, about putting good and positive energy into the world, about being an actual nice and kind person, about looking out for others all the time. He's . . . *unreal.*

"Yes. I remember how you are. Mekhi Carter, the media's beloved Good Guy." I think about how Gigi spit that at Khy like it was his worst flaw. And she really is delusional because it's the best thing about him.

Neyo barks and then nudges my ankle with his head. I glance down at the puppy. He gazes up at the steep ramp I helped Roscoe conquer. I kneel and lift Neyo onto the bottom of it. I keep my hand on his bottom and push as he uses his little legs to scramble upward. When he makes it to the top of the ramp, he's panting happily and his tail wags victoriously. I grin. "You did it, boy! Go you!"

Neyo dashes down the opposite ramp, and I let my stare travel back to Khy. He's gazing at me, too.

Butterflies don't erupt. Something worse happens.

I grin—with my whole body, not only my face—over at Khy. I feel his huge answering smile thrum around me, from my hair to my sneaker-clad feet. A million alarm bells go off inside my head that are too late. I'm not *catching* feelings for

Khy. I have *caught* feelings. *Major ones.* I've been in denial since the tournament, but being in the same vicinity as Khy makes me unable to go on having ostrich-syndrome. *I like you, too. A lot. So much.* My inner voice repeats the mushy, smitten words that I curbed earlier back to Khy.

Ancestors help me! I am in *deep* trouble. So much trouble.

"Since we're back cool, do you wanna schedule our next fake date?" Khy asks bashfully. It's a crime how cute it is that he easily swings between having all the swag to this shy version of himself.

"When are you thinking?" I ask, working hard to keep my newly recognized intense feelings in check.

"Are you free this weekend?" Khy says. "There's another big-press Coven thing coming up on Sunday afternoon. It's a Sundresses and Seersuckers Garden Party. Becca and Naomi are cochairing it. Becca hasn't stopped talking about how awesome you are since the golf course. Naomi keeps mentioning how much she likes you, too—and she usually hates every new friend somebody in our group makes. They'd both love for you to come. So would I. I umm . . . it's the type of thing you'd normally take a date to if you had one."

Whoa. Okay. My stomach does a somersault or two. All right, maybe it does a triple twisting double backflip. Khy has proposed we attend Coven events together before because they make for great photo ops. But this time, it feels different. Heavier. More significant. *Probably because he asked after telling me, explicitly, how much he likes me, and after I've at least admitted to myself that I like him as much back.*

"So if we keep hanging out, will it be more fake dates or . . . real ones?" The question tumbles out. I don't make a conscious decision to ask it beforehand. My mouth and newly recognized feelings, apparently, decide to do what the hell they want.

Khy hasn't stop staring at me in this super-intense, super-unnerving way. It's like he's piercing me with his brown stare. Looking at me and through me all at once. Like he's trying to figure out how I feel about him, if it's equal to what he's confessed.

Tell him it is, a part of me insists. I bite down on the inside of my cheek. Not yet. I need time.

"If I asked for it to be a real date, would you be okay with that?"

Yes! "Maybe," I hedge.

Khy smiles with his whole face, and, unsurprisingly, it shows up the sun that's bearing down on the courtyard. "I can work with that," he says, the hyperconfidence returning.

I roll my eyes. "I'm sure you can." I can't help my own huge grin. I sober quickly when I think about what else is happening this weekend. "I can't go to the garden party, though. The cookout is on Sunday," I tell Khy, and I am surprised by how bummed I am. But at this point, I guess I shouldn't be shocked at all.

His disappointment lasts less than a second. "That's

right," he says cheerfully. "I hope y'all kill it and the turnout is huge."

"It seems like it will be. Just about every media outlet based in Houston wants to cover it, and most have already started publicizing it. Donations have been pouring in!" I grow excited as I catch Khy up on what he's missed.

I can't lie, though; I have a seriously difficult time shaking *my* disappointment that the garden party won't be a real date for us.

Yup, I've definitely plunged into *deep*, unchartered waters.

Chapter Sixteen

"Wow! Folks really showed out and showed up!" Mercedes looks around Emancipation Park, in awe of all the people who've come to the cookout. The crowd includes radio DJs, local podcasters and influencers, several news anchors, and *all* the Divine Nine (the undergraduate and the graduate chapters) from STU.

"It is pretty spectacular!" I exclaim. I'm grinning from ear to ear. The fact that this event has reeled in so many supporters gives me actual hope that bougie witch-types won't get away with wrecking my neighborhood, Dad's business, or other businesses simply because they have globs of money to throw around.

Since we've got all the volunteers checked in and situated at their duty stations (a bouncy house, inflatable slide, silent auction tent, puppy adoptions pens, and food serving tables), Mercedes and I spend the next hour near the entrance of the park working as greeters. We hand out goodie bags filled with perks (spa certificates, coupons for free appetizers or desserts at restaurants, half-priced hair salon vouchers, 20 percent off book purchases at the local independent bookstore, and so on) donated by community businesses to thank attendees for showing them love. When Mercedes's parents walk up, Auntie Vesha announces that Mom sent them over to relieve us from our duties.

"Go have some fun," Auntie Nikki adds.

"We can stay," I say. "Mom or Dad might need y'all somewhere else."

"Yeah. We can work this area all day. No big deal," Mercedes says.

Auntie Nikki smirks. "I wish our child was this enthusiastic about working through chores at home."

"See, first of all, house chore are *eww*," Mercedes states. "And this is fun work. Plus, I get to hang with Cayden."

"Your cousin can come help with chores if that's all it takes," Auntie Nikki responds.

I hold up my hands. "Nah. Leave me out of this."

Auntie Vesha chuckles. "Your mother told us that if you argue, then to tell you there's more than enough volunteers to fill each and every post for the entire day."

"But if y'all just wanna keep working today, then I got a list of stuff I need taken care of at the house," Auntie Nikki says.

"We're good. And you're not serious," Mercedes says

quickly. "Come on, though, before my mama decides that she is," Mercedes tells me. She grabs my hand and drags me away.

She and I end up standing in line at a sno-ball truck, and I take the time to look at what we've put together and watch everyone enjoying themselves. Then I spot the last person I thought I'd see today. Khy, a goodie bag in hand, is walking toward me. Hades is beside him, panting happily while looking around at all the activity like he's just barely restraining himself from dragging Khy, who's holding his leash, into the thick of whatever catches his fancy the most. Khy grins at me and waves. When he does, his dimples flash and my resident butterflies take flight. I wave back, confused as hell.

"Hey," I say when he reaches me. Thank the Ancestors I don't *sound* breathless, but I certainly *feel* like I'm experiencing a sudden lack of oxygen. How the hell does this boy have such a strong effect on me every time I see him? I inhale a small, inconspicuous breath and collect myself. "I thought you had a Cotillion thing?" I ask in what I hope sounds like a chill tone.

Khy smiles. This time, it's his bashful one. "I decided to skip the garden party. This seemed important to you, so I wanted to be here."

Beside me, Mercedes doesn't so much as try not to audibly—and mortifyingly—swoon.

"Oh." It's the only word I can squeeze out. The jittery butterflies dial up to a bajillion. I clear my throat. "That was nice," I manage. "I didn't expect you to . . ." I clear my throat again. "What I mean is you didn't have to . . ." I bite the inside of my cheek, tongue-tied. The true weight of the gesture apparently has made me forget how to form complex sentences. "Hey, boy!" I exclaim to Hades, trying to distract from my awkwardness. In my desperation, I forget that the demon dog and I are nemeses. I lean down to pat his head. He rears back, gives me his doggy side-eye. He doesn't flash his pearly whites, but I'm guessing that's only because Khy fussed at him about it last time. Hades doesn't miss a beat, though, when he sniffs the air near my hand, as if my mere scent being so close is offending.

Khy is watching him, and Hades slants a look his beloved owner's way. After peeping he's under scrutiny, Hades lets out a chuff of air and then—yoooo! Texas is gonna freeze over in June. Hades willingly leans into my touch, rubs the top of his head against my palm. Snuggles it, even.

Khy beams at Hades and scratches behind his ear. "Good buddy!" A spinning ball of water about the size of a golf ball appears in Khy's hand. Hades yips. Khy tosses it in the air. Hades bounds up to grab it and the watery sphere falls apart, splashing Hades on the nose. Hades barks raucously. He nudges Khy's leg to do the trick again. Khy does it once more, then tells Hades, "We'll play more later. Okay?"

Hades whines for a second and then falls silent, nuzzling Khy's cargo shorts.

"Are you a dog whisperer? Or do you and Hades just have a super tight connection?" I ask Khy, amazed. He's done the impossible and gotten Hades to both like me and mostly behave.

"I can't be sure," Khy shrugs. "Hades is my first dog."

"So what made you get him?" I realize I never asked.

Khy ruffles the (admittedly adorable) curly fur atop Hades's head. "My house got real quiet and empty feeling after my brother moved into the STU dorms last year. Since my mom travels back and forth between Houston and DC a lot for work, that means it's only me and my dad in the house a good bit of the time." He says it matter-of-factly, without the tough guy nonsense some guys might try to pull.

"Your brother goes to STU?!" I exclaim.

Khy grins proudly. "Yup. He's the first in our family to attend an HBCU. Our parents and both sets of grandparents and great-grandparents, for as far back as they let us Black folks enroll, went to Harvard. But Rashaud convinced our parents to allow him to attend STU. I'm gonna be the second in our family now that he's made it... *okay*."

I'm near positive the word *acceptable* was what he was about to say instead. But him wanting to go to STU over an Ivy League is so dope, given who he is and how some folks regard HBCUs as inferior to PWIs. "And here I thought you just like walking around in STU gear for clout." I flick a sleeve of the maroon and white STU T-shirt Khy is wearing today. I'm only teasing—partially. Because, truthfully, I did think the STU swag was for vibes only. "I'm going to Howard," I tell him. "That is, if I get in."

"You'll get in," he says immediately and adamantly.

A corner of my mouth quirks upward. "You say that with such confidence, like you can predict the future."

The hyperintense look he wears stays fixed in place. "It doesn't take a Connection in the psychic arts to know that you are amazing as hell and any school you apply to should snatch you up." He sweeps a hand out at the park. "You did organize this whole thing."

"I had plenty of help from my family," I say, grabbing Mercedes's arm. His compliment leaves me a little lightheaded. Woozy even. I casually lean against my cousin for support to play it off.

Mercedes smirks like she knows what's up. "We all helped, but it was Cayden's idea initially, and she sunk a ton of work into pulling this off," my cousin gushes. "Take the praise, Sis!" She gases me up, bumping my hip with hers.

I suck my teeth but cheese hard and say thanks, basking in the fact that we pulled things off so flawlessly.

"Cayden!" I jolt at the sound of Dad's voice. Nearly jump a mile in the damn air. Heart pounding, I spin around in the direction of where I heard Dad. Oh God. He is literally a few feet away and swiftly approaching me and Khy—the witch boy I've been chilling with that he and Mom don't know about.

"Relax, girl. You look guilty," Mercedes whispers into my ear.

"How the hell am I supposed to do that?" I hiss back. "Uhh... hey!" I say when Dad stands in front of us. My voice scales high and sounds pathetically suspicious.

True to form, Jason Jackson misses nothing. He gives me a look, and then his eyes narrow on Khy. My heart tries to thud right out of my chest when Dad's stare takes on a laser-focused intensity that makes it plain he's about to grill the knucklehead boy about who exactly he is and what exactly is up between the two of us.

"Khy, this is my dad. Dad, this is Khy," I say quickly before Dad can start in. "His family adopted Hades from the shelter, and we've been hanging out a little. *As friends.* He brought Hades to the park." *Please pick up on the fact that I didn't introduce you as a witch and say nothing about it*, I beg Khy in my head.

"Nice to meet you, young man," says Dad as he holds out his hand.

Khy shakes it, impressively not withering under the mean mug Dad turns on every boy I introduce him to. "It's very nice to meet you, too, sir." As always, Khy is the picture of manners. "Is there anything I can help out with? My family organizes a lot of similar events, so I know how hectic things can get. An extra set of hands is always useful. So, please, put me to work if you need to."

While Dad's mean mug turns into an approving expression, I try my best not to go rigid. I think I stop breathing when Dad asks Khy, "What types of similar events does your family organize?"

He answers, "Both my parents sit on the boards of a few different charities. So, mostly donor fundraisers and galas. But I recently talked them into spearheading more meaningful community outreach, too. Throwing money at stuff and labeling that as helping isn't enough, you know?" Khy scratches the back of his head when he finishes. There's a slight darkening to his brown cheeks. "I just realized that probably sounded very privileged, very pretentious, and embarrassingly ineloquent. I promise I'm usually better at articulating my thoughts, sir."

Dad appraises Khy, the approving gleam in his stare remaining in place. "No, son. I understand exactly what you mean, and you sound like a very smart young man. Your name is Khy, right?" He motions to Khy's STU shirt. "You an underclassman already over there, or are you looking to apply in the future?"

"I want to attend the college after I graduate next year," says Khy.

Dad nods, appreciatively. "That's what I like to hear! I'm an alumni. Cayden's mom is, too. Our lovely daughter wants to ditch being a legacy and go up north to that other, *I guess*, great institution they call Howard." Dad winks at me. "I like this kid. He makes good choices."

I roll my eyes, relaxing by a billion degrees since the convo has veered away from Khy's family. *Thank you*, I shoot to the Ancestors. Them looking out and working a damn miracle has to be the only reason I'm not in seriously hot water right now.

"Don't be a hater," I quip back at Dad. "My college choice is fantastic, and you know it."

"It's aight," he teases. "You got an idea about a major

yet?" He asks Khy. "Because you sound like public affairs might be your thing."

Khy slides his hands into his pockets. "Actually, I want to be a political science major, sir. After college, my goal is law school."

"My man!" Dad extends his fist out. Khy pounds it with his own. I gawk because Jason Jackson has never warmed up to a boy I like this fast.

"Is that when you plan to fall back on family tradition and go to Harvard?" I quiz Khy, wondering at his answer.

He appears rueful for a second and then says, "Yeah. That's the deal my brother made with my parents. It's the same bargain I'm going to strike."

Khy slashes a nervous glance at Dad like he fears he's about to be judged. But neither of my parents are like that.

Dad only bobs his head and says, "Ain't nothing wrong with experiencing the best of both worlds and accumulating degrees from both." Then he asks, "Are either of your parents lawyers?"

Gah! How did we get back here?! The Ancestors aren't looking out, I see. Instead, they're toying with me. My returned stress must show on my face because Khy gives me this tiny, soothing smile. I swear it says, *I got you.*

"They both attended Harvard Law," Khy says. "They went there for undergrad, too." I brace for him to add that they don't practice at a firm and are in politics instead. Dad will subsequently become curious and ask what they do exactly. And then, yeah, queue the flaming hot mess of a disaster that will ensue. Khy doesn't say anything else, though. Just gives me that same tiny smile as before. I pass him an infinitely grateful look.

Guilt pricks me, though, because I can't even pretend like I'm not majorly lying to Dad via deception right now. I manage not to feel like the complete worst by reasoning that I'm doing it so I don't blindside him in the middle of a crowded park with all the specifics of who and what Khy is.

"Pivoting to an HBCU behind parents who are double Ivy League alumni is quite a choice," Dad muses. "Why STU, son?"

"I've grown up in Houston my whole life," Khy answers without missing a beat. "This isn't me bragging, but my family is very wealthy and I've been extremely privileged. It's important to me to use that privilege I was born to in a way that makes a difference. Houston is my home, and I want to stay in my home city, help uplift others, and affect change right here. And I don't want to go off to college across the country and wait until after I graduate to do it. As for STU specifically, I really dig the level of community and support that an HBCU provides its Black students."

I have to work hard not to gape at Khy. Or drool. He had no reason to be self-conscious before. *Inarticulate* is a term that will never apply to *Khy Carter.*

Chapter Seventeen

Khy wows my mom as much as he did my dad when he meets her for the second time. She immediately remembers him from the rescue, and my absurd mother slides me a thumbs-up in Khy's face. (Yes, it is absolutely mortifying.)

And it isn't only my parents Khy's terrific with. For the entire day, he fits seamlessly into my world. When three of Dad's closest frat brothers descend upon us and bully Khy into a game of Spades simply to talk mad junk and intimidate the boy rolling with Jason's daughter at the cookout, Khy good-naturedly plays. He gets his and his partner's behinds whooped because he's playing against folks who've got decades of experience beasting on a cards table. But he holds his own against the normal ribbing that's as much a staple of Spades as the playing cards themselves. And by the end of the game, he has Dad's fraternity brothers telling him to consider pledging their frat when he gets to STU.

Then, there's the current way he's easily meshing with me, Mercedes, and our school friends at the park. We sit on lawn blankets battling it out in a fierce game of Heads Up—Mercedes and her theater crew against me and my fellow rising senior class Cabinet members who turned out to support me and the event. Khy, the traitor, is on Mercedes's team, and they're kicking my team's butt in the current round where the category is Disney villains.

"Let me find out you're a low-key Disney nerd," I say to Khy after he correctly names, like, eight villains in rapid succession, only needing to listen to his team's hints for a couple of seconds every time.

"It's not even low-key." He grins unashamed as he hands Mercedes her phone we're using to play with. "Me and my big bro, we been high-key obsessed with all things Disney since we were little kids. We make our parents hit up Disney World like four times a year."

Nessa, Mercedes's girlfriend, whistles. "Damn, boy! You're rich, rich! Let me tag along next time. I'll be your sister for the day."

"Bet," Khy says, chuckling graciously. And I sit back and appreciate—drink in really—how he doesn't throw his status around like some snob, walking around like he's better than everybody, but he isn't shy about who he is, either. He embraces *everything* that makes him *him,* and he does so with this easy confidence that contributes to his swag. I love—*it*. Yeah ... *it* was totally what I was about to say.

We play a few more rounds of Heads Up, and my team redeems itself when we pick the Marvel and Black Excellence decks. We're about to dive into a fresh category when Mom's voice rings out across the park. Standing atop the stage a few yards away, Mom excitedly says hello into a microphone. "Thank you all for showing up and showing out!" she exclaims.

Before she can continue, her sorors in attendance loudly cheer her on. Dad's frat joins in.

When they quiet down, Mom goes on. "We all know this cookout has a dual purpose. I am so grateful for the community, family, friends, and volunteers that have always supported the vet clinic and Lucky Paws. I'm glad I can play a small role in funneling that tremendous support behind a cause that affects everybody who lives, works, attends school, has family, or has roots in Third Ward." She pauses for a round of more claps and cheers. Then says, "Again, a huge thanks to you all. But I am not the great Michelle Obama, so my grand speech ends here." Her joke lands, garnering laughter. Mom finishes with, "I'll hand over the mic now to more eloquent orators who have something loud, proud, and powerful to say about the forces trying to drive us out of our community."

Dad is the next speaker. He looks and sounds exactly like the brilliant man with a sharp mind for economics and urban policy that he is. He talks about how the seemingly financial benefits of gentrification and places like The Spell Shoppes coming to Third Ward aren't as advantageous as they appear on the surface. He highlights the negative impact that includes forced displacement, discriminatory behavior by people with more social, financial, and political power, and the emergence of many spaces that exclude lower-income residents and people of color. "But it's not just about what us old heads believe and would like to see for our neighborhood in the future," Dad says afterward. "It's also about what the generation *of the future* believes and wants to achieve. That's why I'm handing the mic over to my and Eva's daughter, Cayden, so she can come up here and tell you what this community's preservation means to her."

There are more claps and cheers. Lots of "I hear you!" and "I know you right!" But I barely hear them because even though I agreed to this beforehand and knew it was coming, I've suddenly developed stage fright I didn't know I had. Which ... all right, maybe since I've never spoken in front of a crowd before I should've considered the possibility. But it's me; I'm usually pretty fearless about most things, so I figured it'd be fine. But ... there are a lot of people inside the park.

"Come on up here, baby girl!" Dad calls out, grinning proudly from ear to ear and waving at me in the crowd.

"Get up there!" Mercedes tells me when I don't budge. "What's wrong?"

"I ... I think I'm terrified," I admit. "There's a lot of folks out here. And how am I supposed to say anything that sounds half as articulate and smart behind Dad's speech? Whatever I say is gonna sound dumb."

"It won't," Mercedes promises. "And a little bit of stage fright is normal. You can conquer it. You got this! You can't just leave Uncle Jason hanging."

She's right. I *know* she's right. But when I try to force my legs to unfold and my body to stand—my muscles refuse to budge.

Mercedes squeezes my shoulder. "Listen to me: you won't sound stupid. You're a mini Uncle Jason mixed with Angela Davis. You'll be amazing."

"She's not wrong," Khy says adamantly. "You'll kill it, Cayden. You're always extraordinary every time you talk about stuff that means a lot to you. But if it helps—" Abruptly, he stands and brushes off his khaki shorts. "Do you mind watching Hades for a bit?" he asks Mercedes.

She wrinkles her nose but says, "Sure."

Then, Khy holds his hand out to me. "I'll come with you and stand beside you for moral support. We can picture everybody in their underwear together—or however that trick is supposed to work." He winks. "Maybe we can switch it up to swimsuits and snowsuits. That would be wild side by side."

His joke does its job. I laugh, nerves lessening a bit. "Okay," I say and stand. When I slide my hand into Khy's, the warmth of his palm works more magic and makes the rest of my jitters vanish.

After we walk onto the stage, Khy drops my hand and

takes a step back to stand behind me and beside Dad. I stand in front of the mic by myself. With my usual confidence fully back in place, I don't hesitate to start speaking. "My dad grew up right here in Third Ward," I say. "Many of y'all already know that he's a graduate of the neighborhood school, Yancey High. He's an STU alumni, too. My mom didn't grow up here. She grew up in Dallas. But she attended undergrad right here at STU, remained at the university for vet school, and chose to open a pet clinic and dog rescue shelter that serves the community. My mom, Eva Jackson, is a good example of how outsiders moving into the neighborhood can do so in a way that gives back and makes a positive impact. Witch corporations who want to construct shopping plazas like The Spell Shoppes and high-end condos that specifically cater to wealthy witches aren't giving back or making a positive impact on our neighborhood's existing residents. They are pushing out current businesses and residents to make room for a very specific and narrow population. I know not all change is bad. I also know that for urban communities to sustain themselves and flourish indefinitely, change needs to be welcomed and embraced. But change that doesn't care about the local businesses and residents being pushed out due to rent hikes can't possibly be the right path."

The crowd erupts into applause and excited hooting and hollering. I'm giddy and buzzing with energy by the time I finish.

"Okay. Damn girl! You were more than amazing," Khy

says when we're off the stage. "You had squat to worry about. You sounded *better* than your dad."

"I did sound pretty spectacular, right?" I grin, still riding the adrenaline high.

Khy cheeses as wide, licking his lips. My eyes, of course, snag on the gesture. I notice how close we're standing then. And that our hands have become laced together at some point. I gaze at Khy, and it's evident he's imagining kissing me. The same image pops into my head. My lips tingle, and I swear I can feel his full, soft lips sliding against mine, even though they aren't. I blink, a little dizzy.

I manage to cobble together some good sense and take a healthy step back. I cannot kiss Khy in the middle of the park with my parents around. Not when I've introduced him as just a friend. But damn if I don't really, really, *really* want to do it. "You're incredible yourself," I say to Khy. I can't believe he not only showed up today but got up on stage with me to help me get over my nerves. It was more than cool—and brave. My entire speech, after all, threw shade at Coven folk, and technically his family, too, since they help govern and promote witchkind's interests. I mentally add *ride-or-die* to the list of things about Khy that makes me *like* like him. And I decide, right on the spot, to just toss any lingering reservations away about he and I dating for real. Khy has proven he's beyond worthy at this point, right? I like him, he likes me, and I want to do something about it so bad my chest physically aches.

"Do you wanna get out of here?" I ask on impulse. We

remain at the foot of the stage, feet away from my mom and dad. Which is a whole problem because..."I really want to kiss you—*a lot*—and I can't do that here," I tell Khy. "So, are you down, Royal Boy?"

His eyebrows shoot up, his mahogany cheeks darkening. He quickly recovers, though, and supplies an answer with the way the rich brown of his eyes glimmers, and he leans in a fraction closer to me. He comes so near, my forehead brushes his chin. I crane my head up so I can gaze into his face in this new position. His eyes dip down to my lips. "Absolutely, I'm with it." He announces this in a hypnotic voice that's deeper than his usual pitch. It's as tempting as chocolate cake, and it should be illegal for him to toss it around. I blink, dazed. Ball my hands into fists at my sides so I don't forget my parents are around, grab Khy's shirt, and drag him closer right now.

My torment must be evident because Khy's stare sharpens with a knowing gleam. Then, I'm treated to a new variety of grin that I've never seen on Royal Boy before—one that's full of mischief. It promises me just how good sneaking off to make out with him is about to be. I go warm all over. I grab his hand, make a quick pit stop to collect Hades, and get us moving, *speed walking* out of the park.

Chapter Eighteen

It is truly a travesty that merely clearing the park grounds isn't good enough, and I can't turn to Khy as soon as we're on the sidewalk and get lost in everything about this boy. My parents are still way too near.

"I'll grab a Lyft," Khy offers, voice uneven and clearly as out of sorts as I am. "Where are we headed?" he asks as he takes his phone out of his pocket.

"Some place not public. My house is around the corner; we can go there." I say it before I realize how it sounds.

Khy swallows heftily. "Ummm..."

Oh my God! My whole face blazes. "That's not what I meant," I tell him quickly. "I meant...that...ummm...there's always a camera somewhere lurking when you're in the equation. And..." I clear my throat and boss up, allowing myself to be real with Khy. "I'd really like this to just be about us,"

I say, "I guess what I'm trying to say is . . . I don't want potential cameras to be a thing we're thinking about, or that even matters. I only want *us* to matter for a while." The truth is out of my mouth before I can snatch it back or rethink it. And though I made the choice to be honest, I'm not sure which I'd rather be subjected to anymore: the mortification of Khy thinking I was propositioning him for more than kissing, or the fear I feel after hinting to Khy how serious my feelings for him have started to become.

"I'd like that, too," Khy murmurs. His words make me go mushy inside, and it becomes hard to focus. Not because his hands lightly rest on my waist (though that's part of it), but because the ache in my chest intensifies and I feel drunk on how much I like simply hanging out with Khy. Kissing or no kissing.

I step back, out of Khy's hold, to catch my breath and try to lessen how intense *everything* has become with him. It's not a bad thing, but it is an entirely new experience that leaves me feeling like the ground was yanked from beneath my feet. "Can we ditch the Lyft and walk?" I ask, hoarsely. Walking will be good. Walking means more time before we make it to the privacy of my house, which means more time for me to get myself together, not feel so much like I've tumbled over a ledge and am falling toward a destination with no bottom.

"Whatever you want," Khy responds immediately. He puts his phone away. Offers me his arm. "You lead."

I take advantage of the tether back to solid ground that

his corny, retro gesture offers. I flick his arm. "Is that one of the things they teach you to do in Bougie Boys Charm School?"

He chuckles. "How many swag points do I lose if I say yeah?"

I smirk. "About a hundred." *But it's cool because you were already clocking in at, like, a bajillion.*

Khy scoffs. Levels a look at me that's playfully arrogant. "Guess I'll have to earn them back."

As we walk down Emancipation Avenue and cross over Elgin Street (*without* my arm looped through his), I ask him something I'm curious about. "Do you hang out down here a lot when you visit your brother at STU?"

"I've mainly stayed around the campus's grounds and places surrounding it," Khy admits. "I realize that's some straight-up mess on my part after hearing your speech," he hurriedly adds before I can return the light criticism he had to know was coming. "I really need to come explore more of the neighborhood beyond the college one day soon."

I don't give him a hard time. Only nod my head. Then, an idea hits me as we come upon Stuart Street. "Let's get you a mini tour in now," I say and grab his hand, hooking a right. I pull him a short way down the block and stop when we're standing outside of Kindred Stories. I point up at the charming historic row house structure of the bookstore. "This is one of my favorite places; there's a cozy lawn space in the back where you can chill and read and that they use for community events. And this bookshop is owned by Black women," I tell Khy. "They close at six so we just missed them, but you should stop by sometime."

"I definitely will," Khy promises. "What's next?" His excitement is genuine when he asks, and it's all the encouragement I need to keep the tour going. Making out with Khy at my house will still be there at the end of it, but walking with our hands laced together and sharing laughter and conversation is its own form of total bliss.

First, we swing by the popular restaurant, Soul Food Vegan, to indulge in their famous plant-based boudin balls. Then, I take him to see Project Row Houses, a community nonprofit based in a collection of restored shotgun houses. All lined up in a row, they show folks the architectural style of the kinds of homes that used to make up the majority of the neighborhood. Actually, they made up the majority of Black wards across Houston and towns in the southern United States in general. I've seen similar row houses when my parents and I have taken trips to Louisiana, Alabama, and Georgia. "The houses are used as galleries," I explain to Khy. "They host all types of events from art shows to neighborhood gatherings with live music to performances."

Khy looks over appreciatively at the small white homes squeezed side by side. "This is so cool. Historically Black neighborhoods aren't celebrated enough," he says low and thoughtfully.

"Agreed," I say.

Afterward, I show Khy a few more significant places in the vicinity. When we finally make it to my house, I suggest we hang outside on the back patio. Inviting Khy *inside* turned awkward the moment he misunderstood me before.

"Your backyard is dope as hell," he says as we sit on an outdoor sofa in the middle of Dad's zen garden. It was created using white sand and black slabs. There's a koi pond in the far corner against the fence, too, with pretty purple orchids around it. Currently, Hades is standing beside the pond, staring down at it and enraptured by the fish, who are probably terrified as hell.

"My dad designed everything himself," I mention proudly. "He and I renovated the backyard together last summer as a bonding project."

Khy sits up straighter, looks around the yard in awe. "Wait—you and Mr. Jackson did this by yourselves?" He then looks directly at me in a similar astonished manner. "Your family gets more and more cool. How many crazy talents do y'all have?!"

"A lot," I say, grinning. "Don't hate." I lean closer to him, knocking my shoulder against his chest. When I do, his arm curls around me, tightly tucking me into his side.

"I wasn't," he responds low. "Everything I keep discovering about you is incredible. *You're* incredible."

I get a little woozy as I'm staring into his eyes while he says it. They twinkle in the same fervid way he uttered the compliment. "So are you," I respond breathlessly.

I'm not sure who moves first. All I know is that when our lips meet, it's better than heaven. It's sheer bliss. And does the entire earth shift beneath me? I'm near positive I feel it. Smiling with my whole body, I wrap my arms around Khy's neck, letting myself get lost in his scent, the perfect way both his arms lock around my waist, and the electric current that shoots up my spine when his hands rest against my back. I float away. I think Khy does, too. Another thing I'm unsure of is how long we stay this way. Time loses meaning. The backyard, the rest of the world—literally, it all vanishes. It's just me and Khy and this kiss that leaves me dizzy when we come up for air. I have to blink several times to get the world to stop spinning. Once it does, Khy and I just sit on the sofa gazing at each other, arms still around each other.

"Can I ask you something?" Khy eventually asks, bashfully. He briefly closes his eyes, his long lashes casting a shadow over his high cheekbones like they often do. When he opens his eyes, *what* he wants to ask—or at least the gist of it—is clear on his face. We're about to revisit our convo about going out on a real date.

I swallow to calm the butterflies that take flight. "Sure."

Khy drags a hand down the top of his hair—which, as always, sports the sexy combo of a fresh fade and glistening waves that could compete with the ocean. He inhales. Exhales. Then he says, "I really like you. I have since we met at the shelter. This might sound insane, but I've felt this really intense connection with you since that day. You're funny and thoughtful and passionate and fierce and super genuine and really smart and gorgeous and . . . really, really special. Which is why I'm nervous about what you're gonna say to me asking you this again, if I ever get to it..." He laughs nervously. Takes a breath. "I'm laying it out. I'd like very much for us to do more than pretend to date in my world and only be *friends who met at the rescue* in your world. I want to be boyfriend and girlfriend for real. I want to *date you* date you, Cayden. Like *seriously* date you. Not take you out on bogus dates as part of some scheme for media attention, but actual dates, which is what today felt like..." He motions around us. "I want to do stuff like this with you, stuff like our mini-tour earlier."

Hearing how he feels about me floods me with jitters and an intense warmth—like curling up by the fireplace on a winter day. *Hell yes! I want it, too.*

I swear to the Ancestors it's the only way I want to respond. It's on the tip of my tongue, but the *yes* sticks in my throat. Blocking its way is the lingering worry about my parents' reactions and past hurts I can't entirely let go of. And I can't help thinking about the Gigi mess. Or about his frigid parents. The former might've been a misunderstanding, but it didn't hurt any less. Plus, I still don't know if I can believe Khy's claim that his parents were only trying to avoid giving the press gossip to spread. What if it was deeper than that? What if Mrs. Carter hates her son "dating" me in the same way Mom's parents hated Dad?

My gut twists and it's a little hard to breathe, not in a good way this time. Because I am painfully certain about one thing: if I go all in and date Khy for real and then something does go wrong, it *will* devastate me. Especially after today. Whatever feelings I had about Khy when I woke up this morning are now ten times more extreme.

The punctuated silence that's sprung up between us while Khy waits for my answer stretches on. His expression never strays from the picture of patience, but there's this mix of hope and dejection alongside it—like he guesses I'll decide I don't want to make things real but wishes otherwise. My phone chirps right then. The distinct tone is Mercedes's.

"Give me a second; I need to check this," I tell him quietly. She might be warning me my parents are headed home.

Khy's arms fall away from me at the same time that I let him go. I take my phone from my pocket. When I see the text from my cousin I giggle.

> Are you somewhere kissing on your Witch Boo still? You better be!!!! GET. IT!!!!!

I angle the phone away from Khy and quickly text her back.

> I was. Then he asked me to be his girlfriend!!!! Now I'm kind of freaking out. WTF should I do????

Her response comes back only a few seconds later.

> Are you high? He's fine AF!!! And you got him all twisted up! And he proved he ain't a fuckboy!!! CUFF HIM!!!

Uncle and Auntie are strolling with the Greeks just so you know. Say yes and go back to making out. I'll text you a heads-up when the parents dip.

I roll my eyes and rest my phone beside me on the sofa to make sure I receive her heads-up as soon as she sends it. Then, I face Khy. "Sorry," I say, feeling bad that I've left him hanging. It's time to put my big girl shorts on, I guess. I fidget with a loose thread along the seam of the couch cushion. Logically, I know what my answer should be if I don't want to eventually get hurt.

"So about your question..."

"If the answer is no, you can just say it," Khy voices, and I don't miss the way he clenches his jaw. The smile behind it is rueful. "What I mean is before, when you didn't answer at first... if you were trying to figure out a way to let me down easy, I'll be bummed. But that's not on you. You don't gotta feel bad about anything, and I don't want you to."

"No! Not at all! It's more complicated for me than that!" I hate that's the conclusion he's come to so much that the words rush out of my mouth without a second thought. My stomach is twisted into knots at the mere thought of not having a reason to see Khy anymore. And my chest, it legit *burns* when I think about this possibly being the last day we spend together. This precise moment is when it hits me exactly *how* bad I have it for Khy. I don't *only* like him. I'm not *falling in love* with him, either. I'm pretty sure I love Khy *already*.

The realization washes over me, and I expect to inwardly revolt against it. To instinctively hurl it far, far away, understanding that nothing but trouble can come of it. But something entirely different happens in that moment. A second truth smacks into me that makes one thing clear: while the prospect of future heartbreak is scary as hell, I already feel wrecked at the thought of things ending between Khy and me right here and now. So, if I'm hurtling toward possible calamity either way, I might as well be bold about it, right? If there's no getting around being crushed, then what am I really protecting my heart from?

I suck in a breath, and tell Khy, "I want what you want. I want to be your real girlfriend and keep dating."

Khy grins with his entire face. "Seriously? For real?"

I grin back so hard my cheeks end up hurting. "Yeah. For real," I tell him, leaning in and kissing my new boyfriend.

Chapter Nineteen

I walk—no, skip—into the bakery the next morning on cloud nine. I swear I'm like one of those sappy characters in a rom-com movie after they snag the guy, and I don't even care. Case in point, I stand behind the register humming a new Summer Walker drop about falling in. Then I move on to love songs by SZA and H.E.R.

Mercedes lets me make it for about an hour until she snorts and stabs me with a look. "Is this you shedding your Tough Girl Era and entering your Soft Girl Era? I've never heard you sing *out loud* and *in public* a day in our lives. Spitting the newest Megan bars? Sure. But not this, Sis!"

I shrug, leaning my hip against the counter. "What if I am?" Obviously, I'm joking. Maybe? I don't know. I mean, I don't entirely cringe at the accusation.

"Damn!" Mercedes laughs. "You do have it bad!"

Formerly, this would be the exact moment that I vehemently deny the mushy stuff to keep my rep intact and remind myself that we never, ever, catch *deep* deep feelings for a boy. But I couldn't fight my goofy smile if my life depended on it. *My cousin is right; I do have it bad.*

Mercedes shakes her head. "I'm glad things are slow around here, for once, this morning. If we were slammed, you'd be no help. Your Witch Boo got you twisted all the way up, babes."

I flip her off. "Kiss my ass."

She cackles like the cartoon version of a witch. "Eww. Nah, I'll leave it to—"

"If you finish that sentence, I'm gonna murder you in this bakery."

My threat only makes my delightful cousin hoot louder.

The door chimes, signaling our first customers of the morning. I turn from Mercedes, prepared to greet what's become the usual opening rush, which is streaming in a tad late. But only two people—an older man and woman—step inside. The man is unfairly tall with dark brown skin and a narrow but sturdy build. He wears a pair of navy slacks, tan dress shoes, and a white dress shirt. The woman has similar coloring; her complexion is only a smidgen lighter. Her dark hair is styled in a sleek silk press that falls past her shoulders. She's wearing a green tweed skirt suit.

My eyes nearly pop out of my head because I immediately recognize who they are.

I choke on spit, then cough for a good ten seconds. *Ain't no way!*

Mercedes slaps my back. "Are you good?" She asks as Mom's parents walk up to the counter. They look identical to the pictures on those profiles Khy sent me. The stuffy, bougie air even clings to them. *What the hell are they doing here?* They can't *not* know who owns the bakery. My name is in huge letters above the door. But . . . *do they know my name at all, though?* That thought is like a kick to the teeth when it hits. I clench my jaw as my stomach twists.

"Yes, are you all right, dear?" the grandmother I've never met asks me.

"I'm guessing you know who we are," the man, my grandfather, Robert Hilliard III, speaks before I can come up with what the hell I'm supposed to say to them.

I nod, mutely. Manage to find my voice. "I'm okay." Wildly, I look between my grandparents, Carolyn and Robert Hilliard. "Sorry if this sounds rude, but what are you doing here?" Actually, I don't feel bad if it does sound rude. They've been rude. My whole life. For Mom and Dad's whole marriage. And when my parents dated. They deserve rude. I should've been more discourteous.

"Umm. What's going on here?" Mercedes asks. "Who are they, Cayden?"

"My grandparents," I mutter.

Mercedes eyes grow as wide as the snickerdoodle cookies resting on top of the counter. "You're for real right now? Those are Auntie's parents?" She tenses up. Squeezes my hand. Her stupefied look vanishes, and irritation replaces it. "Do my auntie and uncle know y'all were popping up?" She asks Mom's parents.

Carolyn's mauve-painted lips press into a guilty line. Robert slightly winces.

"No, they do not," Carolyn says. "We are aware it may be graceless to do things like this, but..." An odd vibe I can't name slashes through her prim energy when she gazes at me. "We tried calling, but Eva didn't answer. We decided to come by since we were already in town." Her intense stare never leaves me. If I didn't know better, I'd say it was wistful. But I do know better. They made it clear in the past they hated Dad. They've made it immensely clear they aren't thrilled about my existence either—otherwise, why not reach out?

"We saw you on the news, Cayden, talking about the bakery," Carolyn says after a moment of awkward silence.

"You are a very articulate young lady," Robert says. Again, if I didn't know better, I'd swear he was radiating pride. "We took seeing you speak as a sign from the Ancestors that it was time to mend our broken relationship with our daughter," Robert continues. His wild claim quadruples my bafflement. Did I truly hear what I think I did? "We didn't know you'd be working here," Robert adds apologetically. "We were hoping to speak with your parents first."

I inhale slowly through my nose to calm how fast my pulse wooshes. Mercedes never lets my hand go. I become infinitely glad because it gives me an anchor amidst all of this madness. I squeeze her hand.

The bakery's door chimes open. Mom walks in. When she sees who is standing in front of her, she stops dead in her tracks. She takes in Carolyn and Robert for a moment longer. And then Mom becomes the most pissed I've ever seen her. She looks at her parents like she'd turn them to ice on the spot if she had that Connection. "You're bullshitting me!" she screeches. "Both of you have some nerve. Why the hell are you here, and why are you speaking to my child? Get out."

Carolyn clutches the slim strand of pearls at her neck. She stares at Mom the same intense way she'd been gazing at me, only it's doubled. And the only accurate way to describe Robert, who has slid his hands in the pockets of his slacks, is *devastated*. "Eva... sweetheart, your baby girl is so beautiful," Roberts says hoarsely.

"What's all the yelling about?" Dad asks, puzzled, as he steps through the kitchen door. Like Mom, he freezes. First complete bewilderment colors his face. Then, he scowls. He looks to Mom with an eyebrow raised. "I guess we have our answer to why they were randomly calling."

Mom shakes her head as she walks up to the counter. She plants herself at her parents' side. "No, we don't. What is this?" she demands from Carolyn and Robert. "Answer my damn question. Why are you here?"

Carolyn stands up straighter. "I cannot believe you're asking me that, Eva. We left half a dozen messages! Are you really not going to accept help for your daughter simply because you remain angry with your father and me?"

"I stopped listening to your messages a long time ago, Mother," Mom says through her teeth.

Carolyn frowns deeply, like *she* has a reason to be perturbed. "Despite whatever differences we may have, we're still family, and family comes together in times of crises. Let us be here for Cayden. We've already hired the best public relations firm in the country to minimize the impact of the fallout from Cayden's very eloquent speech." Carolyn pivots to face me directly. "I promise you, we will squash it, honey. The entire unpleasant business will vanish soon."

"I—I have no clue what you mean," I sputter.

"Explain better than that, Mother," Mom grits out.

"Yes, Carolyn. Please do," Dad says just as tightly.

Mercedes has dropped my hand. Her phone is out, and her fingers fly over the screen. She coughs. A lot. When she looks up at me, she's pale, like most of the melanin has drained from her face.

"What?" I ask, scared as hell myself now.

Mercedes shows me her phone. Mom and Dad lean in to see the screen, too. The first thing I see is a pic of me on the stage speaking at yesterday's cookout with Khy standing behind me. The world seems to grind to a halt—literally, it's like the planet stops spinning on its axis, when I read the title above the picture: **Mekhi Carter Betrays His Coven for New Girlfriend.**

Panic slams into me. I keep my eyes glued to the phone, too guilt ridden, too terrified, too much of a coward to glance up at Mom and Dad.

I blink rapidly at the bold black letters of the damning title that leap off the screen. Stomach clenching in a way that makes me shaky, I read the article beneath our photo.

America's beloved young witch royal seems to be turning his back on his Coven and family, being pulled away by the Mystery Girl he's been dating, who apparently has an ugly and sordid history with Covens. An anonymous source told THE SCOOP that Mystery Girl, whose name is Cayden Jackson, is a witch and so is her mother, Eva Jackson. Mother and daughter come from a prominent witch family that is, in fact, one of the founding families of Dallas's Coven. However, Mekhi's girlfriend's mother broke from her prestigious family and Coven society twenty years ago when she was involved in a scandal, and she continues to hold disdain for Coven witches. It seems that the daughter, Cayden, feels the same if the way she publicly blasted Covens and witch-owned corporations during a rally aimed at smearing the reputation of Coven witches is anything to go by. THE SCOOP's anonymous source informed us that they fear Mekhi's new girlfriend is a bad influence who is convincing him to feel the same way she and her mother do about Coven society. This fear appears true. Mekhi purportedly blew off a Coven event of great importance to attend the anti-Coven rally with his girlfriend.

I am trembling by the time I finish. "This is such a lie!" I yell, momentarily forgetting about the catastrophe that's about to pop off with my parents. "Literally, there's only like two pieces of truth in here. The rest is gossip-site trash!" I ball my hands into fists, barely able to breathe around how furious I am. Are they seriously dragging me like this? And with a totally bogus-ass story!

I catch the first couple of comments visible beneath the last line of the article. I flinch at the vicious things strangers are saying about me.

I bite my bottom lip, feel the tears sting my eyes, warn myself that I better not cry. *I will not cry over this dumb mess.* I wipe roughly at my eyes. Finally, I gaze up at my parents. Angry ain't even the word to describe their energy. They're clearly confused and upset and there's a hundred questions swirling in their hardened gazes that they're demanding answers to.

I swallow, a bitter taste souring my mouth. I inhale a deep breath, and it *hurts*. Yes, I'm pissed as hell that my name is being dragged through the mud. Most of all, I am furious and disappointed with myself—because out of all the ways I feared dating Khy for real could end in a hot flaming disaster of a train wreck, I did not anticipate this. And I should have. He is a famous, beloved witch prince, after all. I am nothing compared to him, right? At least in the public's eyes.

My stomach plummets.

Last night, I came to grips with the risk of getting my heart broken if I dated Khy for real and decided we meant enough to take that chance. But I never considered the crap I'd get from the rest of the world, from media outlets like THE SCOOP if they decided some random, basic, non-Coven girl wasn't good enough for their golden witch prince.

"I—please, just take this away." I wave a wild hand at the phone Mercedes holds. Nausea roils through me from merely glancing back down at it.

"This is awful. Cayden, I'm so sorry," Mercedes says softly as she locks her phone screen. "Do you want me to cuss everybody out in the comments? I'll go *in* on all of them."

"No," I mumble. It's not as if it would do any good and make folks stop talking trash about me.

"I hate that I must add to this unsavory business," Robert says gently, "but this is more than some errant article on a superficial gossip site."

"What do you mean, Robert?" Dad says tersely.

Robert offers me a pitying, if supportive, smile that lets me know stuff is about to go from catastrophic to nuclear.

"THE SCOOP," Carolyn says the name like she's just taken a big foul-tasting bite out of something disgusting, "isn't the only outlet running the story." She tells Mom, "Major news sites, including CNN, the *New York Times*, the *Washington Post*, and the Associated Press, have picked it up since that article was posted this morning. Our family lawyers have already sent everyone running this slander a cease-and-desist letter that threatens a lawsuit if they fail to retract the story."

"Let me make sure I have everything right," Mom says to me instead of responding to Carolyn. "That boy, from the cookout, he's a Regent's son? And you've been dating him, a Coven boy, behind our backs?"

"And not only have you kept that from us," Dad says, "but you outright lied to us, too. You should've told us who he was when we met him yesterday. There is no excuse for not doing so. Lying is inexcusable and unacceptable in this family. Did you forget that, Cayden?"

"No," I mumble. I can't stand how they're looking at me. If they were standing there about to lose their shit and ground me until I graduate, that I could deal with. But it's the betrayal and disappointment and clear grief over me breaking their trust that is hard for me to take.

Tears surge forward again. I bite my cheek. "I know I messed up," I say quietly. "I was wrong. I'm sorry for what I did. I'll never do something like it again."

I can't not cry any longer. I let it out. Mom and Dad immediately swallow me up in a hug. Dad locks his arms around me from the left and Mom does it from the right.

"I'll close up early," Dad tells Mom. "Let's get you home, baby, and sort this out," he tells me.

Chapter Twenty

I slump against my headboard, miserably watching Tik-Toks. I'm not foolish enough to go on any other social media; I know #Mekayden (the terrible couple name for me and Khy the internet came up with) will likely slap me in the face and then bury me under vitriol on any other site. But my TikTok's For You page is well curated, and I can find a safe haven among the Greek strolls, Coming OWT shows, and Battle of the Bands matchups while I wait for Mom and Dad to have a talk downstairs before a family talk I am dreading.

At least I try to find some warped version of sanctuary, a sliver of comfort. But my usual method of numbing my bad mood by falling down a TikTok rabbit hole doesn't work this time. I can't stop thinking about that unfair and completely bogus news article. And all the hate getting thrown my way.

And my grandparents showing their faces after twenty years because of it. And how upset Mom and Dad were when they saw them and found out the truth about Khy.

Tears spring to my eyes, because I messed up. Badly. On so many different levels.

My phone buzzes and Khy's face appears. Seeing his pic is a fresh dropkick. I ignore the call. I'm sure he's seen the article, and I am not in the headspace to go there with him.

Khy calls again. By the third time, guilt eats away at me. I blow out a breath and answer.

"Cayden, I'm sorry!" he cries as soon as the FaceTime call connects. "I'm working on fixing it; don't let it upset you."

"Too late for that," I mutter.

He curses. "I'm so sorry," he says again. "I swear all those stories will go away soon. My mom has her entire PR team and lawyers making sure it happens."

I laugh wryly. At Khy's confused look, I say, "That's near the same thing my mom's parents promised." And it's never been clearer how much they and Khy belong to a wildly different world. Khy being so unbelievably wonderful made me foolishly forget—or ignore, more like it—that dipping even a toe into the world, even surface level, can eviscerate you if you aren't one of its darlings that match up exactly with what's considered the "perfect" Coven witch.

"Wait, what?" Khy scrunches his face up. "You talked to them? When did that happen?"

My smile is drier than a desert. "Literally about an hour ago. They popped into the bakery because they saw me on the news and took it as a sign from the Ancestors, according to them, that they were supposed to finally stop being assholes. They said they had their own fancy lawyers working to squash the news stories because *'family comes together in times of crises.'*" I laugh again. How the hell did things journey into this bizarre of a place? I swear I feel like I'm living out an episode of *Black Mirror*, trapped in my own twisted version of a hellish alternate timeline.

Khy's gaze grows wide. "That's—"

"Beyond insane," I finish for him. I fight against laying my head against my knees, which I've curled up to my chest. I'm tired. *Exhausted* from everything. "My parents, obviously, know about us dating, or whatever we were doing, now," I say. "I'm not sure which they took worst—my grandparents' unannounced visit or finding out I've been chillin' with the enemy behind their backs."

Khy winces, visibly hurt.

"I'm not the enemy," Khy mutters. "I'm not like that."

Aren't you, though? I bite the inside of my cheek hard. He's a Coven witch, and the Coven system and its bullshit hurt my parents. Which means Khy *is* the enemy since he's proudly a part of that system. I barely curb myself from saying it; a part of me puts the brakes on and realizes how unfair and cruel it'll be. But that part of me isn't big enough to stop what I say next. "All this is way too big for you, or your mom's team, to fix," I tell Khy. I cut off whatever he's gonna say to that. "It's not just the ugly media story—it's the whole system. You know my parents are downstairs right now because they can't even talk to me right now? The way they reacted to my grandparents turning up and then finding out about you was brutal. *I* hurt them. And I can't do that again. I won't do that again."

"Hold up. What are you saying?" Khy grits out.

He knows what I'm saying. Otherwise, he wouldn't look so gutted. But I ignore it and my own heart feeling like it's cracking in two. I blink away tears—and damn, I am seriously over crying today. "We're done," I tell Khy. It comes out final, but in a hoarse way I don't mean.

"Cayden, please," Khy begs. "Can we talk about this? Or give it a minute and wait until the media junk is quashed? I'll even come talk to your parents, if you think that'd help. I don't want to lose you, Cayden. I—I love you."

My heart splits down the center. Those three words grind it to dust, and I feel a very real and very savage ache, inside my chest. *I love you, too.* I figured it out last night, and today it's no less true. I bite my lip; I use the sting to hold tears back. Crying will only make this more of a flaming wreck. I wish to the Ancestors that alternate timelines really were a thing. Because in another world, under different circumstances, if my family didn't have so much awful history with Coven witches and Khy wasn't who he was, or I wasn't who I am, then I might reconsider. I might let my heart make this decision for me.

But I can't. Risking my family and ripping open old

wounds for Mom and Dad, or even more scarily, possibly creating a rift between them and me, isn't one thing I'm willing to risk.

Which is why, as heart crushing as it is, I make myself stick to what I told Khy. "I'm sorry," I say. "But this is how it needs to be."

"Hold on a sec," he hisses. "Just...don't do what you always do!"

"And what do I *always* do?" I snap.

Khy scrubs a hand down his face, as if fighting for calm. But I guess it doesn't work, because he waves at me wildly and yells, "You always go from zero to one hundred over every damn little thing! You never give us a chance to have a real convo and figure things out *together*. You just make your assumptions, deliver judgment, and that's it. Done. But it's not fair!"

I narrow my eyes. "Oh, we do not want to talk about what's fair here. And just so we're clear, nothing about my rep being trashed is *little*. It may not be a huge deal for you because you're rich and privileged and famous, and you've got *a team* that you can snap your fingers at and summon to take care of whatever. It isn't *you* who a gang of strangers are talking trash about! This is devastating for me. And the fact that you don't get that, that you're sitting here giving me shit over being rightfully upset, tells me I am making precisely the right choice to end us before things go any further, *Mekhi*."

He flinches. Good. He should. As silence stretches between us, I'm so heated that I start trembling.

"Is that it? Are we done talking?" I ask.

He shakes his head, opens his mouth, and then closes it. "I—we—I really am sorry for everything," he finally says.

"I wish that was enough to change what's happening, the way it's wrecking my life, or the way it could ruin things between me and my parents," I state. Then, I sever ties between me and Khy so that last thing positively won't happen. *It can't happen.* "Have a good life," I tell him. "Bye."

Hanging up should feel good, like a step in the right direction. But instead, it feels like slamming a rolling pin on my own heart.

Chapter Twenty-One

My phone rings again—a normal call. It's Dad. "Cayden, downstairs please," he says when I answer.

"Coming," I respond miserably. After I end the call, I blink at my closed bedroom door. If only it was soundproof; then I could let out the frustrated scream that's dicing my insides apart. I scream in my head to alleviate some of the pressure inside my chest. It doesn't work.

With my teeth clenched so tight my jaw throbs, I throw my phone on the desk, stand, and trudge downstairs to face how majorly I've screwed up.

"Hi, baby." Mom greets me when I enter the living room. She and Dad sit on the sofa. Her voice is all wrong—it's stiff and reedy.

My insides knot.

A round of tears start up as I gaze at my parents and

their stoic faces. "I know how bad I messed up," I sputter. "I'm so sorry. And I told Khy we can't talk anymore right before I came down. We're not friends, or dating, or anything else to each other anymore!"

Dad curses. Mom sniffles. They both rush to me. Dad hugs me tight from one side and Mom from the other. Mom smooths her hand along the top of my hair. "Oh, baby. Regardless of what's going on, please don't cry. I hate seeing you cry; we're going to sort it out. Right now."

Mom kisses my forehead. Hugs me tighter. Dad does, too. "Let's sit down and talk it through," she says gently.

"Maybe we should give her some more time," suggests Dad.

I smile weakly. I appreciate both of them so much, and nothing I've done in the last few weeks shows that. If anything, it shows the opposite. I suck as a daughter.

"I'm fine," I tell Dad. I know they have questions, probably a ton, and they don't deserve to be left in limbo. "I would like to sit, though," I say.

Once we're seated on the sofa, with me protectively wedged in the middle of Mom and Dad, I lean against Dad's broad shoulder, take a breath, and tell them everything. *It's the least I should do.*

I relay the full truth about why Khy and I started hanging out, and how much I've been enjoying spending time with him. I leave nothing out—I even cop to last night. Not our super extended make out session (because that is nothing I ever need to share with my parents), but I tell them about us deciding to try dating for real. That I ended things between us because it wasn't worth all the hurt I caused. I know they *see* how devastated I am, but I express it, too. I admit feeling supremely dumb and naive about ever catching feelings for Khy and finally acting on them.

"Okay. The first thing," Mom says with a fierce rage threaded into her voice, "is I am so sorry you're dealing with all of this, baby."

"That family shouldn't be *working* on fixing things. This mess should already be resolved!" Dad's voice is as angry. But he shakes his head and visibly pulls on a calmer attitude. "None of that matters right now, though. What can we do to make it better for you?" he asks me.

I stare at them both, the astonishment momentarily cutting through the thickest part of my misery. This isn't what I thought the conversation would be after how upset they were at the bakery. And for some reason that makes me feel even worse. That after everything, they're still here for me. "I'm sorry you two have to deal with all this. You guys don't deserve any of it. I was gonna come clean about Khy, I swear. I was just so scared of hurting you both. Part of the reason why I did lie about him is because I was sick thinking it would. I don't, and never did, think Khy was good for me, or the best boyfriend option for me, just because we're both witches. I don't think like that. I wouldn't ever think like that. Dad, you're amazing, and I love you exactly how you are. I don't think there's a better human being on the planet than—"

"Cayden, baby, you don't have to say any of that," Dad

says. "I know my daughter, and I know you'd never think that way. Does it open old wounds for me and your mom? Sure. It would with most folks. But not in the way you're afraid of. Any hurt on our part is because we are crushed *for* you, not because of something *you* did. We remember how rough it was when your mom and I first started dating. The heavy judgments were something serious. The only thing that hurts *us* is to see you going through any of that, too. As for any other choices you make pertaining to who are your friends or who you date, we love you and only want you to be happy."

Dad's words immediately lift a mountainous weight from my chest. "That makes me feel a whole lot better," I say, and I squeeze him around the waist. I squeeze Mom next. "I love you both. So much. Y'all really are amazing; thank you for everything." A peace I didn't think I'd achieve today—or anytime soon—steals over me as I settle back against the couch, the two best people in the world perched protectively at my side.

"Always," Mom says and kisses the side of my forehead. "And I know you didn't say this, but if you were going out with this Coven boy, at least partly, because you've become curious about that side of yourself, then there is *nothing* you need to apologize for, or feel bad about. It wouldn't make us upset. It's not a bad thing if you're interested in what ordinary, everyday life looks like for most other witches. I know we've kept that from you, and we've made you miss out on an entire facet of who you are."

"We're sorry about that," she and Dad both say at nearly the same time.

"Hold on—" I actually have no clue how to respond. *They're what?!* "Everything about this family talk is throwing me for a loop," I finally say. I look between Dad and Mom. "How can y'all be this level of calm and understanding?"

Mom passes me a tiny smile. "The truth? I've looked into Houston's Coven more times than I can count over the years. I don't regret my past decisions; I broke away from my old Coven for my own peace and mental health, but I do miss that part of myself. Sometimes, I miss it a lot."

The surprises really just keep coming. A wistfulness stole over Mom as she confessed to missing being a part of a Coven. It's still there, and right now she looks like she's lost in some of the happy memories from that time.

"Khy says Houston's Coven isn't like some of the other foul ones," I find myself saying because I really want the joyful way she looks to stay. I want Mom to have whatever will make her happy. "I went to a couple of their events, and the people I met seemed cool." The jury is still out on Khy's parents, but his friends were dope. So were the adults I convinced to bid on stuff for the silent auction.

Dad nods and peers at me intently. "It sounds like you had a good time."

"I did," I say honestly. Our talk has made admitting that to them and myself a bazillion times easier.

"That's one of the main things your mother and I talked about while you were upstairs," Dad says next. "She and I made decisions that were best for us, and we should have reevaluated them and considered what was best for you once you were in the picture."

"If you're currently thinking, or if you think it in the future, that you want to get to know your other set of grandparents, or the rest of the witch side of your family, or Coven life, that's all right, too," adds Mom. She clears her throat then. "I actually had a call with my parents while you were in your room. They claim they mean what they said at the bakery about wanting to repair our relationship. And they want a relationship with you as well, Cayden. Your father and I will be having brunch with them tomorrow to discuss how we can move forward. The four of us have our own mess to figure out first before getting you involved, but the choice will ultimately be up to you. As for getting to experience Coven life a little more, maybe you and I can do it together, if you'd like that."

My chest tightens, but it's for none of the earlier reasons. *Do I want those things? Maybe?* I can't lie and say the picture Mom paints isn't nice.

"Can we just start with my grandparents?" I say to Mom. "I think I would like to build a relationship with them."

"Absolutely," Mom says.

Dad clears his throat. "Now back to this boy..." Dad gives me my first firm look since I've come downstairs. "I don't like this mess you mentioned about dating somebody for attention. It's not your job to worry about money and the business. Don't do something like that again. Ever."

"Yes, sir," I say. He's right, and yet I add, "I just wanted to help however I could. The bakery means a lot to you."

"*You* mean more to me," Dad says inflexibly. "And you've clearly had a rough go behind all this media stuff." He smooths my hair back. His tone is softer when he says, "I can see from how puffy your eyes are that you've been crying, baby girl."

I pick at the hem of my jean shorts. "It's been tough," I admit.

"Because of the news stories and the public comments or because you really like Khy?" Mom gently asks.

I hyperfocus on my shorts. The answer is both. I don't want to lie to them anymore, but I don't want to admit how intense my feelings got with Khy. "It doesn't matter," I mutter. I widen my eyes to make the tears threatening to spill dry up quickly.

"You didn't *have* to break up with him," Mom says. "And you don't need to stick to that choice if you're crushed by it. You can try calling him back and seeing if y'all can—"

"I'm fine with the decision," I stress. "All the way." The worlds Khy and I live in are just too different. *We're* too different. Even if my parents are good with me dating a Coven boy, the disaster with the news proves the potential for a greater, more devastating hurt is extremely high if I date Khy. Like astronomically high. Because of who he is, I'd always be judged and made to feel like I'm not good enough.

Mom hugs me tight. "It's all right if you're not okay. You know that, right?"

I swallow thickly. I respond when I get it together. "I'm *good*. Can we please drop the subject of Khy? I don't want to talk about him. And it doesn't matter anyway. Our relationship was fake most of the time. We only dated for real for less than a day; it's not that deep." Or, at least, it shouldn't be.

"Whatever you want," replies Mom. But she and Dad trade a look. I choose to pretend like I don't see it and ignore the fact that they clearly don't believe me.

It has to be over for the sake of never feeling this terrible again, I tell myself. *And that means I have to be all right, regardless. I can't stay a mess.*

Chapter Twenty-Two

I play myself. I, in fact, do stay a mess. A colossal heap of one. It drags on over the next four days. I'm made worse every time Khy calls, or texts, or DMs me to say sorry again, give me an update on stuff getting fixed, or ask how I'm doing. I ignore his attempts to reach out, though, because what's the point? We're over; it's best we stay that way; and us talking will just make everything harder. I've already slammed the door shut on us. For my own good, it needs to stay permanently locked and deadbolted.

I remind myself of that as I lean against the bakery's counter, wishing for a morning rush to keep my mind busy. But ever since the news story broke, business has slowed to a crawl. I try not to blame myself for that, too.

I intently scroll through my feed trying to find something else besides Khy to consume my thoughts. Despite seeing zero content about a certain royal Coven boy, I still can't stop obsessing—wallowing, really. I clench my jaw, irritated with the Ancestors for letting my path ever collide with Khy's in the first place. *Next time I ask for a hot summer fling, please send me an uncomplicated one that there's no way possible I'll fall for,* I silently grumble at them.

I give up trying and shove my phone in the pocket of my shorts. "Nothing is gonna take my mind off Khy and the breakup," I tell Mercedes, voice sounding as raw as I feel. She's standing behind the register beside me. She wraps her arms around me as I lean my head on her shoulders. "If I cry again, will you judge me for being *that person* over a guy?" I ask it as joke. At least I attempt to. But I can't quite achieve the levity I was going for.

Mercedes hugs me tight. "Not at all. In fact, if you cry right now, I'll deny I ever saw it, just like the previous times. Tears? From who? And where? Certainly not my cousin."

"Period," I say, blinking to ease the sting in my eyes. I roughly wipe them at first. Try to hold everything that's too fresh and too enormous—and nothing like anything I've felt before—inside. God, if I wasn't in the bakery I might just finally give up. I am so tired from the effort I've been making this morning. Last night, too. And all of yesterday. Also, the day before.

When the door chimes, I dig deep and pull it together. I cannot be almost crying in front of customers.

When I see who enters the bakery, I swear the Ancestors are getting a perverse kick out of tormenting me. The two people who wave as they walk up to the counter are almost as bad as if Khy had come himself.

"Hey, what are you doing here?" I ask Naomi and Becca, trying my best not to sound too rude. They haven't technically done anything wrong, but if I'm severing ties with Khy, then I should apply the same logic to Naomi and Becca for the same reasons.

"For you and Khy," Becca says, as if it's the most obvious thing in the world.

"Obviously, we read the news stories," Naomi says. "And Khy told us about the breakup. He asked us not to meddle, and we tried to respect it. But he's crushed." Naomi frowns, peering at me intently. "You don't look great either, Sis. So help me understand it: Why are y'all broken up if you're both miserable?"

I wince. "I just can't do the boyfriend-girlfriend thing with him," I answer.

"That's not an actual explanation." Naomi calls me out.

"I don't feel like getting into it, okay?" I say exasperatedly. "Didn't Khy tell you what I told him?"

"Yeah, and I think you're full of it. I get it: your family has a history with Covens. Some old-school ideas are crap. But that has nothing to do with you or Khy. He isn't like that, and neither is our Coven. So does it really have to be that big of an issue?"

"It *is* that big of an issue," I say. "And like I told Khy, it's bigger than me and him."

"That's du—"

"Let it go, Nae." Becca cuts her off. "Cayden's feeling are valid."

Naomi lets out an annoyed huff but drops arguing.

Well, sort of.

"Becca and I are your friends, too," she tells me. "Which is why we came here to check on you. We've been calling and texting, and you haven't answered." Naomi doesn't bother to make it not sound like an accusation.

Oomph. She does not let up, does she?

"I thought it would be awkward to talk to y'all after I broke up with one of your best friends," I mutter. "Plus, I figured you were just calling to cuss me out, Naomi."

Naomi sucks her teeth.

Becca tries to hide her laugh before turning sincere again. "Me and Nae came here to let you know that you don't get to break up with us just because you broke up with Khy. We didn't do anything, and you're our girl now. So Nae and I are just gonna figure out how to be friends with the two of you separately. Okay?" Becca finishes definitively, and in a tone that leaves no room for argument.

I look between her and Naomi, too exhausted for this. "That sounds messy and like it's gonna put y'all in the middle of drama. Won't Khy feel betrayed?"

Naomi shrugs. "Nah. We mentioned it to him already, and he was happy about us staying friends with you. To your other point, I'm a queen at staying neutral and minimizing the messiness. My parents have been divorced for five years, refuse to be in the same room with each other, and I handle their drama like a pro. You and Khy are child's play in comparison. Plus, there isn't even any bad blood between y'all. Like you aren't mad at him, are you?"

"Umm . . . no," I admit. "Khy didn't do anything wrong." He needed to check his tone during our last conversation, but we were both upset.

Naomi smirks. "Then my point is made. So, are *we* good?"

"Please say yes?" Becca adds.

"Y'all don't think that is even a little weird," I counter.

"Nope," Becca shoots back. "And the quicker you say yes, the quicker we stop being pains in your butt about it. Otherwise, Nae and I are gonna keep pressing you." She grins fully unapologetically.

At first, my lips twitch. Then, I give up and all-out laugh. It's my first time in days; it feels good to do so.

"I like y'all's ride-or-die energy," Mercedes, who has been quiet while watching the exchange play out, finally inserts her two cents. "I'm Cayden's cousin Mercedes," she tells Naomi and Becca. "Nice to meet y'all."

Even though we didn't start off on the right foot, Naomi and Becca are pretty lit. And I don't have a gang of friends. I'm not built like that, nor do I have the time for the mess that comes with having a million besties. I have folks I go to school and associate with, but outside of that I only have Mercedes—my single ride or die that I can trust wholeheartedly. But Naomi and Becca seem different. The very fact that they've gone out of their way to corner me at the bakery like this shows it. And if Mercedes is already vibing with their energy, too, then that means it's 99 percent likely that they're *legit* legit.

"You didn't answer our question, Cayden." Becca's assertion cuts into my thoughts.

She, Naomi, and Mercedes all stare at me.

Grinning, Mercedes exclaims, "They've got my approval. Say yes! I like them a lot! We can all hang!"

I roll my eyes, but the "yes, we're cool" comes surprisingly easy. And I realize I mean it. I guess maybe it's because, my dislike of Coven politics aside, I was really excited to hang out more with Naomi and Becca—teen witches like me—after Becca suggested it at the golf tournament. I've never thought I wanted, or needed, that connection to my witch side before. But it felt nice to have a couple of friends that I had it in common with.

The bell chimes and a good number of customers stream in. Mercedes and I both gaze at them, surprised.

"This hasn't happened since that stupid story," Mercedes sputters.

Naomi beams at the customers and then back at me. "You should check THE SCOOP." She winks, then spins around and holds up her phone. "Smile," she orders over her shoulder right before snapping several selfies with herself, Becca, Mercedes, and me in the shot. "Khy isn't the only person that's got social media clout," she says, fingers flying over her screen. "I'm posting this to my Insta story. That way everyone will believe the exclusive interview Khy gave THE SCOOP is all facts and not damage control. If we're seen chilling together, they'll know it's all good."

"Khy gave an interview?" I ask casually. It's normal to be curious if it pertains to me—doesn't mean I am eager to read about what he said or anything.

Naomi and Becca move aside to allow the first customer in the line behind them to step up to the register. "Read the article," Naomi answers with a smirk. "We'll let y'all get to work. Bye!"

She and Becca head for the door, and for the rest of the busy day, the interview Khy gave is all I can think about.

But after we close up at the end of the day, I can't bring myself to go searching for Khy's interview. Naomi said it was a positive one, and I leave it at that. If I actually read it, and he's amazing—per usual—then I might be tempted to rethink our breakup. And I can't afford to do that when this is what's best for my own long-term sake, my parents', and Khy's.

✦

A day later, I'm still itching to read the interview, but I stay strong. Luckily, we have a family BBQ and all the extra help I offer Mom and Dad with grilling and setting the table keeps me busy. The fact that Mom's parents are guests also claims the bulk of my focus. My grandparents and parents had their brunch and the meetup apparently wasn't a dumpster fire. So, here we are.

I'm taking a pan of golden-brown tea cakes out the oven

for Dad when the doorbell rings. I glance at the smart hub on the kitchen counter, and it shows Carolyn and Robert standing on the porch. My stomach twists with jitters. I'm not sure if the reason is excitement, apprehension, or some combo of both. Mom and Dad step inside from the back patio as I turn for the door.

"It's your parents," I tell Mom.

She waves her phone. "I saw." Despite their brunch going all right, I'm still surprised that her voice is clear of any tension. Dad looks relaxed, too.

"Do you want to grab the door?" Mom asks me.

My first reaction is to decline. But something—maybe simple curiosity or possibly a deeper urge—makes me curb it. "Sure," I say, the jitters doubling. I walk to the door and open it.

"Hello again, dear," Carolyn greets me with warmness.

"Hello, Cayden," Robert says, grinning. He reaches across the threshold and squeezes my hand.

My head swims as he lets me go. It's so surreal seeing them at my front door wearing smiles. I glance over my shoulder to my parents in the kitchen. They watch the exchange without looking nervous or upset or even stoic. They look peaceful, completely at ease. The brunch must have gone better than *okay*. Mom did say it was very "healing." I guess she wasn't putting extra sauce on it solely for my benefit. *Alrighty then. So we're really doing this.*

"Hi," I tell Carolyn and Robert. "And ... it's nice to see you again," I say awkwardly. As they're coming inside, two other cars pull into the driveway. Grams and Grandpop get out of the black pickup truck as my aunties and Mercedes emerge from the SUV. I wait for them all at the door, hearing Mom tell her parents everything is set up on the patio. Each of Dad's folks would just walk right in if I went ahead and joined the others in the backyard, but I steal the few moments to fully wrap my head around the sensation that my whole life is shifting on its axis. My maternal grandparents, whom I've only met a few days ago, are sitting down in my backyard for a family dinner! It shouldn't be so rattling since I knew what the day would bring, but being amid everything as it happens is a whole other level of wild.

Grams and Grandpop reach the porch at the same time my aunties and cousin do. Each takes a turn hugging me, then Auntie Nikki asks how I feel about my extra guests. Grandpop grunts when she does, and Auntie Vesha pokes him in the side. She tells him and Auntie Nikki to behave today. He scowls but falls quiet. It doesn't change the way my family gazes at me, all waiting for my answer, though. I know, without a doubt, how I respond will set the tone for their attitudes. "I'm good," I tell them. "Mom and Dad seem cool with it, so I am, too."

"That's all I need to hear not to set it off," Auntie Nikki says. "But I'm still about to stay ready to keep from getting ready." She kisses my forehead and strides inside. The rest of us follow her out to the backyard, with Grams mumbling that if our visitors know what's good, they better not piss off her husband and daughter. I grimace; this can either keep going relatively well or get really bad, really fast.

Once outside, we all gather around the patio dining table, the smell of Dad's delicious BBQ ribs, grilled salmon burgers, potato salad, and baked beans pleasantly filling the backyard. The spread is laid out on the table atop platters, and I've used my magic to keep everything sizzling as if it's fresh off the grill (Grandpop vows it's the only way to eat BBQ, and I agree). Dad's parents and my aunties are seated at one end of the glass rectangular table. Mom, Dad, and Mom's parents are seated at the other end. Me and Mercedes are in the middle. The table is freakishly quiet at first. Clearly everyone is thinking some manner of the same thing: sharing a meal together—at our house, no less—is a big freaking step. It's a huge deal. A grand gesture—on multiple people's parts.

Grams and Grandpop have disliked Carolyn and Robert and talked junk about them my whole life. My aunties, super protective of Dad, have, too. Then there's Mom, who vowed never to speak to her parents again and let them back into her and Dad's life, yet she has. As for Carolyn and Robert ... well, the snobbish Coven witches who told Mom that Dad wasn't good enough to marry are over to their son-in-law's for a very nonbougie BBQ lunch and breaking bread with that nonwitch son-in-law *and* his ordinary family. I look down the length of the glass table, remaining stunned as hell this is happening.

No sooner than I think it, Dad clears his throat. He pushes his chair back from the table and stands. He turns to Robert and Carolyn. "Before we eat, there is something I'd like to say with us all gathered together," he says.

Grandpop emits one of his grunts. Auntie Nikki coughs. Grams stares at Dad with a pinched expression that's fiercely protective.

We all then give Dad our attention, who is holding Mom's hand tightly. He brings it to his lips and lays a kiss to their clasped fingers. Their hands stay laced together as Dad tells Mom's parents, "It means a lot to my wife to have you back in her life. And I think it'll mean as much to my daughter to get to know you. So, I want you both to know, truly, that there are no hard feelings where we stand." He sweeps a hand around the table. "We invited my family here today, too, because strong family bonds are important to Eva and me. And that's because my parents made it so that's how our family always did things. Eva and I want, very much, that sentiment to extend to her parents. You say the Ancestors nudged you toward seeking to mend things with Eva. Please tell them thank you from me because I see the happiness it brings my wife, and that is all I care about."

As soon as Dad finishes his speech, Robert stands. He reaches across Mom and holds his hand out. "You are a bigger man, Jason, and better person than I've been in the past. *Thank you* for being a terrific partner to my daughter."

Dad nods and clasps Robert's hand. Carolyn, who has stood, pulls Dad into a hug. She hugs Mom next.

I smile wide, my heart squeezing as I watch them, a happy thrill buzzing through me. I never imagined this day ever occurring, never even thought about wanting something like this to happen before. But now that it *is* happening, it feels really good. *It feels right.* It might sound corny, but it seems like the Ancestors really have put in some strong work to get everyone to this point, to give my family a little push toward finally healing.

"I'm not sure who's cheesing harder," Mercedes leans into my side and says for only me to hear. "You or Auntie Eva. I'm happy for y'all."

"I am, too," I say. As Grams stands and volunteers to pray over the food, I realize how much I mean it.

"I hear you're a big theater lover and young thespian," Robert says jovially to Mercedes as everyone is loading down their plates.

"I am," Mercedes answers politely.

"Have you caught any of the Broadway shows at the Hobby Center?" He asks.

"I haven't yet. But my moms took me to see *Hamilton* last year in New York. That was my first in-person one. It was spectacular! I want to catch *Les Mis* when it comes to Houston in February. And I've seen just about every Broadway show that can be streamed." As Mercedes starts with the lengthy gush session, I settle in for her to tell us all about her favorite and most disliked shows, her analysis of the overall acting in each one, the directors' creative choices, the impact of the chosen musical scores. I appreciate the effort Robert is making, but this man has no idea what he's detonated.

However, he listens to Mercedes intently, doing more than giving her his courteous undivided attention. His face is as lit up with enthusiasm as hers, and he actually contributes his own opinions about several musicals. I mostly manage not to gawk. Who would've known Mom's dad is a theater geek?

His wife laughs beside him, patting his hand that rests on the table. "Don't monopolize the conversation, dear," she chides lightly.

Robert's cheeks darken a tiny bit. "Oh. I apologize," he says to the table.

Grams has this moment where she eyes Robert, as if sizing him up. "No need to be sorry. This is lovely to listen in on," she finally says with surprising levity. When Robert asks Grams if she's into the theater, she groans and emphatically responds no. "I don't do much besides church that has me sitting for hours at a time," Grams tells Robert.

"My wife lives in the roller derby rink," Grandpop, who is seated beside Grams, says chuckling.

"Really, Yasmine?" Carolyn exclaims, leaning toward Grams with interest. "That seems intense."

Grams cackles. "Only for the other teams. Me and my girls bring it!"

"Perhaps I'll have to catch a match sometime," Carolyn returns. "Roller derby is one of those sports you always hear about, but I don't believe I've ever met someone who plays."

Carolyn's interest seems genuine versus simply making friendly conversation. Grams must pick up on it, too, because she immediately rattles off her next match date and gives Carolyn a few good teams in the Dallas area in a recruitment attempt.

From his end of the table, Robert lifts an eyebrow at Grandpop down at the other end. "Should I be concerned?"

Grandpop chortles. "My man, you've got no idea."

I swivel between my two sets of grandparents who have slipped into a conversation that gives the vibes of the start of a possible legit friendship. If I wasn't already 100 percent sure I was awake, I'd pinch myself to see if I'm dreaming.

Mom, who sits beside her dad, casually asks him how the ranch is doing. He gives her an update that consists of a bunch of numbers and words like gross profit and net annual revenue. He next gives her an update on the welfare of the farm animals themselves. During it, the stuffiness with which he spoke about numbers bleeds from his voice. The way he talks about the animals is full of passion and excitement. It reminds me so much of the way Mom is when she talks about her work at the clinic.

"As much as I love my practice, I do miss farm life sometimes, I have to admit," Mom tells her dad. She turns to me and says, "Hilliard Ranch was such a fun place to grow up." She goes on to talk about how the ranch has been in her family for four generations. It's info I read in the screenshot of Robert's member page, but it is so much cooler hearing Mom relay it. Her whole face lights up as she tells me about

Robert's Connection to magical husbandry and how she used to watch her dad help with the births of calves, foals, and lambs. Mom has clearly always adored animals. And it's clear she was a girl who adored—*hero-worshipped*—her dad, too.

Thank you, I send up to the Ancestors for helping Mom get back what she lost.

"How long you two been in town? Are you planning on staying long?" Auntie Nikki asks Moms' parents.

"Oh, we've only been here a few days," Carolyn answers. "We came down because I'm on the chairing committee for this year's witch Cotillion. We originally only planned to stay in town through the end of next week after the Cotillion ball takes place on Saturday. But Robert and I have discussed extending our stay for a few more weeks." She turns to Mom and Dad when she mentions the last part. "I mean, if that is all right with you and Jason, Evie."

Evie. I've never heard that nickname for Mom before; I didn't even know she had a nickname. Carolyn gazes at Mom and Dad hopefully. Robert looks much the same beside his wife.

Mom exchanges a look with Dad. He covers Mom's hand resting on the table with his own and squeezes it. Mom leans over and kisses his cheek, whispers something in his ear. "That would be really nice," Mom tells Carolyn.

"We'd like to spend some quality time with you, too, Cayden, if you're not too busy," Robert says to me.

"Um. Yeah, sure," I respond. "That'll be cool." It *will*, and

I am excited, but my voice comes out quiet and wobbly. Not because of my grandparents, though. The mention of Cotillion brings my thoughts right back to Khy.

"Oh, Cayden, I'd love for you to come to the ball with us," Carolyn says, not noticing my change in attitude. "We can add you and your parents as our guests. It really is a stunning event and a lot of fun, if I do say so myself." I hear her words, but they reach me as if steeped in static. Or maybe the extra background noise from the flurry of gutted thoughts about Khy. I suck in a breath that does nothing to lessen the ache in my chest.

"I'm sorry. Excuse me." I push away from the table and rush to the kitchen before I do something embarrassing like revealing how much of a wreck I am.

"Baby, are you all right?" I hear Mom's voice behind me as I am leaning over the kitchen sink and splashing water on my face.

"Perfect." I pat my face dry with a paper towel.

I hear footsteps. Then she's hugging me from behind. I twist around in her arms and bury my face in her shoulder. There's no point in trying to pretend like I'm fine when obviously I'm not.

"Sweetie, what's wrong?" Mom asks, stricken. "Is it my parents? Is this lunch with them too much, too fast?"

I shake my head. "No. It's not them. It's ... the Cotillion. Khy ... Khy is participating." By the time I confess what's wrong, I'm crying. *Ugh! Why am I crying?*

Mom kisses my forehead. "Baby girl..." Her voice trails

off like she isn't sure what to say next. Neither am I. So we both just stand there in the kitchen for a little bit, Mom never easing the pressure of her hug.

After a while I admit something to Mom and, finally, myself that the BBQ has made super clear. "I think I messed up," I say hoarsely. I thought Coven witches and regular folks couldn't truly exist together harmoniously. But my family is outside doing exactly that, and it's drama free. "I broke up with Khy even though I loved him because I thought it was the best thing," I sputter to Mom. "I didn't want to hurt you and Dad more. But now your parents are in the backyard and stuff really is good and—I don't know how to fix it. I don't know if I can fix it. Khy's friends told me I crushed him. I made a terrible choice."

Mom smooths my hair back, although it's already in a sleek high bun. "Telling him what you've told me might be a good place to start if you do want to fix things."

I smile bleakly. "But I was horrible to him. *I* wouldn't forgive me. I'd hold a grudge and be bitter as heck."

"That might all be true, but you never know what could happen if you don't at least try," returns Mom.

I internally wince. I admit another thing. "That sounds scary."

"Because love *is* scary, and so is a potential broken heart," says Mom. "But if you're already sad, what do you have to lose?"

My pride, I think. But that's silly, and this isn't about that. This is about me feeling the weight of something too big and too intense to name. It's the same wrecked emotions I've been feeling since I told Khy we were done.

"Just try to talk to him, sweetie, for real," Mom advises again. "I hear you: you're scared it's beyond fixing. Try anyway. I thought the same thing about my rift with my parents, and look at us now. What's meant to be will happen. The universe has a way of setting everything right that should be right."

Mom's conviction settles around me, and it's strong enough to boost my mood. It makes me think about how right she is regarding her parents. Maybe broken relationships don't have to always *stay* broken.

As I stand beside the sink with Mom, a tiny hope ignites that it's true.

Chapter Twenty-Three

I don't call Khy that same night. Or the next day. Or several more days after that. To keep it one hundred, I can't find the nerve. Despite the hope Mom inspired, I can't shake the jitters over possible rejection. I know it's my ego talking, but I've never experienced that in my life, and *jeesh* would it sting. But also, the more time I let pass, the more awkward an attempt to repair stuff will be.

On Saturday afternoon, I sulk on the sofa in my living room, wallowing in torment. I mindlessly watch TikToks. Repeatedly, I click off the app, type in most of THE SCOOP's web address, then close out my browser and go back to TikTok, my safe space.

Mercedes: Have you called your witch boo yet? CALL HIM, CAYDEN!!!!

The text notification from Mercedes pops up on my phone, infiltrating my safety bubble.

Naomi: No she hasn't. Khy hasn't mentioned it. Naomi responds in the group chat that Becca created for the four of us.

Becca chimes in less than a minute later. **Becca:** Girl, just call him. He wants you to call him. Trust me. Have you read his interview in the scoop????

Naomi: You NEED to read it. You need to read today's story about Khy too. And do something about it ASAP. My boy can't go out like this! I need you to make it better, Cayden.

I frown, having no idea what their rapid messages are talking about.

The next messages are THE SCOOP links from Naomi. Two pictures of Khy pop up on my phone. The first is of him in a sky blue polo shirt, fresh fade, and blinding dimples. He's casually leaning against his orange-and-black Porsche. He's looking directly into the camera; it's clearly a shot that was taken specifically to be paired with a feature press article. My stomach aches. Seriously, though, how is looking at a photo this painful? But I've plummeted into misery, so I might as well finally read the interview. It's not like I can feel any worse. At least that's what I think before I click on the link. As I read it, I can barely breathe around the massive pressure in my chest. During the interview,

Khy hella puts himself out there. He answers a bunch of questions about his breakup with Gigi, getting cheated on, and then dating me afterward. I know how badly he hates talking about his ex and how uncomfortable the media harping on his old relationship drama makes him. But he endured it to set the record straight about me. And he says all the right things, tells the truth about me, makes me sound really freaking amazing. My heart squeezes at how he calls me "beautiful inside and out," talks about how I've got "a huge heart" and spend a lot of time volunteering at my mom's rescue and helping Dad out at the bakery, and says I sounded like "a kickass community activist who should inspire everyone" during my speech at the cookout.

I try super hard not to cry for the millionth time in the past few days. I messed up. I really, *really* messed up with Khy. And since I apparently want to keep torturing myself, I go back to my messages to view the second article Naomi sent.

A pic of Khy and Gigi from the tournament is featured in this one. The article's title is a fresh dropkick to the chest: **Royal Teen Heartthrobs Mekhi Carter and Giselle Bernard Reportedly Attending Coven Debutante Ball Together Tonight**

My eyes go wide as if the action will make different words appear on my damn screen. *Ain't no way! Khy's ass better NOT!* And it isn't about my jealousy—well, not all the way. Khy deserves so much better than Gigi being his date. I stab a finger to my screen and open up the article. A quick read tells me Khy and Gigi are only going as "just friends to show the world there's no hard feelings between them." But that doesn't lessen my irritation. Gigi is trash, and Cotillion is something special for Khy. He should have a date that actually gives a crap about him! And who didn't cheat on him and then dump him. *Ugh!*

A date like you? A smug voice asks.

"Yes!" I cry. I've clearly lost my mind because why the hell am I asking my own self questions *and* answering them? Khy clearly has me twisted. Though, not in a bad sense, I guess. I love him. I'm in love with that boy. And I want him back. I want the girlfriend-boyfriend vibe we were gonna try out for real. *Gigi* cannot *be his date. No way in hell!*

First, I text the group chat back.

> **Cayden:** I read that shit and I'm calling him right now. She is so unserious!

Afterward, I do what I should have gotten over myself and done days ago. But Khy doesn't pick up. And I FaceTime him twice.

I frantically text Naomi and Becca that he isn't answering. Then I ask: **Cayden:** I thought y'all said he doesn't hate me?

> **Naomi:** He doesn't. He's been sick about the breakup the whole time. He was just still sick about it last night when we hung.
> **Becca:** Facts.
> **Cayden:** Why isn't he answering then?

It takes all my willpower not to be a stalker and call him a dozen times.

> **Becca:** He's the witch regent's son and cotillion is huge. He's likely got a ton of photo opps and interviews scheduled. And he's gotta get ready. I'm sure Mrs Carter has a big ass team in place making sure Khy is flyer than fly.

Becca's logic makes sense, but it doesn't lessen my panic.

> **Cayden:** What the hell do I do then?

Mercedes's reply pops up before anyone else's.

> **Mercedes:** Pull a move straight out of a movie and show your ass up at cotillion. DUHHHH. GO GET YOUR MAN.

I balk at my cousin's insanity. But then I think about it. What else can I really do? If Khy is swamped and won't answer his phone leading up to the ball, then if I don't lean fully into absurdity, Gigi will stay his date.

Just the idea of that is like a dropkick to the chest, so I swiftly make a decision.

> **Cayden:** Can all y'all come over and help me get dressed. I don't know what to wear. Or how to do my makeup or hair for this or anything.

Obviously, I've done Homecoming before and Junior Prom last year. But the Cotillion ball feels different. Huger. Infinitely fancier—it is put on by elite witches, after all.

Cayden: Naomi and Becca it's ok if you're busy getting ready yourself. I type it behind my plea after I think about it.

> **Naomi:** Be for real. Send me your address and I'll see you at 4. I'll bring you a dress and get ready there myself. We can ride to cotillion together.
> **Becca:** I'm not missing the fun. I'm coming too!
> **Mercedes:** I got you on hair and makeup cousin. I'm heading over right now so we have time to make you bad as hell, Sis.

I text everybody a nervous thank-you and make one more call to ask Carolyn if I can still take her up on her offer to be her guest for Cotillion.

Chapter Twenty-Four

I gape at myself in the full-length mirror on my closet door. The dress Becca and Naomi rolled through with is gorgeous. It's an aqua, strapless gown that's got a structured corset and tulle skirt that flares out at the waist. The frothy skirt has light blue roses (real ones!) stitched on it that cascade the entire way down to its hem. The flowers have been enchanted, and they rearrange themselves into a beautiful new pattern every so often. Mercedes did her thing on the hair and makeup front, too. My ride or die has swept my hair up into a high ponytail and worked her juju on my curls so they're glistening, bouncy, and well hydrated. She left one curly strand hanging down the right side of my face beside my temple. The makeup she applied consists of neutral tones—a shimmering copper eye shadow, golden-brown bronzer, and a mocha lip tint. I look like the same me, but not me. And I can't stop staring because the image is so damn stunning.

"You're a boss!" I tell Mercedes. "How are you this talented?!"

She kisses my cheek, grinning, not bothering to be humble. "It's a gift."

"And is!" Becca decrees. "Thanks for hooking all of us up, girl." Grinning ear to ear, she's looking at herself beside me in the mirror, admiring the glittering orange-and-magenta tones that Mercedes used to accentuate her pretty warm ivory complexion. Becca's gown is coral with sleeves that drape off her shoulders and dozens of glittering pink crystals that shift into a different zodiac constellation pattern every few minutes. Currently, Becca's gown is showing us Scorpius.

"For real, though. Thanks for looking out; I've never looked better!" Naomi gushes to Mercedes. She's sitting on my bed, studying her flawless face card in her phone's camera. Naomi's ballgown is the alluring black of a midnight sky. There are no magical enhancements to it. Made of only shiny satin that hugs her body, its neckline is a halter and it has a high split up the right side. Mercedes did her makeup using black and silver hues, creating a smoky eye effect that I swear could compete with professional makeup artists.

"Cayden, are you girls ready? It's about time to get going," Mom calls from downstairs.

"We're coming down now!" I yell back. I spin to Mercedes, who is standing to my left, and crush her in a hug.

"I'll call you afterward with updates," I promise Mercedes before she can remind me that I had better.

She pops her lips. "Sis, I'll be right here waiting for you to get home. Khy's ass better recognize or I'm coming for his head. I want the in-person recap of how much he loses his mind when he sees you, so I'm sleeping over tonight."

I laugh because of course she is.

"Baby! Look at you!" Mom gasps when I walk into the living room. She and Dad stand beside the front door.

Dad scrubs a hand down his face. "My kid is growing up," he says gazing at me in a weird way. He shakes his head, then smiles. "You look beautiful, sweetheart," he says. "But do me a favor and slow down on me just a little bit, all right?"

Mom chuckles. "You know there's no stopping time, Jason."

"You sure about that?' Dad asks. "It ain't some witch with a Connection out there who has that kind of juice?"

Mom pats his shoulder. "It's okay, honey," she says soothingly.

"Your dad is funny," Becca giggles.

"He's something," I say. I decide to put Dad out of his misery. I go to him and give him a big hug. "It doesn't matter how old I get," I tell him, "I'll always be your baby girl." I pull away from Dad and wink. "But just remember that, Father of Mine, when I go to college and then graduate and get a job and I still call home and ask my wonderful dad for money."

Dad holds up his hands. "Now, wait a minute—"

"Too late," I say and kiss his cheek.

"We'll see you at Cotillion later. I'm going to finish getting ready," Mom tells me. Her parents extended an invitation for her and Dad to come along as their guests, too, and Mom decided it'd be nice to spend more time with them and take the chance to feel out Houston's Coven. "You girls get going so Naomi and Becca don't miss the call time for debutantes," she says, waving us toward the door.

After an agonizingly long ride, Naomi, Becca, and I step out of the limo that they had pick us up. Wedged between them, I gaze up at the Houston Coven's official membership house, where the Cotillion ball is being held. The Coven house nearly resembles a freaking castle. The building's old-world architecture is leagues ritzier than Khy's lake house's aesthetic. The beauty of it all takes my breath away as I ascend the dozens of steps leading up to the entrance with Naomi and Becca beside me. Naomi gives the greeter at the door our names. The guy scans a list. "Debutantes are gathering in the Rose Ballroom on the first floor. There are ushers inside who can direct you if you need help with where to go," he says to Naomi. He tells me, "I'm sorry, miss. But you're about an hour and a half early from when guests are allowed inside. Is it possible to—"

"It's all right. She's a last-minute debutante, too," Naomi rushes out.

The greeter's eyebrows furrow. "I didn't see that information next to her name." My heart feels like it lurches into my throat. I swallow roughly. I need to catch Khy *before* Cotillion—the sooner, the better! The last shred of calm

I've got left reminds me that even if I have to wait a bit, normal guests will be allowed inside well before the ball is scheduled to start. But reason isn't a word in my vocab right now.

"Can you just let me inside, please?" I ask desperately. "My name isn't on the list because I only decided to participate like an hour ago," I say quickly, going with Naomi's lie. I add a bit of truth that will hopefully be convincing. "My grandmother is Carolyn Hilliard; she's on the planning committee. You can look up her name; she's the person who added me as their plus one. I'm sure you see that, right?"

The greeter glances back at his tablet and nods. "You can follow the others to where the debutantes are gathering," he says after a heart-pounding second.

Thank-the-freaking-Ancestors.

The ballroom that we were directed to is mighty (though not unexpectedly) sumptuous for a holding room. The tables and chairs are swathed in gold silk. There are two chocolate fountains and what I guess to be a pair of sparkling cider fountains, from the scent of crisp apples in the air. There's a charcuterie table, too, along the wall where the fountains are.

"I don't see Khy," I tell Naomi and Becca nervously as I scan the room. I do, however, spy Gigi. The Parisian "princess" stands a good distance away with a group of girls. She notices me near the entrance and if a look could impale, I'd be skewered to the wall. Her hands clench at her sides, and she marches my way.

"I've got this heifer," Naomi says, stepping in front of me.

I step from behind her and stand back beside Naomi. "I appreciate it, but I can handle Gigi on my own."

Naomi folds her arms over her chest as Gigi reaches us. "Okay. But I'm right here and will tell her about herself if you need me to." Naomi states it while smiling directly at Gigi.

Gigi rolls her eyes. "What are you doing here?" she sneers at me.

"Where is Khy?" I ask straight up. I'm not about to waste air or time dealing with her crap.

She clenches her jaw. "Why is he so hung up on you?" Gigi spits the question at me like the mere idea in intolerable.

"You mean as opposed to tripping over *you*, the girl who cheated on and dumped him?" I retort. *Okay, maybe I am about to take a second to get back with her; somebody needs to check her, for real.* "If that's what you're on, you're high," I say. "Who the hell with a shred of self-respect would still want anything to do with somebody that played them?"

Gigi stiffens. She flips her hair—styled in a bone-strait silk press—over her shoulder. "Girls like you *wish* you could be me. But you, especially, never will. Like I said, *you're* a nobody. You don't belong mixing with Coven witches, and you for sure don't belong with a regent's son. And Khy's a smart guy; he knows how our world works," she says sickly sweet. "He'll decide to stop slumming it soon enough." Her smile sharpens. "Or maybe you're just his latest charity project."

"Oh, you've lost your damn mind—"

"Nah, I said I got this." I cut Naomi off. Then I tell Gigi, "My guess would be you're the current charity project. Your new boyfriend is too busy to be your escort tonight, right? And knowing Khy—and yourself—you manipulated him into feeling bad for you. It's actually pathetic that you only got him to agree by making yourself into a pity project, and you're okay with it. Me, personally, I've got too much pride. But hey, that's just me.

"Oh, you thought I was finished?" I cut her off when she attempts to retort. "I'm not yet. Nobody, but you, of all people, don't get to tell me where I do and don't belong. You don't know squat about me, and your opinions mean less than shit, boo."

Naomi cackles as Gigi sputters. Naomi slings an arm around me. "Yup," she says to Becca on my other side, "I'm super glad we've gained a new bestie!"

When the three of us stare Gigi down, she does that ridiculous hair flip and walks off.

She can go stroll right off into the sun.

"Oh my God. I don't think I've seen Gigi be placed on mute before," Naomi says, still cackling to herself.

"Becca! Naomi!" Darius shouts his friends' names as he, Geo, and Jordan rush up to us. The guys are dressed in the same suave black tux that the debutantes who don't have on dresses wear.

"Ummm... what the hell are *you* doing here?" Jordan cries to me.

"Really?" I snap. "You too! I thought we squashed our beef."

"He doesn't mean it like that," Geo says in this weirdly stricken manner. "But you cannot be here, Cayden. You're not supposed to be here."

Okay. I'm getting sick of people telling me that.

"What is going on?" Becca demands of the guys.

Geo curses.

"This is so damn twisted." Jordan laughs dryly.

Okay. I'm more scared. "Is Khy okay?" I stress. "He isn't sick or something, is he?"

"No," Darius answers. "Khy arrived here with us a little while ago, but then he left to go find you, Cayden."

I didn't hear him right. I couldn't have heard him right. "Khy did what?"

"He ditched Cotillion *for you*," Darius says slowly and enunciating every syllable like it's super important I understand. He gets this dreamy look. "It's really sweet, if you think about it. Khy is crazy about you. He was trying to respect your decision to break up, but tonight he was all *Broody Sad Boy* from the time our limo picked him up from his house. Then, a few seconds after we'd gotten inside, he said he couldn't do this if everything it was founded on made you feel you couldn't be together. So, he left, Sis. To go get his girl back—to go get *you* back."

At first, all I can do is stand there speechless while what Darius said really sinks in. When it does, if I wasn't made of solid flesh and blood, I'd melt into a puddle of mushy goo on the spot. As grand gestures go, it's so like Khy—so selfless and considerate and earnest and incredible. Unamused exasperation hits behind the mushy feelings. *Why are the Ancestors perpetually torturing me with this boy?! Do they—or the Universe—hate me?!*

I rub my head. "Jordan's right; this is so damn warped," I mutter. I jerk my phone from the pocket sewn into my dress and book a rideshare to my house. "Is there anything any of you can do to stall Cotillion from starting until I come back?" I ask Khy's friends. "I'm gonna go get Khy. I don't want him to miss this." He shouldn't miss this huge event in his life for me—or for anything or anybody.

"That, you don't need to worry about," Naomi says. "If we tell Mrs. Carter that Khy left and you went to get her son, she'll *make* everyone wait until he shows up."

I inhale in infinite relief, realizing how ironic it is that I silently thank the Ancestors that Khy's mom sits at the apex of bougie witch society and has so much influence.

My phone vibrates with a notification that my rideshare is three minutes away. "If things with Mrs. Carter don't go as planned," I tell Naomi just in case, "figure something else out. Do whatever it takes for things not to start until Khy gets here."

The forty-five-minute drive to my house is pure torment. I swear it feels like the seconds crawl by and like we get stopped at every single red light when we aren't on the freeway. Knowing how important Cotillion is for Khy keeps my stomach knotted the whole time, and I worry we won't make it back in time.

When the car pulls up to my house, it parks behind a white stretch limo. I bolt from the car, run to the limousine, and bang on the back window.

"Can I help you with something, miss?" a man calls out. I look toward the direction of the voice and the limo's driver has his head poked out the front window.

I realize how unhinged I probably seem. Which is why he's looking at me with an equal mixture of concern and wariness. "I'm looking for Mekhi," I say. "Is he back there?" I squint at the window in front of me, but it's no use. The tint is too dark to see anything.

The driver shakes his head no but doesn't give up any further information.

"Where is he, then?" I ask frustrated, checking my porch and not seeing him there either.

"Who are you?" the driver asks, more guarded.

Ugh! We don't have time for this! "Cayden Jackson," I say. "This is my house. He came here to see me, and I'm here to take him back to the party. Satisfied? Where is Khy?"

Understanding dawns in the driver's expression; his suspicious demeanor evaporates. He points up at my house. "Inside."

Mercedes snatches open the door as I'm punching in the lock code. "Both of y'all are insane! What the hell is going on?" She yanks me inside without waiting for an answer. She hitches a thumb at Khy standing in the middle of the living room in a black tux with his hands stuffed in his pockets. "He got here a few minutes ago. I told him where you were, and I was just about to call you. Why are *you* back?"

"For him," I say and rush to Khy. "You need to get out of here and make Cotillion." I grab his hand to pull him toward the door, but he doesn't budge.

He blinks rapidly at me, takes in my dress, and his forehead creases. "You went to Cotillion for me?"

"Yeah," I say hurriedly. "I was going to surprise you," I admit. "Come on." I tug his hand. The boy stays planted. "I have Naomi making sure things don't begin until I get you back, but we should still go right now. If it does start and we're not there, at least you won't miss the whole thing."

"Cotillion isn't what I care about," Khy says. His forehead remains creased. "And I decided I can't vibe with what it stands for if institutions like that hurt—"

"I don't have anything against Cotillion," I say. "Nor do I feel some type of way about your specific Coven. You, Becca, Naomi, and the rest of your friends have shown me that I really can't judge an entire group by the past actions of others in it. Darius filled me in about why you're here, and I do want to hear it directly from you. I have things I want to say to you, too. But Cotillion *is* super important to you, and I'm not about to let you miss out on this experience you only get once in a lifetime because you're trying to prove something to me. So, let's go. We can talk on the ride back," I promise him to get him moving for the door.

This time when I pull on his hand, he takes a step forward. *Thank the Ancestors.*

Once we're inside his limo, Khy and I sputter words at the same time. My "I'm sorry; I made a mistake" tangles together with Khy's "I don't want to lose you."

We both fall quiet. "I'd like to go first," I say, purposefully. Khy always puts himself out there first; he has been since we met. It's my turn now.

Khy graciously nods. "Whatever you want. I'm listening."

I take a deep breath in. "You haven't lost me. I like you, so damn much. To be honest, I more than like you. *I love you.* You told me you loved me at my house after the cookout. I didn't say it back then because I was scared. And I was letting my fear get the better of me when I said we were through. But I think I was just making things extra complicated and extra impossible when they don't have to be that way. I thought we were impossible because of our differences, but I showed up at Cotillion tonight because I realized we're not. I've had some really deep talks with my parents; they genuinely only want me to be happy, and what *I* want is *you*. I want *us*. And I'm pretty sure that's been the case from the first moment I met you, even if I was lying to myself about it. You said you've felt this intense connection between us from the first time we met at the rescue. Same. I've been falling hard for you since that day." If I'm keeping it one hundred, fighting catching feelings for Khy was a lost cause from the time I saw him walk into the dog spa in cool sneakers that he didn't even care got ruined.

As I ride with Khy in the limo, everything out in the open, the two of us gazing at each other, my heart feels like it's been replaced by a dang hummingbird. My hands have grown clammy as hell at some point during my grand speech. I've never been this emotionally open, or deep, with a guy before. It's terrifying, and I feel exposed, with no idea what comes next.

Khy, on the other hand, has some ideas about the last part. He leans forward, murmurs, "I love you so damn much it hurts," and kisses me. Thoroughly. It becomes hard to breathe and my heart crashes against my chest for a new reason. Like the last time we kissed, I find that I don't really care. I don't need air. Drawing oxygen into my lungs is completely unnecessary. I lean into Khy when his arms curl around me and hold him the same way.

Eventually, it's Khy who ends the kiss. He rests his forehead against mine, both of us breathing heavy. "I really want to return to that," he says, a smile curving his lips. "But first I need to say things back to you. I'm sorry that there were ever times of miscommunication and stuff that hurt you to begin with. I should've anticipated a lot of things, and I should've approached us differently than I've approached other relationships. Because you're different. Remarkably so. I should've recognized that me being who I am, and my mom being who she is, and you being who you are was going to make this relationship a lot different from past ones. I should've protected you from being hurt by my world better. I suck for not doing so. Will you forgi—"

I kiss him, cutting off his absurd words. I break this second earth-tilting kiss to quickly tell him, "There's nothing I need to forgive because you didn't do anything wrong." Then, I seal us back together. Kiss my boyfriend who I'm crazy in love with for the entire ride back to Cotillion.

When we get to the mansion, I almost regret it. A completely self-indulgent part of me wants to hunker down in the dim interior of the limo and spend the rest of the night doing nothing except making out with Khy.

Our minds must be operating on the same wavelength because when the driver opens the door, Khy only partially ends our latest kiss. His lips stop moving, but he leaves them lightly pressed to mine. He locks eyes with me, doesn't spare the mansion a glance, and says, "We really don't have to go inside. I was already dead set on skipping out."

Okay! Thirsty Cayden wants to jump at the offer. *Tonight is important to him*, I remind myself. Which is why I let better sense prevail, and I pull away from the boy who has captured my entire heart so intensely that it leaves me dizzy thinking about it. I climb out of the limo and hold my hand out to Khy. "Let's get you to your ball, Prince Charming."

Chapter Twenty-Five

I stand outside the double doors of the Cotillion ballroom nervous as heck, with my arm hooked through Khy's. I'm in a line of Coven debutantes, all of them waiting to hear their name called as they're introduced to Coven adult society as its newest "mature" members. The debutantes' order isn't alphabetical—it's impossible since some of them decided to be each other's escorts, others chose to be introduced without one, and then there's some, like Khy, who have escorts who aren't participating in Cotillion themselves. But Khy has been placed right up front as number one, given the fact that he's America's prince and the United States is this year's host country. Gigi is solo behind us. The petty part of me is infinitely smug about it since I can practically feel the heat of her staring a hole into my back. I wipe thoughts of Gigi, though, because, like I told her before, she's utterly insignificant to my life.

"I'm really glad you're here," Khy whispers in my ear as he squeezes my hand.

His grin that eclipses the sun is on full display. I grin back. "I am, too!" I tell him. "I'm happy I can share your big moment." He bites his bottom lip. My stare gets trapped on the kissable fullness of it. I mentally shake myself, pull my gaze away, and face the closed door. Sadly, it'll be entirely inappropriate and awkward to kiss him right now.

Moments later, an older witch, a beautiful Latina woman wearing a violet mermaid gown and whose job is to direct the debutantes inside, opens the door and waves Khy and me forward. I expect at least a trickle of fear to rise as we stride through the doors. But utter joy and a sense of rightness—and a thrill—is what washes over me. Once Khy and I are inside the ballroom, I follow his lead and halt a few feet beyond the doors. The deep baritone voice of the announcer, who stands at a podium to the right, booms out. "Ladies, gentlemen, and esteemed folks of witchkind, I present to you Mekhi Carter of the Houston Coven, son of Allison Carter, born Allison Tremaine, and Graham Carter." Deafening applause rings out for America's witch prince. I assume that's the end of this part, but then when the applause dies down, the announcer says, "I also present to you, Mekhi's escort, Cayden Jackson, a witch with an Independent distinction, and the daughter of Eva Jackson, born Eva Hilliard, and Jason Jackson."

The claps begin again. I turn toward Khy, startled. "I didn't know I'd be announced, too?"

"Why wouldn't you?" he responds. "You're standing right next to me, aren't you?"

"Yeah... but I'm not a debutante. I'm just your date. Who I am doesn't really matter."

Our arms still hooked together, Khy tightens his hold on me as we walk down a shimmery gold runner toward a stage. "Of course it does. You're not *only* my date. You're a young witch participating in Cotillion, too, and it deserves recognition. So, I asked my mom to request that the announcer make a last-minute change for you and the other escorts who aren't debs."

I'm glad he's the one guiding us forward because all I can do is stare at him, stunned and swept away by how amazing Khy always is. "And you had them include my dad."

"Without a doubt, including both parents' names is tradition," he says, like it's no big deal. But it is. Because he really went out of his way to make sure a nonwitch was paid an honor within witch society; he made sure my ordinary dad was recognized as every bit a special and integral and worthy part of my life as my witch mom is. And *his* mom agreed.

Between this realization and Carolyn and Robert's change of heart, I think about how Mom mentioned checking out membership in Houston's Coven together. Maybe that's something I *would* like to do.

Khy and I reach the stage. As we walk up its steps, I set

the topic aside to reconsider later. Khy's mom stands behind a glass podium on the stage. America's Witch Regent is dressed in a champagne-colored ball gown with emeralds sparkling at her throat, wrists, and ears. She steps back from the podium and hugs her son tightly when he reaches her. She turns to me next. "It's very nice to see you again, dear," she says super nicely, collecting my free hand in hers and squeezing it. "When you join our dining table later, I'd love to get to know you better."

"It's nice to see you again, too," I say shyly. "And thank you."

She smiles and directs Khy and me to take up spots directly to the right of the podium. She turns back to the crowd, and Khy and I stare out at the ballroom, too. The announcer is calling the next debutante, but I barely hear it. My attention is snatched by who sits at a table in front of the stage. Khy's dad, his brother, Carolyn and Robert, and my parents. All four of my people give me excited waves. It feels so unreal that I blink several times. Yes, I knew my parents were coming. But actually seeing them here, at a Coven ball, seated beside my grandparents and looking as if they're perfectly comfortable and are having a good time . . . taking that all in is everything.

"*I love you, sweetie,*" Mom mouths. Dad winks at me, then tips his head at Khy before giving me a thumbs-up. I bite my cheek so I don't laugh. Jason Jackson isn't serious; my father is trying to embarrass me.

I wave at my parents. She and Dad have hands laced together and resting atop the table's gold cloth. My grandfather catches my gaze, and his eyes are full of love. My grandmother beams while dabbing at her eyes. I'm so happy Mom and her parents are finding their way back to each other.

After all the debs are announced, Mrs. Carter, Khy, and I join the table where our families are gathered. Mrs. Carter drops into an empty chair beside her husband. Next to Khy's mom are two empty seats between her and my dad. Khy and I sit there.

"Y'all look *good* all dressed up," I gush to my parents. Dad is in a tux and Mom is wearing a stunning red gown. It's always fun seeing them in fancy clothes. Especially Dad, since most of the time I see him in an apron and dusted by stray bits of flour. I brush invisible lint off his collar. "Don't hurt 'em, Jason Jackson," I tease.

Proving he's always gonna be himself, no matter his surroundings, Dad hits a shimmy in his seat and says, "I do clean up nice, don't I?"

Mr. Carter chuckles. "I didn't know you're a Kappa man," he exclaims to Dad. "Some of my closest friends are Nupes. You should come catch a golf game with us sometime if you're up for it. If our kids are spending all this time together, I figure we should get to know each other more."

Dad passes Mr. Carter a nod. "I guess you're right. Just let me know a time and place."

I swivel back and forth between them. Khy must read

the astonishment I try to hide on my face because he leans into my ear and whispers, "See, I told you my parents weren't uptight."

"How's your night been so far?" Mrs. Carter then asks Mom.

Mom looks around the ballroom wistfully. "I've been sitting here remembering my own Cotillion like it was yesterday *and* thinking that I feel extremely old," Mom laughs.

Mrs. Carter does, too. "That, I can agree with. I can't believe I have two children old enough to have participated in their own." She eyes Mom for a second and then says, "But there's plenty of experiences and memories us older folks can still make. Our Coven has a robust social calendar in case you're interested in that now or in the future."

"*Mama!*" Khy says. "Can we not—"

"It's all right," my mom cuts in. "To be honest, I have been thinking something along those lines. There are things I do miss." She tilts her head in Mr. Carter's direction. "And Graham here has been filling me in on your Coven's core values and the vision for its future." From the appreciative way Mom mentions it, it's clear she's impressed with what she's heard.

"We'd be elated to have you as a new member," Khy's dad says earnestly.

"You've nearly sold me," Mom responds.

"I am glad to hear it," Mrs. Carter says genially. "So, are you two a real item now?" Khy's mom then asks her son and me. She raises a knowing eyebrow.

"We are," Khy states, a cheesy smile on his face.

My cheeks grow ridiculously warm. And they become hotter when Mrs. Carter says, "Well, you're a lovely young lady, Cayden, and very eloquent, too. I saw that from your fundraiser speech. I'm sorry that was taken out of context. For what it's worth, I appreciated what you had to say. It gave me and this Coven's Matriarch Elders a lot to think about. In fact..." As she eyes me, I can't help being a bit anxious under the older woman's gaze. Khy's mom takes elegant and queenly to the max. "If your mother is considering joining our Coven, does it mean you are as well? You'd also make a delightful addition, and I'd love to see you help create change from the inside."

"I—I thought you didn't like me much when I met you the last time." In my total shock, the word vomit spews out before I can keep it in.

"Oh, I doubt that's true. What's not to adore about you?" It's Carolyn who says it. She keeps her tone light but passes a look to Mrs. Carter that I don't miss.

Khy's mom takes it in stride, though. "I assure you there is no need to turn the infamous Carolyn Hilliard wrath my way," she tells my grandmother. "I meant it when I told Cayden she was a lovely girl. Khy has mentioned that his father and I might have come off a bit cold at the golf course," Mrs. Carter says to me. "I apologize for our disposition wounding you, dear. There were paparazzi around that day and our public masks were on." She scowls. "I can't express how much I dislike handing the media anything to spin tawdry gossip from."

Mrs. Carter's sincerity makes me decide that I like her; she seems super cool. So does her husband.

"Thank you for saying that," I tell Mrs. Carter. "And thank you for helping to set the record straight about my speech in the media."

She waves me off. "No thanks is needed. I would've done it for any of my people. It's my very job as Regent to look out for and advocate for all Coven folk."

"But I'm not in a Coven," I say.

Allison shrugs. "Official member or not, you're still a witch who dwells within the US *and* within my personal residential city, which means even if you don't claim us back, *I* claim you as one of us." She looks at Mom and then Dad. "That goes for the both of you, too." When Dad turns as startled as I am, Allison shakes her head firmly. "I don't ascribe to some of witchkind's antiquated and misbegotten purity politics. Neither does Houston's Matriarchs or most of our wider Coven members. If your wife and daughter are witches, and you're their loved one, then that makes you a part of *my* people and my Coven as well. You should know that up front." Mrs. Carter turns back to me. "I don't believe I ever got your answer, dear."

Khy groans. "Mama, can you *not* be pushy? Let her breathe, please?"

Khy's brother, Rashaud, cackles. He speaks up for the first time. "Have you met our mother?"

Khy winces. "I have. Sorry," he says to me.

"No, it's all right," I reply. Then, I give Mrs. Carter an

answer that I don't need to think about all that much anymore. "I'd love to explore that option."

"Excellent!" Mrs. Carter gets up from her seat and steps over to me. "May I hug you?"

I say yes—albeit awkwardly, because what in the hell—and she swallows me up in a *Mom Hug*. "The invitation extends to you as well, Jason," she says to Dad. "The media's whole ugly smear campaign with Cayden galvanized me and Graham to push a new policy through that'll allow non-witch spouses of members to formally join the Coven. We hope ones in other cities will follow the precedent we set."

"Carolyn and I will certainly advocate for the same change within Dallas's Coven," my grandfather speaks at once.

"Absolutely," my grandmother says, gazing at my mom intensely. "My husband and I have been a part of perpetuating damaging ideas. We'd like to be a part of eradicating them moving forward."

Mom makes a sound that's between a gasp and a cry—not a sad one, though. She hugs Carolyn and says, "I love you, Mama."

"Your initiative is noble," Dad says to Khy's parents.

As servers set the first dinner course (tiny and delicious-smelling bowls of lobster bisque) in front of us and the whole table digs in, Dad and Mr. Carter end up in deep conversation about urban policy and politics once they realize they're both huge nerds for the topics; my grandfather, Rashaud, and my grandmother talk excitedly (and with fervor) about if the Texans or the Cowboys are the better football team—a staple debate around a lot of dinner tables in Texas; and Mom and Mrs. Carter (two badass girl bosses, obviously) swap stories about what it's like to be a doctor and a regent. The conversations keep up through the remaining dinner courses. Me, I'm unusually quiet because I'm taking in the surreal, unbelievable scene. Matter of fact, I'm pretty sure I'm still having trouble processing everything that happened tonight. Khy, charming as ever, flits between chatting with everybody and quietly asking me if I'm okay because of how silent I am. But I promise him that I am more than okay.

A little while after dessert is served, Khy leans into me and whispers conspiratorially, "If we slip away, do you think they'll notice?"

I swallow a smile, putting the fork down that I just ate a bite of frosted lemon cake off. "Hmm. I'm not sure," I whisper as mischievously. "You can excuse yourself to the bathroom, though, and I'll do the same a couple minutes later."

We both laugh. Then, he stands and holds out his hand.

I place mine in his and let him pull me to my feet. "Cayden and I are going to find Nae and the gang," he tells his parents. "I think they're somewhere over there." He motions to the crowd of people who are now on the dance floor. There's a ton of teens, but a good bit of adults mixed in. Everybody's hitting the "Cupid Shuffle," a song and dance that transcends any class or age boundary that exists when you live in Houston. It's one of those songs that's gonna get played at everybody's and they mama's functions. Hella coolly, the string musicians are showing out with their classical cover.

The adults at the table all slide us some variation of "have fun."

Rashaud smirks. "Have fun *dancing.*"

Khy's brother might be cool people, but he's still a jerk. I serve him a side-eye. In the middle of doing so, a tingling sensation swirls around my legs. I gasp when my dress shortens to above my knees. I stumble back a step. *What in the heck?*

Mrs. Carter and my grandmother chortle at the same time. "Don't you love a Helen-Marie Mayfield gown?" Carolyn asks Mrs. Carter.

"I sure do; Mayfield gowns were my choice for every ball when I was younger," Mrs. Carter responds wistfully. She pats the emeralds at her neck. "That's perhaps the sole thing I don't love about being regent. My wardrobe these days is a quite deal less flamboyant." She eyes the significantly shorter length of my dress. "I'm assuming *dance* triggers the spellwork for your gown."

Sure enough, a moment after Khy's mom offers up her suspicion, I feel the tingling and my dress elongates. "If that starts to exasperate you," says Khy's mom, "then every Mayfield gown has the word C-E-A-S-E woven into its spellwork as an auto shutoff."

"Good to know," I say gratefully because, oh boy, perpetual tingling and shifts could be a pain.

I leave the dress at floor length since I think it's prettier that way, and then Khy and I wade into the thick of the dance crowd. And, up to no good as we mutually agreed, we keep walking right on out of it. We sneak out of the ballroom and find an empty terrace on the second story. We stand under the stars and end a perfect night with perfect, blissful, yummy kissing.

A lot of it.

I didn't aim to gain a boyfriend this summer, but I'm glad my hook-up only plans got obliterated. Because Khy isn't just a boyfriend. As I drink in everything about him, about *us*, and let myself get lost in the earth-tilting intensity of how much I'm in love with him, a gut-deep feeling washes over me. The extreme curve my summer has taken, and not just with me and Khy, but gaining a second set of grandparents in my life, Mom reuniting with her parents, and Mom feeling free to rediscover her witch side—it all feels like greater forces might've truly been at work to nudge us all toward providence. As for me and Khy, specifically... I don't know if it really was the Ancestors making subtle moves to bring two people together that would automatically click, or fate, or simply a chance meeting, but I do know that Khy, he and I, *we* feel like destiny in the best of ways. The two of us ending up deliriously in love—so much so that it's hard to breathe—feels like it was always inevitable from the first moment our orbits crossed.

Acknowledgments

Love Spells Trouble is my fourth published book! I never in my wildest dreams thought I'd end up here. Okay, that's not actually true. Back before even my first published book was released, I dreamed (A LOT) of getting to this incredible place in my career where I'm fortunate enough to be publishing multiple books! However, there was also lots of crushing doubt—and lying in my backyard gazing up at the sky in existential angst. So, I am incredibly grateful for everybody who has uplifted me along the way and believed in my stories, including my own ride-or-die bestie. Whitney, you've been reading my stories for over the last decade and you've always encouraged me to pursue any and every dream I have related to writing and publishing. I seriously would not have come this far without you. The same goes for the rest of my family, including my siblings (Janeé, Elana, Lauren,

Desiree, and Avery), my mom, my dad, and my husband, Courtney. I so appreciate that you all are always ready to be sounding boards for new ideas and I appreciate your endless yelling about my books to any and everybody you meet. To my daughters, Iyanna, Carmen, and Cydney: thank you for weighing in on the cover art and providing incredibly insightful feedback that truly made it pop!

I also must extend a very special thank you to my entire Bloomsbury team and my incredibly brilliant editor, Alex Borbolla. I am so grateful for everyone's support and enthusiasm for this project! Alex, I am forever grateful that you saw something special in this story, which is a "heartfelt contemporary fantasy romance with a side of social commentary," as you've phrased it. This description really, truly just gets my vision for Cayden and Khy's love story—it's about the two of them, but it's also about community and family ties. A huge thank-you as well to my rock star agent, Caitie Flum, who has always been a cheerleader for me and my work.

As always, this latest book would not have come together without my extraordinary friends, who are also my writing gang: Traci-Anne, Shari, Kwame, Andre, Davaun, and Brent. I am always grateful to you all for taking the time to read pages, provide feedback, or just be an ear to bounce ideas off. To Jennifer Chen, another amazing writer and friend, the biggest of a thank-you for being one of *Love Spells Trouble*'s very first readers back in its earliest form and giving me feedback about the development of Cayden and Khy's romance.

Lastly, to any readers who may be coming to this story after reading my previous books, the hugest of THANK-YOUs for picking up this next story and continuing to come along with me on this journey!

JUL 2025